EL DORADO

A HAIM BAKER MYSTERY

JOEL SHAPIRO

For Leon Dahl. The Air Cav chopper pilot. The outdoorsman. The guy who inspired me, showed me guns and drop top Brit cars, blondes, and pinatas. The guy who was a little boy's replacement for the dad I never had. The guy I looked up to, the guy I knew was a real hero. You still are. Always will be. Even without much of a roof over your head.

Thanks to John, one of my best friends and a real inspiration. A ladies' man who loves the good life and lives it to the fullest. The dapper guy who turned me on to Cubans and Chartreuse and plied me with exciting stories of controlled debauchery. May you live on for many years sampling the haute cuisine of life while having fun within the pages of adventure.

PROLOGUE

Suddenly Manny heard music. It was some old-timey stuff, with a white guy singing—"crooning" was what he'd heard some country club bitch call it before he shot the fucker in the face. Yeah, it was the kind of crap old white people seem to like, like they never got past the old days when whiteys ruled the world. Manny knew eventually these crackers would die off, taking their weird and stringy and croony lame music with them. Manny knew he was the future. Manny was gonna rule the world someday.

Someone finally pulled the black canvas off his head. Manny found himself attached to a strong, slatted wood chair—it felt like the kind he'd seen in backyards and patios and pool parties of those upscale houses above Sunset. He knew he must be in the hills somewhere like Brentwood or Beverly Hills. Figures.

Manny tried to look around, but it was dark, too dark. Then he heard a finger click something on a phone or iPad and a single beam of light hit his face as quiet footsteps padded up behind him. Manny had a swelling bruise on the back of his head where he'd been knocked out, and he'd also bitten his tongue when they took him from behind. That too was swollen, mixed with the metallic iron taste of blood that coated his dry mouth, and worst of all, his head was throbbing. Damn. If he only had some Advil.

"Hey man, can I get some fucking Advil?"

Then he felt the measured breath on the back of his aching head.

"Sorry." The voice said.

"You're the fucker who's gonna be sorry, asshole. You got no idea who you're fucking with." Manny turned his head left, then right, to no avail. He wanted to see this fucker.

"I know exactly who you are, Manny."

"How you know my name?

"I know everything."

"Yeah? So where am I? And who the fuck are you? I can't fucking see you. What you hiding? Pussy." Manny tried to spit, but his mouth was far too dry.

"You're in La La Land" The voice purred close to his ear. "And if you saw me, I'd have to cut off your head."

Something about the way the guy calmly said that line freaked the hell out of Manny. But that was bullshit. Manny knew this was just cartel wannabe bullshit. Sure, if he was back in Durango with the heat and the flies and the stink where no one gives a shit, then yeah, he'd probably have his neck cut in two. But here, in Cali, in the hills of LA—this guy had seen too many episodes of *Breaking Bad.* Sounded like a white dude anyway. Manny didn't have nothing to worry about.

"Hey asshole, real life ain't like *Breaking Bad.* And if you don't want some fucked up shit to happen to you and your family, you better cut me loose now, cuz I'm the real deal."

"They could have squeezed at least two more seasons out of that show. But that's neither here nor there."

Manny was really getting tired of this shit. "So what the fuck is here and there? What you want from me, asshole?" Manny was losing his patience.

Why, you're going to do something for me, Manny." The voice said.

"I ain't doing shit."

The man moved to the other side of Manny, still staying in the shadows, which were made all the darker from the bright light closing down Manny's pupils.

"I appreciate your bravado. I can certainly see why Patterson trusted you so much."

The man felt like he was getting closer—very close, but still in the shadows. Manny could feel it. The dude was close enough to touch. Big mistake.

Manny figured he had one shot. He strained, hard as he could, the tight leather binding ripping and stinging the skin off his wrist, as he reached out hard as he could. And for his effort, he was able to touch the fabric of a man's suit. It was soft, firm, silky smooth. Rich. In an instant, Manny grabbed a sleeve with his two fingers to hold the dude, and with his right foot struggling against a similar binding, gave the biggest kick he could muster, moving the heavy chair ahead with the force of his leg. He made gentle contact with the guy's shin, maybe grazing it at best, certainly not enough to even leave a mark. But enough to send a message: don't fuck with Manny.

"You shouldn't have done that, Manny." The voice warned.

"Yeah? Well Imma gonna fuck you up.

He heard the dude sigh, then, "Oh, Manny..."

"How you know my name, asshole?" Manny's moxie, his cajones, had gotten him through tough spots before. Just scare the sons of bitches, let them know you're the bull, you're the predator. Maybe this white rat fuck with the money threads will think twice about fucking with Manny. Manny wasn't just a tough kid. Manny was a fucking Sicario.

"Like I told you, I know everything, Manny. Everything."

"Oh yeah? Then you know my boss is gonna fuck you up. You a dead man, whitey."

Manny tugged at his leather binding again, but then they began to tighten as the shadowy man quickly, methodically, pulled the straps even tighter, making Manny's hands and feet instantly go numb.

"What the fuck you doing? I can't feel my hands."

"That's for your benefit." The man said.

"What? What the fuck is going on? The fuck do you want?"

"I simply wanted you to give a message to your employer. That's all. But now you've changed the game. Now we do it the hard way. For you, that is."

He heard the man move away and come back. The guy had something in his hand.

"You've just given yourself a brief lifetime of grief." The man said.

Now Manny started to worry. There was something wrong with this weird dude who seemed to know everything about Manny. Suddenly a new song began playing over the speakers. It was loud.

Oh the shark babe. Has such teeth dear. And it shows them, Pearly whites...

Manny's bravado began to weaken. He couldn't feel his feet at all. Manny began to sweat.

Just a jack knife. Has old MacHeath, babe. And it keeps it. Outta sight...

Manny yelled over the music. "Okay. Yeah. Sure. What the fuck you want me to say before he comes and rips off your head?"

Manny heard the snap of a leather retainer coming loose. Then the whisk of metal. Then the flash of metal presented before him in a very big, very expensive, custom-made, golden blade.

In front of his eyes, in the prick of light, Manny saw the word that suddenly frightened him to his very core. He began to shake, to sweat even more. He could barely hold himself together. In fact, he started to shit his pants.

On the giant gold-plated knife held in front of his eyes to see was simply a lone inscription:

"El Dorado."

Manny couldn't even say the name. He could just barely utter his profuse apologies. "No, no, oh God, I'm sorry, man. I'm so sorry. Please... I didn't know. I didn't know!"

"You touched me. With your hands. With your feet, Manny. You know what that means..."

The man turned the knife back into darkness and instantly Manny heard the brief crunching of bones.

On the sidewalk. Oh, sunny morning. Lies a body. Just a-oozin' life...

And like a surreal dream, Manny nearly fainted when he saw his own right hand cut cleanly off his numb wrist, the Man dangling it in front of Manny's widening eyes. Blood dripping, echoing onto the dark concrete floor, in concert with the song. He saw it drop to the floor in front of him. Manny began to shake. Piss began to stain his crotch. Then, as the music played...

And someone's sneaking round the corner. Could that someone, be... Mack the Knife.

Crunch! The big blade was razor sharp, and since all the blood was blocked from circulating through his hands, Manny didn't feel the next cut either, but he began to turn white from the shock of seeing his left hand now dangling in front of his face, the man holding it by Manny's middle finger. Drip. Drip. Drip.

Manny suddenly heard screams of terror. Of real horror. The kind that blared loud and shrieked from those slasher flicks he liked so much.

Five'll get you ten, old Macky's back in town.

And when the Man held up Manny's severed right foot, Manny realized those horrible screams were coming from his own throat.

That is until his left foot was shoved into his screaming mouth...

CHAPTER ONE

I couldn't tell if it was the buzzing of those Goddammed fluorescents, flickering that ugly blueish light above my head, or if it was my opiate-fed tinnitus serenading me intimately in my left ear, or maybe it was those fucking little brown gnats that somehow sneaked through the ventilation system, but my anxiety-fueled and Oxy-colored thoughts were flying like a bored and blueprinted four-twenty-six Hemi. Man, I was going batshit crazy.

I'd been cooped up in this depressing beige jail cell for three days with nothing but a drunk male escort named Kimche, and a smelly homeless guy who kept yelling at the gnats while talking to some graffiti scratched onto the cinderblock wall. Eventually we had a big black guy lock in with us who said he was pinched for selling a kilo of heroin to an undercover cop.

Kimche was out in an hour, the homeless guy got picked up by social services, and the black dude was on bail right after he took over the lower bunk.

But me, I was still here in the new El Cajon county jail. I'd been moved into an interview room and had been sitting behind a metal table for at least three hours. And I didn't fucking know why.

Until that bastard walked in.

The blue Paul Newman eyes, the grey pony tail, the silver belt buckle, the Richard Mille watch. A billion dollars of attitude and privileged conceit that comes from living on the highest peak in East County.

I was on him in seconds, my fists flying. Now don't get me wrong, he was fast, especially for a man his age, but I was able to connect a quick uppercut to his jaw before Detective Opp rushed in to knock me back. The Old Man barely flinched.

"What happened to the gas chamber!?" I screamed.

"Haven't had the gas chamber since the '80s, Baker." Opp said as he struggled to hold me back. "Let it go."

"I'll kill him myself," I yelled.

I hated Patterson Nobel so much I couldn't even look at the sun-drenched, svelte man who ran the biggest human trafficking ring in San Diego. The same sonofabitch who'd killed his own wife, Mrs. Nobel. The woman who saved my life. The most beautiful creature I'd ever seen. Now she was six feet under and her murderer was standing six inches in front of me. Same killer who also shoved a 500 Magnum up the birth canal of my best friend and blew her insides out—not to mention shoving the same giant gun barrel up my virgin ass, fortunately without the same results.

"Just give me five minutes with him, Opp."

In a flash the detective pulled me back and cuffed me to the bolted-down metal table.

"Sorry," he said. And then Opp left the room without looking back. And just like that I was incapacitated. Again. Facing a psychopath. Again. Same old story.

Patterson Nobel finally lifted his right hand, and with the back of his manicured fingers, slightly rubbed what was probably a burgeoning bruise forming under the perfectly trimmed white beard that covered his thick crimson lips. Those lips parted. They arched a smile, then he licked them. They were cracked from being outside in the relentless El Cajon sunshine, unlike my formerly violated pasty-ass, which had been in jail for days. The irony was not lost on him.

"Our fortunes appear to have changed, Mister Baker."

CHAPTER TWO

First thing I needed to do was find a gold star flophouse to lay my bones, and believe me, up in La La Land that's a tough call on the budget of an unemployed private dick. I decided I didn't want to catch fleas or bed bugs, so I gave my old friend Kerry Foot a call. He and I met as interns at an ad agency down on Hudson Street fresh out of college. He was a big, heavy black guy with a high voice and thick mustache, and after getting berated over and over for drinking too much coffee and dating every available female employee with minimum size D breast, and realizing he wasn't going to get to actually write an ad for Volvo or New Balance, he abruptly quit the ad game and immediately went over to med school at NYU where he at least would be doing something to help people rather than encouraging them to spend money they didn't have on overbuilt sedans and ugly sneakers. Besides, there were plenty of size D co-eds to "study" with.

Kerry moved to Cali for his residency and went on to become a head and neck specialist, taking a job as the only black surgeon at the VA over near the big UCLA campus. But Dr. Foot found out that being the token black guy wasn't all that it was cracked up to be, and when he blew the whistle on his boss for deleting thousands of patient cases in order to make it look like everyone was seeing doctors instead of waiting months and years to get a checkup, the entrenched management decided to fuck up his career. After a trumped-up charge of sexual harassment, Kerry was quickly fired and forgotten about until he sued and won a wrongful termination suit, proving harassment and retaliation, giving my friend a nice five mil payday. But then the big man discovered his new double-D wife was secretly screwing the married VA director, and had bugged their house to help VA management get the goods to file a countersuit against my doctor pal, which is still being adjudicated to this day.

With a messy divorce and no kids, Kerry Foot was left alone in his Spanish style villa up North of Montana, where the cheapest listing is an easy four mil. But Dr. Foot had let himself and his house go, filling up the four bedrooms and dining room with stacks of memories—especially the backyard, which was littered with the discarded toys from the children that never came and the soccer balls from the AYSO teams he coached.

When I called, Kerry said he was more than happy to have me come and crash in his empty, filled house. I knew he was just being polite. I knew he preferred to be alone, his understandable paranoia not allowing him to trust anyone, even an old pal like me.

Dr. Kerry Foot reluctantly made room for me on the new black leather Crate and Barrel couch in the living room under his new big screen Sony TV (his bedrooms were either stuffed with Godknowswhat or were being "remodeled"). He wouldn't put me in one of his four bedrooms, because holes dotted most of the bedroom walls like Swiss cheese. Kerry'd sucker-punched the plaster during the divorce, then sledgehammered it later when he'd found the audio bugs and decided, on sudden inspiration (fueled by too much tequila so soak up the sorrow of his wife's cruelty), to "open up the place" for more unneeded space.

I pulled my dented, beetle-like, brown '67 Saab into his driveway, right next to Kerry's new, already-dented Kia SUV (he was a terrible driver). Heck, the car didn't even have plates on it yet.

Thanks to his plethora of paranoid security cameras, when I drove up, Kerry was already in the driveway, greeting me before I had the bullet-ridden Saab door open (I didn't have the cash to fix the dozen or so 9mil holes from the shootout in El Cajon—but I also kinda liked the street cred it gave me—besides the funny sideways looks I got in this ritzy 'hood right below San Vicente Boulevard).

After I shook his big, black, meaty paw, Kerry invited me to go grab an IPA over at the R&D bar on Montana Ave. He was wearing his trademark, food-stained Adidas sweats and size 14 Jordans—a black man-child with a sweet personality mixed with the lack of presence of an absent-minded professor. He was an excellent surgeon, but outside of the OR, he was a bit of a mess. Kerry was constantly losing or misplacing his keys or wallet or whathaveyou. So, while we sat on barstools and he searched his many pockets for his wallet, I paid for his Monkish Hazy, quickly insisting on a Yellowspot for myself before the guardian angel on my shoulder had a chance to open his mouth or shake his head.

"Damn, Baker, thought you were on the wagon, bro?"

"That why you wanted to buy me a beer? You've always been a bad influence, you big bastard." I razzed him.

As the glasses were set in front of us by a distracted bartender, Kerry gave me that cockeyed smile, stuffing some mixed nuts from a community bowl into his mouth, several rolling down his chin onto his Adidas belly.

"Thought you were just gonna drink, you know, a beer or soda," he said, talking with his mouth full, picking the nuts up off his stomach, pushing them past his lips right before chugging his beer, chewing and drinking at the same time. I couldn't watch the stream of IPA dripping down his chin anymore, so I stared at the neat golden liquid in the shiny glass patiently waiting before me, as I studied the way the LED track lighting twinkled through the Irish single-malt.

"Fell off the wagon after El Cajon." I couldn't say any more about that case, other than, "It just never ended, Kerry. Never ends."

Kerry's doctor's inquisitiveness saw right through me, and his curiosity took the better of his social manners (not to be confused with his questionable table manners). He gave my shoulder a reassuring squeeze as he sensed the edginess behind my scruffy face and worn fedora.

"That why you're here? I mean, you just showing up in LA isn't like you, Baker. You hate LA." He drained the rest of his glass. "Unless you're on a case."

Staring at the Irish whiskey, I decided I just wanted to jump into it and not answer any more goddamned questions. So I ignored him and pressed my glass to my lips and let the amber nectar slide over my tongue, relishing the slight burn and savoring the smoky, sweet, acrid paradise that dilated my pupils and shot up to the pleasure center of my addict brain. When I opened my eyes, the glass was empty and I wanted more. Damn I wanted more. All of it. I'd already ordered another before I took a breath.

I saw Kerry's eyes register his mistake, bringing me to this place of whiskey and whathaveyou. He gave me a slight nod and stuffed a handful of nuts into his mouth. Then he turned to me as I quickly finished off the next single malt in seconds, trying to get the bartender's attention for yet another.

"I thought you were a Vicodin addict?"

"I was, 'til the fucking Tylenol they put in it almost killed my liver—not helped by my penchant for grain alcohol. Now I've moved on to a more sensible habit, (besides the whiskey), to Oxycontin!"

I saw Kerry lose his smile. He knew better than to scold me about my addiction. He'd already used that approach for years with no effect. But I didn't like the look he was giving me now.

"What?" I said.

Kerry suddenly turned darker. "I don't think I want you sleeping on my sofa, Baker."

I couldn't tell if the good doctor was serious or not, so I pretended he wasn't and laughed. But when I looked into his eyes, I realized Kerry wanted something more for his generosity, wanted an emotional fee for letting this troubled, flawed, scarred, forty-something, directionless addict, struggling with sorrow and self-hatred, flop on an overpriced Crate and Barrel sectional. The painful cost of which to Dr. Foot, was that my sorrow and pain in some way disallowed Kerry to wallow in his own personal sorrow, which no doubt pissed him off deep down inside his fake jolly personality.

"Why? Why are you here, Haim?"

With my bar tab now soaring well past the lone hundred dollar bill I had, and pushing the limit of my worn credit card, I reached out for Mr. Yellowspot tumbler number three, but Kerry's big hand was there to stop me. I didn't know if it was to keep me from falling further into my personal ditch or if he simply wanted to know the truth. I hoped it was option #2, so I pulled my hand, flipped my Stetson back, took a breath, then grabbed a few nuts, shaking them around in my closed fist.

As *Tequila Sunrise* began to play on the bar's Spotify speaker, I turned to him. "Don't have a choice, do I?"

He stared at me.

By the time I was finished telling him the story, the nuts were crushed into powder and my clenched fist was shaking like it was going through withdrawals...

CHAPTER THREE

"I admire you, Mr. Baker. You're a man of action. A man of fortitude. A worthy adversary." Patterson Nobel smiled.

I watched the old, thin, muscular, rich man with grey Ted Nugent hair pace before me as I strained at the handcuff binding me to the metal table in the interrogation room, knowing Detectives Opp and Ugelstaed were no doubt watching me through the two-way mirror.

Or were they?

Why let a man who killed his own wife and was under suspicion for a host of federal crimes stand unmolested before the restrained private dick that took him down? I hadn't had time to think about that as my rage drenched all my senses. But now I was starting to calm down as I struggled to figure this shit out. And what I was figuring was not smelling good at all.

I knew right away, as soon as my head cleared, what kind of cesspool I was in. I should have guessed. A billionaire in blue collar El Cajon can buy anything. Certainly his freedom. And easily my incarceration.

"But let me not say that," he said.

"—Did you spend even a fucking night in jail?" I spat.

He ignored me. I knew he was escorted out of the ECPD building before he even set foot inside a cell that night. Why was I so stupid? He had Captain Sapper in his pocket. And Sapper ran the El Cajon police with an iron fist—backed by the hard, green cash of Patterson Nobel.

What the hell did Nobel want? Why not just taunt me and go off to rebuild his demonic empire of child and teen trafficking while paying a judge and jury to have me rot in jail? Why would a busy billionaire spend even a moment, face to face with the very guy who single-handedly cost him millions, if not billions?

As if to answer my flying thoughts, he smiled his thick lips almost wistfully.

"I'd almost say you have the mettle to be a partner, an associate. And if I may say, perhaps, in some way, a friend, Mr. Baker.

"Are you fucking kidding me?"

"Not at all. You like fast automobiles, as do I. We have the same taste in women. And besides, I prefer friends who are contrarians, who are resourceful. Men such as yourself are a rare find, these days." He said that as if I were some jungle animal he'd captured on safari and brought back to his compound to admire behind thick, bulletproof glass. I answered him with a smirk and a middle finger from my free hand.

He ignored my gesture as he stared into my eyes, as if boring into my soul. For some reason he lost a bit of his smile.

"But you're also a romantic, and that makes you soft in some ways. I don't mean physically, obviously," as he rubbed his bruised chin. "But from where you sit you cannot, ever, it seems, see the Truth. The Truth of those above us. The truth of our fate. The truth of Being."

"The "truth" is you fucking set me up." I spat.

Patterson Nobel finally sat down at the table and crossed his legs, showing off his crimson, hand-made cowboy boots. He opened his mauve leather sport coat, pulling out a gold metal case, and with ritual perfection, flipped open the top to reveal 20 black Treasurer London Luxury Cigarettes. Hard to find a more expensive hit of lung-filling tobacco anywhere in the world.

He put the 18k gold leaf tip to his mouth, pressed a small metal torch, and lit the noir tip. He sucked in a mouthful of nicotine, then strolled around the table to get within striking distance of me. He pulled the exclusive cigarette from his moist lips and began to approach me with his hand, wanting to put it, no doubt, in between my own lips. My squinting eyes told him to reconsider that bit of homoerotica, so he instead placed it in between the fingers of my free hand, knowing he'd piqued my curiosity and quelled my anger, at least for the moment—knowing a blue collar stooge like myself would rather sample the rare experience of sucking down a $60 cigarette instead of trying to take another swing at the old man.

And he would be right. Besides, I knew I'd eventually have my go at Patterson Nobel. But for now I was tugging sweet, aged, English high tobacco into my eager working class lungs, marveling at the shiny gold foil and dark black paper.

"I have a proposition, Mr. Baker."

"Fuck off, Pat." I quipped as I took another drag.

He smiled. Got up, moved to the two-way mirror. Staring out at whomever was watching. Or not watching. I mean, no way would ECPD allow anyone to smoke in this pristine, barely month's old interrogation room, replete with a red "No Smoking" sign above the door. No. Standing there was a billionaire king who had all the power. And I was a fucking pawn whether I wanted to believe it or not.

"I want you to think back to our last encounter, Mr. Baker. Painful as that may be, for both of us. You see, my lovely wife was murdered..."

"Yeah, I watched you blow a two-inch hole in her heart with a fucking 500 Magnum revolver."

He turned to me.

"Why Mr. Baker, was it not YOU who was wielding my gun when the police arrived? Just in time, I might add, to rescue me from your murderous intentions."

Now I was really pissed. I stood up best as I could, attempting to toss the cigarette at him—before changing my mind—why waste a fucking gold-tipped cigarette? I instead threw hate at him from my bloodshot eyes as I squinted and sucked in some more golden nicotine.

He wisely stayed out of reach as he studied me and my thirst for revenge. He didn't have to say anything else, because he knew I'd already figured it all out.

Of course he'd framed me for the murder of Mrs. Nobel. Yes, I was holding the gun on him that night, ready blow a hole through his smug face to match the one that killed his wife. And had Detective Opp not rushed in to stop me, Patterson Nobel would be decomposing right now instead of making me wish I had about 20 tiny white pills of Oxy to thwart the dreadful realization now making its way down my spine, right to my sphincter.

Even though I saw him murder Mrs. Nobel, of course it was my word against his. And what person on an El Cajon jury was gonna believe me? I mean, who wins this case, Haim Baker or Patterson Nobel? A drug addicted dick with a dark past and an overworked public defender, or an upstanding citizen of the community who no doubt gives plenty to local charities and the police athletic league and retains the best law firm in San Diego county? I was fucked. He knew it, I knew it, and he knew I knew it.

"You see, you have a problem, Mister Baker."

I glared at him, simmering. What else could I do, my mind was flying for answers—and coming up empty. I was indeed fucked. I stared at the cigarette in my hand, feeling it burn my fingers.

"But I may have a solution. A solution for both of us." He opened his case of gold tipped treasures and lit one for himself. He relaxed, just for effect, and drew in the tobacco like he had all the time in the world.

Finally, through a ring of smoke he whispered, "As I said, I admire you and your rather... unique talents."

I whispered back, "Get these cuffs off, Pat, and I'll gladly show you what my talents can do."

In my mind I was already going through the exact way I was going to kill this bastard. I'd kick out his knee til it cracked, grab his neck and twist it and squeeze til it was broken and he was dead. Or maybe I'd just put a lead slug into his cold heart. But hopefully, in my fantasy, a bit of blood would leak out of his mouth an he'd taste the iron tinge of my caustic revenge before he died and went to hell.

But he knew what I was thinking and was quick to put a stop to any more of my heroic fantasies.

"Mister Baker, I'll be frank. I'm the only chance you have at avoiding a rather nasty prison sentence. You see, I... I am your savior."

He sat on the table, easily within reach, just to make his point. "Hurting me will only destroy you. And as you are no doubt self-destructive, I doubt you are that unintelligent."

I sucked in more smoke like I had all the time in the world, blowing a cloud into his smug face.

"Why don't you tell me what the hell is going on, Patty? Why you're here, fucking with me, plying me with gold cigarettes and more of your billion-dollar-bullshit?"

He took a moment before he spoke.

I immediately noticed something was wrong with him. And it wasn't the smoke in his face.

Patterson Nobel's demeanor had changed, just a bit, but I saw it. There was an unconscious flinch as he spoke.

"You see, I too, have a problem, Mister Baker. A rather serious problem, thanks to you."

There was a flash behind his steel eyes.

I knew what it was that twitched within that normally calm and assured visage. Something I'd never seen from this man who had it all. The most powerful man in East County. The King of San Diego.

What I saw in the face of Patterson Nobel was *fear.* Real, genuine fear.

I finally started to relax. This was getting good.

"So what's the deal?" I quipped.

Nobel paused, then gazed at me, right in the eyes. "I require your services, Mister Baker."

"My services?" I replied, taken aback as I blew more light grey smoke his way.

"Mister Baker," Patterson Nobel said, "I need you to find someone." He paused a moment, then his face dropped with serious emphasis:

"I need you to find... El Dorado."

El Dorado...

I had heard that name whispered on the streets for years, from New York to LA and places in between. To the underworld, to the street people, to the criminal class, *El Dorado* was a legendary figure. A ghost, a demon, a killer, perhaps the Devil himself—a real-life Keyser Soze. To even speak the name risked having your tongue ripped out by unseen hands. According to underworld mythology, those who were unfortunate enough to lay eyes on El Dorado had their pupils cut out. To touch him risked your hands being cut off by his legendary blade, forged as they say, by Satan himself. *El Dorado,* the folktale goes, is unknowable, unseeable, and untouchable. To those on the street, the name sparks terror, and I could sense that terror hidden behind the formerly smug demeanor from the man concealed behind a puff of dissipating cigarette smoke, thinking I wouldn't see.

I sat back and relaxed. I now knew I had the upper hand. At least for now. If El Dorado was bullseyeing Patterson Nobel, the old man may only have days to live.

Again, he seemed to answer my thoughts.

"You have one week to find El Dorado, Mister Baker. Seven days."

He inhaled the nicotine from his cigarette, then after staring at the black and gold treasure, calmly crushed it on the table, smashing the gold foil end until it split in half. He finally exhaled and looked me in the eye.

"And when you find El Dorado, I need you to kill him."

CHAPTER FOUR

I woke up in a big, comfy bed, high off the floor. This really threw me off because I thought to myself, "wasn't I supposed to be sleeping on a couch?" Maybe Kerry really didn't want me on the couch? This certainly wasn't his living room.

I looked up and saw some sort of fresco on the domed, yellow ceiling—angels and flowers and shit like that. I knew Kerry pretty well, and though he made about $300k as a doctor, he had a plethora of court fees and tax problems, so about half that income went to taxes and IRS and Franchise Tax garnishment. And the five mil settlement had been gone for a few years now. No, free-spending Kerry could never afford to have an Italian fresco like this put on his ceiling. Nor would he. He'd spend it on hookers and food if he had the cash.

My gaze tilted down to a man in a picture frame—wearing the stern-looking face of mild disappointment mixed with a bit of hope—as long as you played your cards right. At least that's how I interpreted that face. It was the face of Jesus.

Christ, what the hell did I get myself into? I was alone, naked, and clueless, and was now being judged by Jesus himself. I looked over next to me—the Egyptian cotton bedsheets were flipped back and the beige MyPillow was indented. At some point, I wasn't alone in this bed, I deduced. But who or whom had been next to me?

A cool breeze tickled my face as I watched the billowing sheer curtains dancing in the wind from an open window. I sat up and turned to put my feet on the floor, but that rattled my head like a sledgehammer. How much of that damn Yellowspot did I polish off? My brain felt like a John Bonham drum solo. I put my foot down onto the soft carpet and immediately felt a slimy squish.

A used condom.

Hopefully it was mine. First thing I did was feel my ass. I was praying I'd been partying with a woman, but knowing how I am when I get on the booze, anything was possible.

I was happy to find my anus was as uptight as ever, and I breathed a sigh of relief.

I found my clothes spread out on the floor and quickly checked out my sport coat and t-shirt. I breathed out more relief when I saw, lying over my shoes, my aged brown leather shoulder holster and my black, sinister looking H&K Mk. 23. I quickly checked the mag—none of the rounds were fired and there was still a Fort Scott copperhead .45 bullet in the chamber. Thank you, God. I can't tell you the number of times I've found bullets belonging to me in walls, beds, pets and people during my many bouts of blackout buffoonery. And now that I was carrying those new tumbling defense rounds, the likelihood of any animals on four legs or two surviving an errant, drunken, stupid, stupor shot from me were very low. Unlike hollowpoints, these little spun copper killers begin to tumble once they hit soft tissue, increasing the wound channel exponentially. Add that to a giant .45 calibre hole, and you get blown-off appendages, shredded arteries and mangled vital organs. No, you don't want to get hit by one of these bad boys.

I pulled on my patented old hipster private dick uniform: Calvin Klein undies, vintage Rock and Republic jeans, a John Vavartos v-neck tee, and an old wool Hugo Boss jacket, all in shades of black and grey of course. I slipped into my blood red Campers and tapped on my fedora, looking in the mirror, catching my three-day's growth of cool scruffiness until my vision began to blur.

Like the heavy recoil of my Mk. 23, my head was pounding from a massive hangover. Or was it? Maybe it was fucking opiate withdrawal again. And then I remembered: I checked the pocket of my sport coat—and there they were, my beautiful little white pills. I quickly dosed 5 tiny Oxies. Then came to my senses and shook five more into my dry, hangover mouth. I couldn't swallow so I ran to the kitchen and drank a gulp of H2O right out of the faucet.

As I leaned on the counter so I wouldn't fall, waiting for the feelgood to kick in, I saw a note on the little Pottery Barn kitchen table:

"Gone to work. Call me. Thank's for last night, it was beautiful!!!!—Luv Jessie."

Now, it wasn't just that I had no idea who this Jessie person was or what her phone number was or the fact that she spelled love "LUV," or even that she used a heart to dot her "I," but the woman I'd apparently just slept with actually drew a series of emojis after her name. *Emojis!* She fucking drew them with a colored pencil. What a psychopath!

Jessie must have been some sort of wannabe artist, because she took the time to craft a set of lips, an eggplant, a taco, a firecracker and a happy face with a wagging tongue and spiral eyes. What the fuck!?

I tossed down the note and stomped to the door, passing the living room. There I saw a portable stripper pole, and realized why I must have came home with this woman. Maybe I <u>would</u> see her again?

As I thought more about Jessie, I was suddenly feeling a little better about this emoji-stripper-girl. She was fit. She was artsy. And more importantly, she seemed to like me after booze and sex, which was a rare occurrence in my experience.

As I thought about Jessie, I began to feel warm, like I was standing in a soothing hot tub. My headache disappeared and a smile rode my face. No, it wasn't Jessie or her stripper pole. It was the Oxy. Those porcelain pills had finally kicked in and suddenly I could think again.

As my mind started to clear, I vaguely began to piece together the disparate images from last night—sort of like someone tossing down Polaroid pictures on a coffee table. I couldn't remember the entire flow of the story, as I only saw bits and pieces.

Oh yeah, I remembered now—Jessie was a good-looking brunette with a big nose, short hair and a twinkling smile. She twinkled alright. No wonder she used emojis. She was about thirty and wore a short, form-fitting burgundy dress with matching high heels. I must have shared drinks with her until Kerry got fed up and left, driving his new, dented Kia back home, leaving me to figure out how to get back to his place on my own. I wouldn't have blamed him. And since Jessie barely had B cup breasts, he'd never be interested in a threesome. Can't remember if I offered or not.

I figured I'd schedule an Uber to get me to Kerry's, but when I walked down the stairs and outside of Jessie's condo, I found myself just below that bougie, overpriced, Farms Deli-Meat Market off 21st and Montana. Heck, I was only about five blocks away from Kerry's villa, so I decided to walk.

It's always fun to stroll by North of Montana mansions, staring into the windows at the stay-at-home moms or paid-off divorcées in their personal pilates and yoga studios, with their white Mercedes or silver Teslas parked in expansive driveways, hosting the ever-present construction and remodeling crews, made up mostly of illegal immigrants—huffing tile and new fixtures and lumber and plaster for daily under-the-table cash from overpaid contractors sitting pretty in their overpriced homes over in in El Segundo and Huntington Beach.

It didn't take me that long, maybe twenty minutes. But when I finally got near Kerry's place, something was very wrong...

CHAPTER FIVE

As I approached the long driveway where my brown Saab and Kerry's white Kia were sitting, I noticed right away it was eerily quiet. Too quiet. Kerry always had CNN or ESPN blaring on his big screen over the sofa in the living room, right next to the front door (which is why I wasn't happy with the couch sleeping choice).

My spidey senses starting ringing in my ears along with my tinnitus. Something just wasn't right. I've learned to trust my instincts, and after 20 years of dealing with low-lifes and bad guys as a so-called "investigator," I've had plenty of experiences to earn that trust.

I waited for Kerry to come out and greet me as he always does, but nothing was stirring in that house. I stepped up to the Saab and saw the door wasn't shut all the way. Could I have left it like that? I didn't lock the car because the net worth was so high in this 'hood that there were plenty of better options for a car thief than a bullet-riddled fifty-year-old relic. No, someone had gone through my vehicle. I opened the door and looked inside—it all seemed kosher. Then I popped the trunk and checked my suitcase. Didn't look like anyone went through it. Everything was still in place and all my clothes were still rolled up. No, nobody had looked through my trunk. I thought everything was untouched until I opened the glove box. My registration and insurance card were slightly out of place. Shit. Someone was IDing me, and now they knew for certain I was here. Shit. I quickly looked up at Kerry's security camera. The lens was covered in black spray paint. Shit...

I had my gun in my hand in seconds, right before I tried the front door. Unlocked. I didn't know whether to yell for Kerry or to remain silent. I figured no one had heard me so far, so I decided to go the quiet route and clear the house, room-by-room, assuming the bad guys might still be there. It took me about ten minutes to hit every room and closet and doorway, gun ready, until I reached Kerry's bedroom.

When I quickly, silently opened the door, I nearly pulled the trigger of my HK out of reflex:

Blood had splattered like a Jackson Pollock painting all over the east wall, with a smattering of small holes mixing with Kerry's collection of fist punches, making a sort of violent, crimson modern art expression next to Kerry's poster bed. Kerry's pajamaed body was slumped on a chair in the middle of the room, with his duct-taped hands keeping what was left of him from sliding onto the blood-stained rug. He was missing three of his fingers on his right hand, neatly cut off just below the knuckles, and blood was staining his groin area. I didn't want to look there, or anywhere else for that matter. I knew my friend had been brutally tortured. Tortured to give me up. And knowing Dr. Foot's ironic fear of blood and pain, Kerry would have talked as soon as the bad guy pulled out a pair of bolt cutters—if not before. But my friend was tortured anyway, probably just for sport. And when the killer was finished with his fun, he pulled out a short, pump action 12 gauge, maybe a Mossberg Shockwave, and blew off the top of Kerry's head, leaving only his bottom jaw and a flap of his left ear.

This told me Kerry was murdered by a pro, but not just any killer—this was a Cartel assassin. A *Sicario*. The kind of psycho that takes pleasure in death and torture because they're trained as small kids to do so, taken from their family and raised by the Cartel to be immune from empathy, to be cold killers with no remorse and no feeling. Those that don't cut it or show too much humanity are quickly, viciously murdered by the others, so only the very deadly, the very evil, remain.

And this guy wanted to know where I was because I was his target. All Kerry could have told him was that I was staying on his couch for a week and was on a case, and that he'd left me at R&D last night with a brown-haired chick with short hair, small breasts and a big nose...

Shit. I had to warn Jessie before the Sicario found her!

I checked my phone, hoping Jessie'd given me her number or had texted me, which she hadn't. I jumped into the Saab and got the hell out of there, making sure to rub down my prints and erase any evidence of my presence before I left.

I figured the killer came in the early morning, with the least chance that anyone would see him. Probably wore a mask and a backpack to carry his shotgun and torture tools, and I guessed that the guy would have avoided or disabled most of Kerry's security cameras. I was amazed he didn't take Kerry's phone, which was sitting pretty on the dresser, still hooked up to its charger. I had quickly grabbed it, knowing the security video would be on it in an app and maybe I'd get a look at the guy who murdered my pal. I'd find out how to unlock Kerry's Galaxy later. Right now I had to save Jessie.

CHAPTER SIX

It took me all of six minutes to drive to Jessie's condo. I didn't have her keys so I picked the lock to the front lobby door, ran upstairs to pick the lock to her door that I'd just left less than an hour ago. But I didn't have to.

The door was open. I was too late. Or too lucky.

I again pulled my gun, but I needn't have. The place was ransacked and the killer was long gone. I was either one step behind this guy or he was one step behind me. I checked out the window. Didn't spot any strange vehicles or people waiting to whack me. So I had a little bit of time.

I had no idea how to contact Jessie, so I started hitting the speed dials on her landline until I hit jackpot and the Gen Z voice of a young secretary answered.

"Tieger and Anderson Architects, how may I help you?"

"Can I speak to Jessie, please?" I was hoping this company was small enough to only have one Jessie, since I didn't know her last name.

"Jessie who?"

"You know, the pretty brunette with a cute bob?"

"You mean Jessie Debost?"

"Yes!" I guessed. "I was on a date with her last night, and wanted to say hi, if it's okay?"

The young secretary giggled knowingly. Obviously she'd heard all about Jessie's adventure at R&D Bar And Grill on Montana Avenue last night. "You must be Harry, hang on."

"Harry" was the name I usually gave girls I didn't plan on spending more than one or two nights with. Especially when I was drunk. It was just far easier to say "Harry" than to explain my first name, especially to perky brunette shiksas. I had grown damn tired of the usual "What kind of name is 'Haim'?" bullshit. Besides, if I actually got on with the chick, then I could tell her only my best friends call me Harry, which would make her feel special. That would usually squeeze another week or two out of the usual doomed relationship before it all fell apart, as usual.

"Hi, Harry!" A chipper voice came on the line. "You got my note! Beautiful."

I got right down to business.

"Listen, Jessie, we have a problem."

"We do? No we don't. I had a great time. Just don't tell me you're married!?"

"Yes. No. I'm not married but I'm very serious. There's someone trying to find me, someone dangerous."

"Dangerous?"

"Yes. A Sicario. And he's already broken into your home. You need to get out of work right away and get yourself somewhere safe. Do you have a friend or relative you can stay with for about a week?"

After a quick pause, she suddenly burst into laughter, which threw me off, then said, "Harry you are sooooo funny. I luv you!"

This was the type of gal who threw around the terms "luv" and "beautiful" like they were expletives. I felt like I was talking to Amy Grant at one of her mall concerts in the '80s.

"I'm serious, Jessie. You're in danger."

"Whaaaaat?" I could hear her tone lose some of the perkiness.

"Remember my friend I was with last night, Kerry? The black guy?"

"Oh yeah, sure. He was a doctor and had to rush off to the hospital or something... Hey, did he just say that so I'd have to take you home?! You little devil!"

"Kerry was murdered this morning."

I felt the wind go out of the conversation.

"Murdered?" She said quietly as it all began to sink in.

"I'm a private investigator, Jessie. You must have seen my gun and holster under my jacket."

"That wasn't real. It was a fake, right?"

"Fake? A fake gun? Why would I carry a fake gun???" I couldn't believe this woman. "Listen, Jessie, a very dangerous person wants to kill me, and if you hadn't rushed off to work and I hadn't left and found Kerry's body, we'd both be dead right now."

Silence. She then began to sound like she was going to cry.

"What, what should I do? Oh my God... Did you call the police?"

"No. They can't protect you from someone like this. We need to get you safe. Now listen closely. I need you to tell your boss you have a family emergency or you don't feel well or whatever, but tell them you need to leave for the day, maybe more. Can you do that?"

"I guess."

"Good. Tell them you're going home. But don't actually go home. I mean it, not even for a change of clothes or a toothbrush. Go to Target or Goodwill and grab whatever you need, but <u>do not</u> go home.

"But..."

I'm serious. I want you to find a safe house. A friend, or..."

"My brother has a cabin in Big Bear."

"Perfect. Go there, but do not tell anyone, I mean don't tell *anyone* where you've gone. Not even your brother. Do you understand?"

She paused. Then, "I think so." Her voice quivered.

"Jessie, are you sure? This is very important. Anyone you tell is at risk of being hurt. Hurt badly. Probably killed. You too"

"—Killed!?"

"Yes. You need to stay away for a week."

"A, a, week?"

"Yes."

"Oh my," she stammered. Her mind rushing to catch up with the fact that she was fucked, and not in a good way.

She paused to take in a yoga breath or something to calm herself. Then Jessie seemed to get angry. I didn't blame her. In fact I expected it. Hell, I almost got her killed. Still might.

"What is this? What's this all about, Harry?"

"It has to do with a case I'm working on. That's all I can tell you."

"This is NOT alright, Harry!"

"I know, I know. I'm sorry. Sorry about this." I tried to sound compassionate. "And by the way, my name's not Harry. It's Haim."

I heard her suck in a breath. Like she was just punked. No doubt she wanted to tell me off, wanted to throw me some real expletives. I figured I wasn't going to get another "Luv" or "Beautiful" coming out of those thin, burgundy-tinted lips.

I waited while she contemplated what she was going to spew over the phoneline, as I made ready my usual apology—that I was generally a fuck up, a cunt or whatever, and yes, she was better off without me, yada yada yada. I'd already come to terms with the fact that I'd never see Jessie again. Just hoped it was because I was an asshole, and not because she was dead.

But then I heard her voice, the tone not quite as angry as I was expecting. I found myself quickly hanging up the phone after she said,

"What kind of name is 'Haim'?"

CHAPTER SEVEN

I needed answers. I was sick of innocent people getting hurt because of my fuck-ups. And having a good pal of mine getting his head blown off really stuck in my craw. "El Dorado," whoever the fuck that was, already knew I was here in LA looking for him. I contemplated bagging the job and driving back to San Diego and putting a bullet in Nobel's head. But Pat was certain to expect that. Besides, Nobel promised to convince Captain Sapper to drop all charges against me if I'd take out El Dorado. Killing Patterson Nobel was a life sentence in a maximum security prison. I had to play that asshole's game whether I liked it or not. At least for the time being. And the game had changed now that Dorado's guy just killed my sweet friend Kerry. I was pissed and hellbent on seriously ending the life of the biggest crime lord and human trafficker in North America—the overlord of Patterson Nobel and the leader of all the other evil cartel bosses from Canada to Mexico.

Kerry and Jessie and me were all just insects to be squashed by the big players kicking over the ant hill has they fought one another for dominance. But I was tired of being stepped on. I was sick of being low man on the totem and decided I needed to climb the pole to get on top of these fuckers and do my own kicking.

El Dorado might scare the shit out of those who make their living stealing and killing and fucking over the rest of us, but I'm the guy who happily stands in their way and I was getting really tired of this shit.

I was gonna find this Dorado guy. Let him try to burn out my eyes or cut off my hands. Go ahead and try, mutherfucker. I was gonna kill that bastard, and then I was sure as shit gonna put my fist or a bullet through the smug face of Patterson Nobel.

I just needed a plan. I needed to talk to Ricky Rizzo.

Ricky was a low-level mobster from Bay Ridge. Back in Brooklyn, Ricky was known by his given street name, "Ratso" because you could never, ever trust Ratso Rizzo.

When Frankie Cannazzaro paid him 25k to reveal when Silvio Bongino was gonna be visiting his cousin in Philly, Ratso then squeezed 30k from Silvio to warn the big guy that Frankie was gonna hit him. Cannazzaro got whacked the next day, which started that big mob war. Bongino got it a week later when Frankie's boys somehow knew Silvio was gonna spend the night with his mistress, who also got hit. Legend has it that it was Mrs. Bongino that gave Silvio up. But I know it was Ratso, who somehow stayed on the sunny side of the grass with an extra 55k in his pocket. That was coincidently about the same time Ricky Ratso decided to make haste and ditch the increasingly unhealthy mob intrigue in Brooklyn and move across the country to the new world and easy money of La La Land.

Ricky Rizzo was a lanky Sicilian with long stringy black hair and a fu-manchu mustache that fell down below his mouth so you couldn't see his lips or bad teeth, and, along with his shaded Sicilian skin, his dark eyes were rimmed with drooping eyelids that made him look perpetually sleepy. But he almost never slept. Ricky Rizzo had a penchant for meth, coke, angel dust, amp, or anything that could keep him going, keep him in the game. And for The Rat to win the game, Ricky "Ratso" had to know what everyone else was doing. Ratso thrived on information.

Now he was in LA, getting the dirt on the Hollywood types, playing the blackmail game when he wasn't working as a fixer for some of the dirtier producers and agents and mobsters. Ever wonder why a certain actor or actress or director suddenly decides to do this or that movie or TV show? Sometimes it's a deal they can't refuse. That's the world and purview of Ratso Rizzo.

I figured if anyone knew where I could find El Dorado, it would be my old friend. But I'd already called Ratso several times and got a full mailbox with no return message. I added a bunch of texts without reply as well. I hoped he wasn't dead, which was likely, since Ratso had more than a handful of enemies. I also knew there was more than a good chance that it was Ricky who maybe gave me up to El Dorado and the Sicario. But I didn't care. I needed to destroy the legend of El Dorado, and then destroy Patterson Nobel—all without facing a life sentence. I'd sort out the bodies afterwards. But since Ratso was currently incommunicado, I went to plan B.

By now it was evening, about 6pm, and it was still a balmy eighty degrees and unusually humid for SoCal. And after making sure I wasn't tailed, I drove the Saab down steamy Hollywood Boulevard, never getting out of second gear, pumping the clutch and rumbling through the stop-and-go taillights of busses, taxis, Ubers, tourists in rentals, and waiters/actors/models/writers/whatever on their way to work the late shift—those determined denizens that populate the City of Angels, spending their days auditioning and dreaming of stardom and success while slaving away at night to pay the exorbitant rent, high interest car loans and overpriced drugs that you just have to have when you live in La-La-Land.

I looked over at the Walk of Fame. By now the tourists were mostly gone and the street people were taking over. Hobos, hookers, trannies, dealers, and pimps strolled the sidewalks and streets and lurked in the doorways.

I saw a guy dressed like Spiderman getting a blowjob from Wonder Woman in the shadows of the Egyptian theater. Two teens were shooting up near the Wax Museum and a plethora of homeless zombies were pushing or pulling their piles of personal trash in shopping carts and bike trailers, shuffling down the Street of Dreams to nowhere.

Finally I hit Hollywood and Vine and pulled over into a red zone. There's no street parking here within a two mile radius, and that's on purpose. The city makes a huge cash flow from the crazy expensive parking lots and on ticketed and towed vehicles due to the incoherent no-parking signs. I knew this ahead of time, so I purchased a fake handicapped sign for my rearview, hoping that Johnny Cop wouldn't look too closely at it.

I heard Willis before I saw him.

"Star maps! Staaaaar maaaaps!" He yelled at anyone and everyone. "Find the homes of the famous stars. Even ones who aren't famous!"

Willis carried a stack of photocopied yellow cardboard maps and pushed his fake, outdated directions at anyone who ventured close. Most people steered away from the weird dude, or ignored Willis completely.

I got out of the Saab and walked over. "How much?"

"Twenty bucks, buddy." He didn't look at me and kept barking "Staaaar maps!"

"I remember when they were a buck." I said.

He turned. I wasn't sure if he recognized me yet or not.

"I remember when they were two-bits. I, th-think." He said.

Willis was about 50, but looked older and plenty grizzled. He was one of those guys on the spectrum but could function enough to work and eat and dream like the rest of us with his stutter and his weird personae being the only apparent clues that he was a special-ed guy. He was thin except for a beer-belly, and wore wild, reddish, curly, balding hair, a hooked nose, and thick glasses that looked like they were purchased from a dime store thirty years ago. His clothes were dirty but he had a brand new Marlboro hanging from his lip.

I slipped him a $20. He tried to hand me a map but I waved him off.

"I need information, Willis."

He pocketed the money.

"Gotta light? They don't trust me with fire."

I pulled out my zippo and hit his cig. He pulled in a quick puff. Let it out and coughed. Then he sat down on the dirty curb.

So did I.

"Since when do you smoke?"

"Since I got these." He showed me several sealed packs of Marlboros in his coat pocket. Probably stolen. "Sell ya one for ten bucks?"

I shook my head. How could I ever go back to domestics when I've tasted those gold-tipped Brit Treasures?

"How you doing Willis?" I asked.

He blew out more smoke, replete with more coughs.

"Been five years, two months and eleven days and twelve hours. Where've you been, Baker?"

Willis had a photographic memory and was a wiz with numbers, probably part of his spectrum thing. "You were supposed to buy me a beer." He added.

Shit, that was over five years ago.

"I'll buy you a beer, Willis. You want some Coors?"

"I, I d-don't believe you a-anymore." He pulled out some doublemint from his pocket and chewed it along with the tip of the Marlboro. He glanced up at me and generally looked sad.

"I, I missed you, Baker."

I felt for the guy, I really did, but he was a nutjob and well, he was *Willis*. He was prone to rants and crazy talk and thanks to drugs, both prescribed and purchased on the street, he could come off as crazy if you didn't know him, and maybe even if you did. Probably why he didn't have many friends.

"I was on a case. Then I was on a bender. A long bender. Here, buy yourself a six pack." I gave him another $20 out of guilt. He quickly pocketed it. Willis was already up and walking away. I shot up and followed.

"Can we talk?" I wasn't sure if I'd just been conned or not.

"N-no." He rambled.

"Come on, buddy. Just like old times."

Willis might be non compos mentis, but he always had an ear to the ground. And if you caught him in a lucid moment, he could give you answers to just about anything.

"I need your help, Willis."

"No." He said as he looked down at the broken sidewalk. "You d-don't understand."

"What is it?"

Suddenly a glaze went over his eyes, and when he looked up at me, it was like I was talking to different person.

"They're trying to keep me out of the Screen Actor's Guild." He murmured.

"What?"

"They're using black magic."

"Black magic? You sure you haven't already drunk a six pack, Willis?"

Willis continued as if I wasn't even there, rambling on to an unseen audience.

"Charlie Sheen. Charlie Sheen and N-Nicky Sixx. They're using black magic to keep me out of the Guild because they want to kill me because they know I'm Scottish Royalty."

"Huh?" This was weird, even coming from Willis.

Suddenly Willis threw some of his maps like they were frisbees, spinning around, looking for unseen assassins lurking in the shadows and the sky.

"The Crown. English Crown is not legitimate and they know it. You see they have to go through Scottish Royalty to be legitimate royalty which is why Prince Harry married Meghan Markel who is Scottish Royalty, because they want a back door to Scottish Royalty and the Screen Actor's Guild knows it too. They use black magic. They always use black magic but the cops don't know anything about magic anymore since it isn't illegal anymore but I have white magic. They want to keep me out of SAG. They know I'm related to King George. They, they destroy people with their magic but I have white magic to keep them back but they're following me all the time, the helicopters and planes flying above my, my apartment, and, and Charlie knows..."

I was perplexed. "What the fuck are you talking about?"

"They know. They know who I am, that I'm royalty, and they're trying to stop me. Charlie Sheen, he hates me..."

Willis trailed off, as if he'd suddenly run out of things to say. Then he looked over at me with those crazy eyes. But before he could start up on another rant, I stopped him.

"Willis." I said emphatically as I put my hand on his shoulder.

"Y-Yeah?"

"I need to find El Dorado."

The glaze quickly went away and Old Willis came back.

But Willis was back with *fear*. Willis was downright terrified when I said that name.

"W- What did you s, say????!"

"I need to find El Dorado. Can you help me?"

"NO. Oh no. No, no, no, no, no!"

Willis began to sprint away like I'd just become a half-Jew version of Charlie Sheen. I chased after him as he ran down Vine Street, stomping on each Walk of Fame plaque, as if to punish the SAG members for his delusion, pushing away the errant tourist or street person to get to each square until a big black, shirtless, homeless man took offense to this scrawny white guy getting in his personal space, and shoved Willis to the ground.

I picked up Willis, who looked at me with wild eyes, then over at the fat, sweaty black man, thinking this was finally his feared assassin.

"S-see, they're after me!"

"Fuck you up shithead," the homeless man barked.

"Leave him alone pal, he's not right in the head." I tried to dissuade the guy who was wearing the typical homeless uniform of bare, sweaty torso with stained, low-riding grey sweatpants that showed off his dirty Walmart underwear, and worn, ripped basketball shoes. But he had his sights trained on Willis—assuming this skinny white dude was an easy target for his delusional anger.

The big fatman took a step towards the petrified Willis, who stumbled and fell back. As soon as the Goliath took a swing, I stepped in, blocked it, grabbing his fist, twisting it behind his back in an armlock. Again I tried to calm him down.

"Let it go, brother."

"I ain't your fucking brother, whitey!"

"Why's everything about race these days?"

"You don't like me cuz I'm black."

"No, I don't like you cuz you're fat and you smell."

This guy had finally had enough of me.

"Fuck you, cracker!"

He spun around and tried to smack me with his other hand. I moved in close, blocked it, hit him with a knee to the groin and an elbow to the face, then another to his nose. Blood begun to gush from his nostrils. But that only increased his anger and the 350 pound, dirty, smelly monster suddenly jumped on me, pinning me to the ground under his fat stomach.

"Hey!" I said, as his large man-boob quickly flapped into place and plastered against my open mouth. "Black lives matter!" I mumbled under massive boob-flesh, trying not to sound too sarcastic.

That just made him more pissed off as he screamed at me while blood dribbled down from his nose onto my forehead.

"I'ma gonna kill you honkey!"

I squirmed enough to get my mouth away from his boob, but wound up getting my nose stuck in the crack of his sweaty underarm. His B.O. was beyond bad. My turn to scream.

"Aaaaarrrrghhh! Next time you steal some Twinkies from 7/11, make sure to grab some deodorant too, will ya!?"

"I'ma make you shuddup!"

"No, you're gonna make me *throw* up!" I coughed.

He obviously didn't take to my comments regarding his personal hygiene, so he began fishing around underneath his torso, trying to find my neck with his paws to squeeze the whiteness and insolence out of me.

I avoided his hands by squirming around, also attempting to miss the crimson drops rolling off his nose, while trying to hold my breath as not to smell his sweaty, overwhelming stench.

Finally, I couldn't take it anymore. I gathered all my strength and gave the fatman the hardest headbutt I could muster—right into his battered nose.

He reared up and screamed in pain. That gave me just enough space to wiggle out from under his blubber, thank God.

I stood up and tried to catch my breath, bending over at my knees—wanting to breathe in anything other than his potpourri of putrid odors. Even the concrete air from the dirty Hollywood Boulevard sidewalk would suffice.

As I was huffing and puffing, I noticed him wallow a bit on the sidewalk like a beached wale, then somehow roll back onto his feet.

Light-headed, I gasped with an open mouth trying to fill my body up with oxygen. But when I looked up, he was already barging towards me like an angry hippo with murderous intent.

Shit. I stumbled back until I ran into an old Chevy Impala. I was trapped. I looked around for an escape—but I was fucked, as the stinky, sweaty, obese African American "unhoused person" barreled towards me, gaining speed with savage, bloodshot eyes, screaming through his gapped front teeth.

Thinking quick, I reached back and grabbed the Impala's antennae, snapping it off. As soon as he got in range, I began using it as a whip, striking they guy's hands and face and bulbous body until the welted fat hobo couldn't take it anymore and finally tumbled away, yelling incoherently, already targeting some bewildered USC coeds for his wrath.

I hate LA.

As I tossed the antenna, got back my breath, and picked up and punched my fedora back into shape, I looked everywhere, but my old pal

Willis was long gone. There was a circle of gawkers who were already trailing off into the night, but the person I needed to talk to was nowhere to be found. Fuck.

Off to plan C. Except I had no plan C.

But that didn't matter, because after the blue flashing lights scared away the last of the street people, a blinding spotlight suddenly hit my face...

CHAPTER EIGHT

For the second time in as many days, I found myself handcuffed in a police interrogation room, albeit not in the new, pristine, freshly painted version in El Cajon. No, I was in the infamous dank, dirty, Hollywood Division station, where a century of smelly hobos, prostitutes, trannies, dealers, rapists, thieves and killers had passed through, each one adding to the dirt and dust and urine and feces and cum that litter the floors and walls here—stuff that lingers even after the contracted janitors do their tepid weekly cleanings—giving this claustrophobic place its bad mojo. The room smelled like must, mold, piss and bleach. I wanted out, but the two stone-faced detectives across from me had other ideas.

Detective Hazard was maybe fifty, and looked like he might be an ex-marine, with a taught workout body, square jaw, flat-top, and angry eyes surrounded by the bags and lines and creases that come with years of stress and lack of sleep. He never smiled and seemed to take everything far too seriously. His partner, Detective Sanchez, was a thin, quiet hispanic female wearing a pony-tail and minimal makeup. She was younger than Hazard by maybe twenty years. Both displayed badges from the City of Santa Monica. I knew right away this had nothing to do with the sidewalk dustup with the fatman. I put my cuffed hands on the metal table.

"You gonna tell me why I'm here?" I already knew the answer.

Hazard simply stared—more like scowled, waiting for me to incriminate myself or something. I guess he was used to idiots confessing to anything just to get out of this windowless hellhole.

"At some point you have to indict me or let me go. And don't forget I have a phone call. So, you mind giving me back my expensive iPhone 6? Before the battery dies. Again?"

They had taken my phone, Kerry's phone, and of course my gun. Hazard shifted in his seat, but kept his eyes lasered on me. Maybe he was trying to gauge my personality or something. All it did was make me more insolent.

"I've got some great porn on there, but then you already know that. Guess that's why you still have it?" I winked. "How about my gun? Can I get that back? I'd like to clean it, you know. Just feels good in my hand. Especially in a cop station."

Nothing from the two detectives. Then I said, "How about taking off these cuffs? With my free hand and my phone, I could at least have some personal fun while I wait for you guys to figure out what you're gonna do with me."

Sanchez looked uncomfortable and seemed like she wanted to say something, but she decided to defer to Hazard, who finally spoke.

"Mr. Baker, where were your whereabouts last night?"

"Isn't that kind of a redundant thing to say? 'Where were your whereabouts'? I mean you could just ask where I was last night without trying so hard to sound intelligent and well-read, which I can tell you're not."

Again he ignored my comment.

"I need to know your location from twelve midnight to nine a.m." He barked.

"I was at R&D on Montana Avenue. At some point I left, but I was drunk, so I don't remember. I don't remember a lot about last night."

I could see Sanchez taking notes while Hazard continued to stare at me with hard eyes.

"Do you know one Jessica DeBost?" Hazard queried.

My face fell. "Is she okay?"

"Ms. Debost claims you told her that one Dr. Kerry Foot was murdered last night."

That emoji-loving idiot called the police. Probably told her brother too.

"Did you murder Dr. Foot, Mister Baker?"

"No, I found him this morning with his head blown off after *someone else* murdered him."

Finally Sanchez piped in. She had a small voice. "Why didn't you call in his murder if, as you said, you found him dead?"

"Because the Sicario that tortured and killed Kerry is after me, and I don't like being a target. And being a private eye for as long as I have, you learn not to trust the police."

Hazard leaned in a bit. "What makes you think Dr. Foot was murdered? I'm sorry, *how* was he murdered, did you say?"

"He was shot by a 12 gauge at point blank range, blowing his brains all over his bedroom, or did you not see the little red paint job on his wall? If you check the floor you might find his missing fingers."

Still the bland face from Hazard, who finally sat back and relaxed.

"After Ms. Debost called 911 to say you had told her about Kerry's murder, we sent a patrol car to his residence and found nothing out of the ordinary. No blood, Mr. Baker. And certainly no fingers on the floor."

At this point Hazard would have laughed or at least smiled, but since he seemed totally immune to levity, he simply drummed his stubby fingers on the metal table and waited for my reply. I closed my eyes—what an idiot I was.

"Of course. El Dorado, or the Sicario had the crime scene bleached. They cleaned up the killing." Oh boy was I fucked now.

Hazard furrowed his brow and Sanchez stopped writing.

"Who is El Dorado?" Hazard pressed me.

"You know, the infamous *El Dorado,* the head of all the cartel crime lords in the Americas. You haven't heard of El Dorado?" I stood up.

Sanchez looked up at me and tapped her pen on her notebook for emphasis. "El Dorado is a myth, Baker. There is no *El Dorado.* I suggest you find yourself another person to blame for your troubles." Before I could reply, Hazard pointed at my empty chair.

"Siddown, Baker. We're not through with you."

I figured I wasn't going anywhere with these handcuffs on anyway, and they weren't coming off until these two crackerjacks got more out of me. So I sat. Hazard continued.

"Dr. Foot did not show up for work today, Mr. Baker, and he seems to be missing. Do you perhaps know where he is or what may have happened to him?"

"Yes! I told you what happened to him. He was murdered by a Sicario and was no doubt rolled up in a plastic bag, along with his severed fingers, and is probably burned or buried or weighted off the Pacific by now."

I saw Sanchez feverishly taking notes. I turned to her.

"That's what *cleaners* do, cleaners who work for organized crime. Not me. I didn't kill Kerry. You have to know I didn't kill my friend." I started feeling less sure of myself.

Hazard pressed me, thinking he was gonna get a confession or something.

"I'm thinking you might have indeed murdered Dr. Foot, Mr. Baker. And then you pressured Ms. Debost to drive to a secluded cabin in Big Bear, warning her not to inform anyone of her whereabouts, not even her family. And she said you specifically told her not to contact the police."

Hazard got up from his chair and leaned over. "Were you then going to kill her too? Maybe rape her first? No one would know, and no one would suspect you, now would they, Mr. Baker? Was her body supposed to end up rolled in a plastic bag with missing body parts too?"

"Look, I was trying to protect Jessie. The Sicario might torture or kill anyone I talked to just to get my location. He'd already done that to Kerry, which is how he found Jessie's place." I began to sweat. This was not going well.

"Mr. Baker, you're currently under suspicion of murder in El Cajon, California. I think it best you let us know where we can find Dr. Kerry Foot or his body, or else you will be under suspicion of murder in Los Angeles county as well."

"I think I'd better speak to a lawyer."

Satisfied so far, Hazard and Sanchez stood up. I didn't know what else to say and decided to clam up before I got myself into more trouble. Until I remembered, yes!—Kerry's phone.

"Wait!"

They sat down again. Sanchez got out her notebook and began writing as I talked.

"Listen, I left Jessie's condo after she'd gone to work. I walked to Kerry's house, found the door open and then found his body in his bedroom. He was tied to a chair. He was missing three fingers and his head was blown off."

Hazard sat back and folded his arms. "You said that before, Mr. Baker, but facts do not corroborate your statement."

"But I also took his cell phone," I said, "it's a Samsung, which has his Ring app on it and it should also have all his security camera footage from last night. I'm guessing maybe it captured the killer's image? Just open up his cell phone and look at the app—maybe you'll see what happened to him and who did it." I hoped.

Hazard looked over and nodded to Sanchez, who put away her notebook. Then he unlocked my handcuffs.

"Mr. Baker, you're the prime suspect in potential foul play involving Dr. Kerry Foot. You are not to leave the Los Angeles area." He slid my phone back to me and the two detectives moved to the door. "We'll be in contact with you soon and will let you know when we have more questions. Where will you be staying?"

"I dunno. Could go back to Kerry's house, but that would be morbid, wouldn't it? Considering *someone else* splattered his brains all over the bedroom."

Sanchez pulled a business card from her coat pocket. It was from a motel on Wilshire Boulevard.

"Stay at this address, so we know where you are. Just show this card to the clerk" She said. "Unless you wish to spend the night in jail?"

I took the card, then shot up from the table. "Hold on, I need my gun back." Sanchez stared at me blankly, then shook her head. "Look, I'm telling the truth. Kerry's dead and the same person who shot him is coming for me." I emphasized.

Hazard turned before leaving. "We're keeping your gun, Mr. Baker. We have red flag laws in California, and they allow us to confiscate firearms from any individual who we may consider a threat to himself or to others. And y*ou*, Mr. Baker, are a viable threat to the community. After six months, if you haven't been convicted of a felony, you can petition a judge to have it returned." He said this last part with a smirk, as if anticipating the red tape I was going to have to run through to get back my H&K .45.

And just like that they left me alone, undefended, and a perfect target. But I don't like having a bullseye on my head, so once I got outside into the humid night air, I made a phone call. Surprisingly, the old iPhone still had battery power.

CHAPTER NINE

I walked the six blocks back to the Saab, which, thank goodness, was still sitting untouched by the meter maids. A few flyers were stuck on the window, including a copy of Willis's star maps. I pulled them all off and tossed them on the passenger floor and made the drive down Vine, then to Sunset Boulevard turning left, driving over the 101, past the endless traffic, and kept straight where the iconic street branches down to hipster Silverlake. I kept on the seedier Sunset Drive route until I hit the end and went left on Sanborn Ave until I found a dark alley and cut the engine.

"Frenchy" La Rue was what you'd expect from an illegal gun dealer. He was huge, built like a linebacker and looked a lot like Steve "Jonsey" Jones from the Sex Pistols: tats all over his body including his knuckles and neck, a big mane of unkempt hair which he kept in a shaggy pony tail-man-bun-thing, and a long beard with a constellation of those silver viking beard bead jewelry bits that kept his thick facial hair in a long, tight point. His dark eyes were covered with square framed glasses. He saw the Saab and hit me with a flashlight beam.

La Rue and I go way back. He too was a transplant from New York, by way of Marseille, where his ancestral family used to run the docks until they fled to Red Hook when the Vichys took over and the Nazis decided to become the top mobsters in the French port. His clan then ran Red Hook until the Italian mob muscled in and forced him to become a freelancer. But he'd done well for himself, selling guns and whatever to whomever—as long as they weren't Nazis or Frenchmen. Years ago he decided the mob game was getting dangerous so he went semi-legit, becoming an armorer on Hollywood films and shows, supplying the firearms and blanks for those action shoot-em-ups. If the movie people only knew that his guns were all stolen and illegal and many had been used in crimes, including murder, they'd flip their biscuit. But then the actors and directors and producers probably wouldn't have cared anyway. Knowing these Hollywood snowflake wannabetough types, they'd probably think it was cool to be handling illegal guns on camera.

Back in Brooklyn, I'd gotten Frenchy off a bad rap when another gun dealer had set him up, and later, when I heard the Feds were going to pinch him, I gave him a heads-up, giving Frenchy time to take an extended vacay in France until the heat cooled down—which also facilitated his desire to move to California and start a new life.

La Rue was waiting in the shadows next to his restored 1963 Chrysler 300. As soon as I walked over, he stuck his key in the trunk and opened the giant metal lid, revealing all types of used rifles and pistols, all with their serial numbers filed off.

I nodded to him and told him what I wanted. "I need a handgun with a lot of penetration."

He immediately fished around in his trunk, sifting through various pistols—all business was La Rue.

"Revolver or semi auto?"

I figured I'd be getting into more than a few gunfights, so the time-consuming reloads of a revolver were out of the question.

"Semi."

"You'll want either a 5-7 or a 10mm for penetration." He said.

La Rue's heavily-tatted arms pulled out two black guns. One was a plastic FN Dutch number called a Five-Seven with a long barrel that fires those small but fast armor piercing rounds with long mags that carry up to thirty bullets. The other was an old-school German Sig Sauer P220, ten millimeter version, all in metal with lots of wear marks on it. I tried each one, racking the slide, dry firing. The 5-7 was light as a feather, barely two pounds. The Sig reminded me of my old H&K that I figured I wasn't going to see again for a very long time.

"The five-seven will go through body armor, but it's a small wound channel. The ten hits harder but you get less rounds and it's heavier." La Rue said in rote, as if he were reading from a manual.

"But it will easily kill a man, right?" I mused.

"Will it kill a man? You can fucking kill a goddamn grizzly bear with a ten." Frenchy said with a sudden laugh.

"I'll take the Sig." I said.

"The drawback is the 220 only holds 8 bullets with this magazine. But I'll throw in a ten-round extended."

He took back the 5-7, let me keep the Sig, then fished around in a cardboard box full of gun magazines until he found a long, slim metal mag with an extended plastic bottom. I slipped it into my pocket.

"What about ammo?" I wondered, knowing that I didn't have the time to wait for a gun store to open. I also figured that, with my current trouble with the law, I probably wouldn't pass the stupid California ammo background check anyway, let alone purchase a legal gun with the idiotic California ten day waiting period. I'd be long dead by then.

"Have any Fort Scott?" I hoped.

He opened a big plastic case in his big Chrysler trunk and handed me a white box. Then looked back at me, knowing my penchant for trouble, and gave me another.

"No. But this Underwood Penetrator will do the trick. It also tumbles in soft tissue. All I have in defense ammo for the ten mil right now anyway."

I pocketed the two boxes, giving me forty rounds of copper jacketed badassery.

"How much?" I wondered.

"How much you got?"

"Maybe $500?"

He stared at me, looking like he was about to grab my shoulders, turn me upside-down, shake the gun and mags and ammo out of my jacket and pants and kick me hard in the ass.

"Hey, this is at least two grand." He cried as he took back the gun.

I opened my wallet and pulled out a wad of bills. I've got...five hundred...thirty two dollars..." I shook out a quarter, "...And twenty five cents."

I was counting on some of his rare compassion for a down-and-out, down-on-his-luck dick like me, and hoped The Frenchman remembered all the good things I'd done for him back in Brooklyn.

He scowled, then took the money, handing me back the gun and the thirty-two bucks. "You need some money for booze. But I'm keeping the quarter for laundry."

"Thanks Frenchy. I appreciate it." Relieved, I turned and walked back to the Saab as he closed his trunk and called back.

"Hey Baker. We're even."

CHAPTER TEN

I pulled into the Wilshire Motel, near the border of Santa Monica right off Bundy Boulevard. The place consisted of a gaggle of small, cute pastel bungalows ringing a tiny parking lot sandwiched between Ralphs and some new overpriced luxury apartments on Wilshire.

The motel was far more upscale than I figured I was going to get. I rechecked the card Sanchez gave me. Yup, I was in the right place. I parked and stepped up to the office next to the sidewalk. By now it was nearing midnight, as I slipped past the unlocked door and rang the little bell on the counter. Rang it again.

A young night clerk eventually appeared, looking tired. She was early twenties, had pink and blue hair, wore heavy eyeliner and those big fake eyelashes that are all the rage, and had one of those big, ridiculous nose rings pierced under her thin schnoz that made her look like a two-legged cow. I felt like attaching a chain to it and leading her out to pasture. Did she really think that made her look attractive?

"Well?" she said, sounding bored and tired. "You need a room or what?"

I showed her the business card and told her SMPD told me to stay here. She nodded as if she did this all the time, and handed me a key.

"You're in Room 22. Across the way. I need to see your driver's license first, though."

I showed her my ID. She nodded and pushed the guestbook to me. "Sign here."

"Can you please give me an extra blanket and two extra pillows?" I said with a hopeful smile.

She stared at me, like I just pissed on her sofa, shook her head and disappeared into the back room. I saw her tube of purple lipstick sitting on her desk, so I snuck around the counter and snagged it, hoping she wouldn't be rushing back. But after about five minutes, I wondered if she was actually coming back at all.

After a few more minutes she finally appeared with a brown blanket and two pillows. She wouldn't give them to me until I signed, pointing to the guestbook.

I scribbled a signature, thanked her and stepped back out into the night air. I walked carefully over to the lime green bungalow and sat the pillows and blanket on the little bolted-down wooden loveseat sitting next to the tiny garden in front of the door. I then got back into my Saab and backed it up, parking it on the street in case I needed a quick getaway.

I walked back to the bungalow, pulling out my Sig, and after I made sure no one was casing me, I then slipped the key into the lock and immediately stepped away to the right, just in case someone was waiting with a 12 gauge to greet me. But no one pulled a trigger, so I quickly entered, flipped on the light, and pointed my gun at every corner in the single room. Just a bed and a chair and a desk, with a Nescafe coffee maker on it. The only other room was a bathroom directly behind the bed with a door on the side. I checked it. Empty. It had one of those fiberglass shower/bath combos in it and a toilet. Perfect.

I went over to the front door and looked at the bed, then at the wall, behind which was the tub and shower. I stepped to the bed, then counted my steps to the edge of the bathroom wall—six steps. Then went into the bathroom and recounted those steps, which led me approximately to the middle of the shower/tub. I drew a four inch circle with the purple lipstick on the shower wall about where I figured where the door and the middle of the bed was directly behind it.

Now, it was my experience that I could trust cops as far as I can throw them. Even when the police are clean, those that rise to the top in command are usually compromised before they get there—or perhaps that's why the powers that be allow them to attain the office of Captain or Chief in the first place—Captain Sapper, case in point. So, no, I don't trust the cops. And I found it a bit suspicious that Sanchez so quickly set me up in a motel like this. This place was too nice and certainly wouldn't be turned down by lowly scum like me. In fact, it was more than a step above the usual seedy So-Cal flophouse.

Something just wasn't right. The room was comped, it seemed, which was strange, coming from a limited police budget, especially in the 'defund the police' era. More likely scenario was the powers that be didn't expect me to wake up in the morning. I also took notice that the little night clerk never asked for a credit card. That too was a bad sign.

I made my bed in the tub, right under the lipstick circle, trying my best to be comfortable with a too-soft pillow and a thin blanket. For assurance, I held my new Sig tight, with a bullet in the chamber and ten more in the extended mag. The loaded 8-round spare was in my pocket. I kept on my clothes and shoes.

It was about 3am when I heard a key quietly slipping into the lock in the front door. I silently got up, stepped carefully out of the tub, and aimed at the circle. A moment later I heard the door open and seconds later: BLAM, KA-CHINK, BLAM, KA-CHINK, BLAM, KA-CHINK!

As soon as I heard him rack the shotgun for the third time, I pulled my own trigger, BLAM BLAM BLAM BLAM BLAM BALM BLAM BLAM BALM BLAM BLAM! emptying all 11 rounds of 10mm slugs, firing an uneven pattern through the purple circle. Bits of plaster and fiberglass blew back as I literally put a softball size hole through the wall and headboard, which exploded into the bedroom and hopefully into the Sicario. I prayed those penetrator rounds lived up to their name.

I quickly dropped the empty mag, slid in the 8 rounder, racked the gun, and ran out into the room, which was now filled with gunsmoke, wood, and plaster chips from me, and polyester and feather bits and pieces that had flown up when my would-be assassin blasted the human form of pillows and towels I'd stuffed under the covers of the bed instead of yours truly.

But there was no body on the floor. Just a broken shotgun—one of my bullets had cut the gun in half, but not only the gun—I smiled when I saw the killer's severed left thumb was also lying on the floor. That one's for Kerry, mutherfucker.

I'd also put several rounds through the front window and the open door and the outside wall and apparently into one or two parked vehicles, as car alarms were already blaring in the parking lot. I hoped I hadn't hit anyone except the bad guy, but I didn't have time to think about that as I rushed out the door. I looked around and and saw movement on the ground—a man wearing a black hoodie and a black backpack, was crawling towards the sidewalk, leaving a trail of blood.

I ran to him, pinned his arms, which were also bleeding, and put the 10mm Sig to his head. He turned to look up at me, and I saw that I'd blown half his face away. He kept trying to feel for his missing cheek with his bloody tongue, but his cheek was gone, just a few flapped, ripped muscles and blood dripping down from his missing eye and missing nose. It was if the bullets had ripped off the flesh on half his face, leaving just skull, bones and some muscle. Hell, he looked just like Two-Face from the Batman comics!

It also looked like he was eerily smiling, with that skeletal, clicking jaw, as he barked at me, squeezing out three words from his raspy, dying breath.

"You dead, Baker."

I shook my head, knowing that this guy was gonna be gone in a few seconds. I actually felt sorry for him, watching him start to go into shock.

"Not today, pal."

I pulled the trigger, blowing a hole through his head. Brains from his tat-covered face splattered the sidewalk.

I quickly reached into his pockets—empty. Checked his bullet riddled backpack and pulled out a thick wad of cash, his burner cell, and a wicked folding knife, putting all of it in my pocket. There were shears for cutting fingers, a sharpened screwdriver for poking out eyeballs, a bottle of black spray paint and a roll of duct tape. I left that stuff. Then I ran into the office. But I was too late.

The nose-ring night clerk wasn't there -until I checked behind the counter and saw her body.

A heavy knife slash on her throat had bled her out. Her dead, mascara eyes were looking up to the ceiling, her glue-on eyelashes askew. The nose ring, however, was still in place.

I grabbed the phone on the desk, dialed 9, then 911, telling LAPD that multiple shots were heard at the Wilshire Motel and two people were dead. Then I hung up, ripped off the page I signed on the guest register, and got into the Saab, pulling away as I began to hear multiple sirens coming fast in the distance...

CHAPTER ELEVEN

I headed west down Wilshire Boulevard until I hit the promenade overlooking the Pacific Ocean. I turned right, then drove onto Highway 1, heading up to Malibu, hoping to disappear into the world of beach bums, middle-aged surfers, and the more reclusive millionaires and billionaires who prefer the salty ocean air and the relative remote privacy of beach and bluff living to the pretentiousness of Beverly Hills and Bel Air.

Soon after I had jumped into the Saab, there was a text on the Sicario's phone: "Jack in the Box Malibu" was all it said. I was surprised I'd guessed right about the location. I cut the lights and pulled into the parking lot. I was surprised not only that the fast food joint was open, but that there were a handful of people eating greasy burgers and fries in the middle of the night. I reached into my coat, drew my bottle of Oxy and popped a handful. Once I warmed up from the opiates, I put on a smile and left the confines of the vintage Swedish car. With the big O giving me steel and bliss, and my now-proven metal Sig giving me confidence, I opened the door to the greasy joint.

Inside I saw a homeless dude at the middle booth, asleep with his tattered suitcase and a pet dog on a leash, who was sleeping along with him on the bench. There were two teenagers on a date at the front table, and there was a man sitting alone in the back booth where it was darkest and he could watch the door. I walked up to him and as soon as he saw me, his dark face turned white. "Baker..." he gulped, like he'd just seen a ghost.

"Hello Ratso. Been a minute." I showed off my Sig as I sat across from my old "friend". His left hand held a large styrofoam coffee cup that looked like it had gone stale, with a ring of errant bite marks on the soft cup edge from his nervous nibbling. Rizzo's right hand slipped under his jacket, going for what I assumed was his Gat. I shook him off as I cocked the hammer on the Sig. He compliantly put both hands on the table as if I were a cop interrogating him. One thing about Ratso, he was crafty and clever, but he was about as tough as a wet noodle.

"B, Baker. Good to see you, man." His beady eyes looked for a quick exit. To dissuade him, I put my gun on the table, pointing at his chest.

"Hey, it's cool, friend. You don't need to do that." He said, as he took a sip of his tepid coffee with a nervous hand. "How'd you know where to find me?"

I looked at him cockeyed, which caused Ratso to chuckle and then laugh as he built up the courage try to impress me.

"Oh, but you know how to find anyone, right?"

"Everyone but El Dorado."

"El Dorado?...Trust me, man. You don't want to know. Forget about it. Bad news, man. You don't want El Dorado."

"That's why I'm here. But then you probably know that already."

"Whaaaaat?" Ratso feigned innocence. Then his eyes flicked past me as a Jack in the Box employee, a kid who seemed to quiver from too much coffee or meth, walked over to the table. The kid's eyes went wide when he saw my 10mm pistol.

"It's okay. I'm a detective. Licensed to carry." I assured him.

That seemed to calm him down a bit. Then he tried to force a smile. "You need to buy something to sit here. Sir." He said, keeping a twitching eye on the gun in front of me. "Want some fries?" He suggested.

"Just gimme a cup of coffee. Black." I pulled out the Sicario's wad and peeled off a fiver. "Keep the change."

That seemed to make him feel better about me and my gun being there. He nodded and left. I turned back to Ricky Rizzo who almost certainly noticed my wad of cash as I put it away. I glared.

"You gave me up to the Sicario, Ratso."

"What d'you mean?" he protested.

The methhead employee dropped off my coffee. I heard some more people enter the place as I popped the coffee lid—too hot to take a sip, so I blew on it, then looked up at Ratso.

"The Sicario, who now has a big hole in what's left of his forehead, just got a text on his phone sending him here. To meet you. For the rest of his payment, I'm assuming." I showed him the text on the phone and leaned towards the thin Sicilian. "Did you put the hit on me, Ratso?"

"No! No way, Baker. I don't know nothing about no Sicario. No Way," he exclaimed.

"So it's just kismet that you're here at this hour?"

"No. It was my boss told me to wait here for him. A meeting. That's all. I got a text from him. Just like you. But he hasn't shown."

Ratso didn't show me a text, and he seemed to feign more innocence about setting me up. But since he always lied, you couldn't ever tell if The Rat was sincere or not.

"Man, don't you see, Baker. *I* was the target. *ME*," he declared. "That Sicario was supposed to be here to hit ME. Thank goodness you offed him. My boss musta set me up cuz I was a frienda yours." He seemed frightened about the Sicario, but then you could never be sure with this guy.

"And who's paying you these days, Ratso?"

"Lotsa people. But mostly I work for Eddie Schwarma," he said. Then Rizzo relaxed a bit, smiled and drummed his fingers on the table. "Better think about that, Baker. Better think about that."

"Why do I give a damn? I don't know who the hell Eddie Schwarma is, nor do I care. This town's full of Eddie Schwarmas." I replied.

"You'll see." Rizzo suddenly chuckled, then pulled out one of his silly trademark Owl cigarillos, lighting it with a flick of his skull and bones Zippo. As he exhaled the nasty vanilla-flavored tobacco, I realized something had made the usually nervous Ratso Rizzo relax like he'd just had a massage. In fact, he sat back in the booth as if he wasn't afraid of me or my gun at all. The Rat took a bold sip of stale coffee, then began to smile, showing off stained teeth through his unkempt drooping mustache.

Right then I knew I'd blown it. Dammit. My back was to the door. Rookie mistake. I'd heard the soft footsteps as we were talking, but they didn't register. Must be getting old.

I tried to quickly spin around, but big, muscular arms were already snaked around my neck, pressing hard against my carotid artery, and my gun was twisted out of my hands before I had a chance to get my finger on the trigger.

"You don't mess with Eddie Schwarma," Ratso said.

That was the last thing I heard before I blacked out.

CHAPTER TWELVE

It was the slap that woke me up. I figured when the world went black, I'd never see the light of day again, that the moment had finally come when one of my many mistakes had at last put me six feet under.

But the hot sting on my cheek quickly opened my very-much-alive eyes and brought me back from the netherworld. Then I smelled a weird mix of vanilla and lavender aromatherapy stuff—the kind you plug into the wall—mixed with plenty of overwrought men's cologne—a sort of nasal potpourri of pretentiousness. I knew I was still in LA.

I looked to my side and saw I was lying on a hard surface in an all-wooden, cavernous space, surrounded by three pairs of feet clad in Air Jordans and draped in male versions of Lululemon joggers.

When I saw the cash register in the background, I figured I was in a trendy retail establishment, and it was probably long after closing time in some sort of hipster clothing store/overpriced restaurant/bar/cafe. A few of the recessed lights were on, and as my eyes unblurred, I could now see racks of clothes with the trendy gay rainbow prints all over them, along with a well-stocked wooden bar with little metal round tables and their little round chairs set atop like they do when the restaurant closes for the night. I guessed that the big windows faced the busy, buzzing Highway 1 and realized I was actually inside that fashionably remodeled Malibu Inn, literally right next door to Jack in the Box.

I looked up from the hardwood floor that had been my bed for the past dozen minutes or so and saw three big guys peering down at me with menacing looks on their faces—one white, one black and one hispanic. I chucked, thinking these must be diversity thug hires—big dudes of different races with a minimum weight of 250.

Then, like Moses parting the sea, the trio drifted back, and another face glared down upon me. It belonged to a small, thin dude wearing a pencil mustache, a pair of gold earrings, an expensive gold jacket, and garish appliqué shoes with no socks. He looked a lot like a young, fey Stanley Tucci, albeit with sculpted eyebrows, a full head of hair and too much jewelry. I could also tell this dude was trans, which seems to be all the rage these days in the rainbow world of La la land.

His synthetic, testosterone-fueled, lisping voice pierced my eardrum as he bent down and babbled in my ear and I realized that the annoying, expensive, Calvin Klein-type cologne I was smelling emanated from him—I guess to prove a point that this was a "real guy" and not some confused girl who decided to squash her breasts and try on a suit and testosterone injections.

"So you're the tough guy. Don't look so tough from here." He smiled, showing off the pricey diamond grill over his bleached, veneered teeth. This had to be Eddie Schwarma.

"Haven't had my coffee yet," I quipped.

Eddie turned to the black thug. "Hey Bobby, the little dick wants some coffee. Why dontcha get him some?"

Black Bobby stepped over to the bar and brought back a pot of black coffee. I prayed it wasn't freshly made, because if it was hot, in a few seconds I was going to have myself a very wicked Malibu skin peel. I closed my eyes and held my breath as Eddie poured a bunch over my cheek. I couldn't help but think of the irony that I'd just blown off the Sicario's cheek, and here Eddie Schwarma was going to burn off mine.

"How's that, little dick?" Eddie laughed.

Thank God the coffee was cold. Probably left over from last night.

I licked a bit of stale joe off my lips, then nodded.

"Thanks. I'll be on my way now", I said, brushing the rest of the black liquid from my face as I stood up, hoping to keep myself out of the coffee puddle that had already soaked my collar.

"Hear that boys? The little dick wants to be on his way."

I grabbed my fedora just as Eddie snapped his fingers and the two other thugs lifted me up by my shoulders and unceremoniously dragged me to one of the tables. Black Bobby pulled a chair off the tabletop, righted it, and Tweedle-Dee and Tweedle-Dum sat me down.

"Got a cigarette?" I asked.

"Gross." Eddie's voice cracked, sort of like an adolescent boy going through puberty—which is no doubt what was chemically happening inside little trans Eddie, which might be why he seemed so petulant. "Nobody smokes anymore." He grimaced.

"Then how about some eggs Benedict?" I asked, nonchalantly, trying to brush the coffee stain off my fedora. I could see Ratso standing at the front door with that nervous look on his face.

"You ask too many questions." Eddie said, as he fiddled with one of his many gold rings and checked his gold Rolex, like he wanted me out of here as soon as possible.

"That's my job."

"Not in LA, it's not. Not anymore."

"Then why am I here?"

"Ahhhh." Eddie walked around to my other side. "Now we're getting *existential.*"

"Okay Jean-Paul...

"The name's *Eddie,* you dolt," he spat like he was famous.

"You gonna go all ironic and Sarte-like on me and say there's *No Exit* or something you think is clever?" I said, trying out a literary reference on Eddie's small brain.

Eddie quickly jumped back in my face and was suddenly very serious. "There's only one exit for you, little dick, and here's how this play is gonna go: you're going to take your unshaven old face and unclean and unfashionable old clothes, stumble out to that ugly old brown jalopy of yours, and get the hell away from my establishment and out of LA county." He spat. "Or else..."

He nodded to one of his thugs, maybe the Latin guy, who yanked out my chair and pulled me to my feet.

"And don't ever come back, or there will be no exit for you, Mr. Baker, *ever.*" He warned.

"Why's that?" I challenged.

"Because Eddie Schwarma says so."

"Who's Eddie Schwarma?" I teased.

"I'm Eddie Schwarma! You idiot!" he screamed. "I run Malibu and no one fucks with me."

"So you speak about yourself in the third person? That's pretty lame." I said, goading him on.

He was getting frustrated and I was making him pissed, which is what I usually do to most people eventually.

Eddie's face twisted in anger as he nodded to the Latin guy. The dude quickly slapped me again, knocking off my hat. I picked it up and turned to Tweedle-Dee.

"Don't ever do that again, pal." I warned.

He sneered at me. I took a breath. Looked at Eddie.

"Can I ask a question?" I said as I noticed Eddie glancing again at his watch.

"No. I told you, no questions."

"Who wanted me on ice?" I asked anyway.

"Everyone wants you dead, Baker. You need a list?"

"Now we're getting somewhere."

Eddie shifted, his face suddenly curious. "Why do you say that?"

"Because you didn't call me 'little dick.'" I replied, sardonically.

"Get out of LA, Baker!" he growled in his boy-voice.

"Out of LA? Where am I supposed to go? This place is kinda growing on me." I quipped with my usual sarcasm.

"Try San Diego. You might find somewhere down there to play tough guy. Yeah. Go back to El Cajon."

With the Latin King still holding my arm, I put my fedora back on my head and checked my pockets. "Can I have my gun back?"

"Don't think so," Eddie spat as he shook his head.

"Then how about my cash? You know, the wad of bills Ratso took from my pocket after your thugs choked me out."

Eddie turned to Ratso Rizzo, who could barely hide the guilt in his face. "That true, Ricky?" Eddie asked.

"Oh, oh yeah!" Rasto feigned. "Sorry, boss, forgot about that." He pulled the money roll from his pocket, like he just happened to remember, and tossed it to Eddie, who gave Ratso a scornful look.

Eddie turned to me, smiled an apology with his diamond teeth, and dropped the cash back in my pocket.

"Rizzo is sorry for forgetting to give it back"

"I bet he is." I couldn't hide the sarcasm in my voice.

Eddie's faux-hard demeanor quickly softened with a bit of embarrassment, as if ripping me off wasn't in the script and the director was gonna make him play the scene again.

"That won't happen again." He said apologetically.

I realized I've always had a problem with these LA types—pretty people who cycle through emotions like a washing machine. Hell, the way things go out here in Hollywoodland, in five more minutes Eddie'd probably be inviting me out to coffee to discuss a movie deal, and Ratso would be angling for a cut.

I shook my head at Eddie. "When you've got Ratso Rizzo around, you gotta keep him on a short leash."

"Fuck you, Baker," Rizzo exclaimed.

"Shut up, Ricky," Eddie called back to him, still in apology mode.

I was getting tired of being held captive in this wooden rainbow bubble by wannabe bad guys. I tried to move, but Latin man gripped my arm tighter.

"This meathead gonna to let me go or what?"

For some reason Eddie took offense at me insulting his hired help. Or maybe it was me taking control of the scene, *Eddie's* scene. After all, Eddie was no doubt thinking this was all his show.

"I don't think like the tone of your voice." Eddie said, as he looked me over again. "Yeah, I don't know that I'm done with you yet."

"First you beg me to go away, now you wanna sing sweet nothings in my ear? Know what, you little tranny..."

"*Trans!* It's called '*TRANS,*' you 'phobe!'" Eddie screamed.

"...I'm tired of you LA amateurs." I spat, as I began to twist out of Tweedle-Dee's grip, but he held me tight, now using both arms and all of his steroid strength.

"Well I'm tired or your insolence." Eddie threatened. "You're in my town and you need to learn some respect."

I watched Ratso smile, waiting for Eddie to have me slapped again. Eddie lifted up his manicured hand and ceremoniously snapped his little fingers. Fortunately I had finally managed to twist just enough to yank myself free from Tweedle-Dee's muscular arm, now that the big guy had released his other hand and was bringing his big arm back to bitchslap me yet again. Eddie watched the scuffle with excitement. I could see the anticipation and pleasure in his brown eyes as he licked his thin lips.

But by now I was over the many indignities I'd endured since my brief stint in Malibu. Plus I was furious at myself for fucking up in the first place, allowing these idiots to get me into a compromising position. And at this point, even with my low self esteem, I just couldn't handle another degrading bitch slap.

So before Tweedle-Dee could smack me, I reached in and grabbed his middle finger, bending it all the way back, until I heard a 'crack', and in seconds the Latin Goliath was kneeling on the floor in front of me in tears. The Caucasian thug, Tweedle-Dum, tried to make a move to hit me, but he was slow and I was expecting it. I kicked out his knee as soon as he was in range, tearing out a couple ligaments and knocking his tibia way out of joint. And just like that, Tweedle Dum was on the floor reeling in pain, cradling his cockeyed leg. Two big men in tears in less than five seconds. Tweedle-Dee was literally crying like a baby, so I finally let his finger go. His hand was already swelling up like a grapefruit. Then Black Bobby started to move towards me but Eddie shook him off.

Eddie turned and looked at me with newfound respect as I picked up my fedora yet again, set it on my head, and walked to the exit. I glared at Rizzo, still guarding the door like a good boy. He looked at me, then to Eddie with his shifty eyes, hoping that Eddie wasn't going to order The Rat to do anything that might get himself hurt.

I knew by now that it wasn't Eddie who put the Sicario onto me. Eddie was no doubt simply taking orders down the line from the Big Guy. This entire evening was crafted to send me a warning. That's how I knew I was getting closer to El Dorado. So I decided I wanted to send a message of my own.

"Do me a favor, Eddie?"

"What's that?"

I stepped up to Ratso, who was trying his best to block the door. He flinched as I reached into his inside pocket, pulling out one of his flavored white owl cigarillos. I lit it with his zippo, tossing the lighter back (he dropped it, of course, but stayed dutifully in front of the door). I drew a big inhale, then let out the vanilla smoke, adding some theater to my impending exit. I turned back to Eddie.

"Tell El Dorado I'm coming for him."

Eddie froze for a second, thinking over the ramifications, as if no one had ever dared to say such a thing before. I gave Rizzo a threatening look, and he quickly moved aside as I opened the door to the pink dawn sunlight that was slowly brightening the crashing waves of the Pacific only yards away across the highway.

Eddie looked up and then seemed to nod—maybe to tell a worried Ratso it was okay to let me go, maybe as a promise to inform the real-life Keyser Soze about my threat, but maybe also in admiration—seeing Rizzo twitching in fear while two of Eddie's big enforcers writhed in pain on the ground—all due to an old, unarmed, unshaven guy with unfashionable clothes.

"Gotta hand it to you, Baker, you've got balls."

I flicked away the white owl (I forgot how much I hated those things), turned back to Eddie Schwarma and nodded in agreement. "Yeah. Too bad you don't have any."

I closed the door, quickly shutting out the loud, high-pitched expletives now being thrown at me by this tumultuous tranny crime boss, and got the hell out of Malibu before Eddie Schwarma decided to start lobbing bullets at me as well.

CHAPTER THIRTEEN

I hadn't slept all night, but I wasn't tired, amped up by winning the recent altercation with the Malibu crew, along with the exhilaration of making it out of there alive. I knew if this was Brooklyn, I'd already be buried in concrete.

And as I drove down the Pacific Highway, fleeing the night and welcoming the dawn, I thought about Eddie Schwarma, the wannabe heavy with a made-up name and a made-up gender. Eddie was like so many people in L.A., living versions of themselves that they pretend to be, like the dreams they see on the silver screen—or on the TV or the xbox or the device or whatever it is people watch stuff on anymore.

I longed for the days past. Maybe this brave new place we're now forced to live in, full of rainbows and transitions and pretend avatars, maybe now it all belongs to the Eddie Schwarmas of the world. It certainly feels like the rest of us old guys and gals who grew up in bucolic days past are simply being relegated to reruns of old movies. But hell, I like old movies.

It was now about 6:00am and my mind was swimming. I automatically reached into my pocket to grab a fistful of Oxy—but my pocket was empty. Fucking Ratso. Of course he snagged my little white pills. I wasn't yet in opiate withdrawal, but I knew it would eventually come. I decided not to think about it as the sun peeked over the horizon, right into my eyes, helping me try to forget that I was an addict, beholden to pills and drugs and booze to keep me sane and happy. But I wasn't sane or happy, and I knew eventually I was someday gonna eschew the Oxy and jump right on the horse, and quickly run to the fentanyl, and then sprint to a fast, early grave. I decided again that this was a really bad train of thought so I ordered my anxious brain to stop thinking about this shit and to instead focus on the next task at hand.

While I wasn't tired, I was pretty damn hungry, and more importantly, I wanted to talk to someone real, someone who wasn't pretending to be anything but themselves. Hard to find in LA, but I knew just the place.

As I pulled off the 1 (in SoCal, local custom dictates that every highway is preceded with "the," as in "*the* 405" or "*the* 5" or "*the* 1"), and onto Main Street, I sputtered the old Saab through Ocean Park, my favorite neighborhood in Santa Monica, admiring the beautiful blonde spandex-clad joggers, maniacal cyclists with $14,000 bicycles, and upscale eateries and boutiques, just now starting to come back after those stupid, devastating BLM riots.

I found a parking place across from Buffalo Exchange and walked over to The Place To Be. The cafe wasn't quite open yet but Matthew, who was setting up the outside tables, saw me right away, slapped my back and nodded me inside, where his wife Sandra was just pulling out fresh, authentic French croissants from the oven.

"Bonjour!" she said with her sparkly face and heavy French accent. Sandy and Matt were transplants from Paris and their cafe baked the best croissants and brioche this side of New York City.

"Monsieur Bak-ier, you move back in LA, non?" She said eagerly as she bent over the counter and gave me a kiss-kiss on my cheek-cheek. Sandy had long blonde hair and was tall and thin, and although she was north of 40, she had the spunk of a teenager and little pert breasts that she let fly free in her knit top, in that lovely French, unabashed way.

"No, no," I said. "I came back just for your croissants."

"Non, non, non, you can't fool me, you silly man. I believe you are on a case, Monsieur Bak-ier!"

She already had a flaky, warm pastry on a plate and in my hand before I could reply with a wink, sans the nod.

"Como cafe?" She handed me a cup of joe as the morning customers began filing inside. I couldn't say no, of course, and gave her a $20 off the Sicario's money roll. While she and Matt were the best bakers around, their coffee was crap, but I never had the heart to tell them, so I grinned and sipped the "merde" and made the best of it as I pulled up a stool, closed my eyes, and sniffed the intoxicating aroma of the baked butter and flour jewel on the plate in front of me.

But just before I could take a bite...

SLAP

"What the hell?!"

I know I didn't tell Sandy her coffee was shit, out loud anyway, so it couldn't have been her that struck my poor, abused cheek. I opened my eyelids and spied Sandy and a few customers glancing my way, but they quickly averted their peepers when I looked at them, as if I were in some sort of lover's spat.

Lovers?

It was then I looked up and saw the skinny, pretty woman with a big nose, a brown bob, and a twisted face full of anger glaring down at me.

"Jessie?"

"That's my name. But then again, I only have one name, so it's pretty easy to remember, even for you. Of course I don't know what your name is today. Is it "Harry"? Or "Haim"? Or something else? Hmmm? "How about 'Herbert'"? You look like a Herbert.

"I do not look like a Herbert!"

"Maybe I WILL call you Herbert!"

"Coming from the girl who draws emojis on her love notes." I shook my head as I rubbed my aching face.

"I happen to like emojis."

"No kidding," I said sarcastically.

"Is that why you wanted to murder me?"

"Murder you?"

"Yeah. You're a, a *serial killer.*" She posited, as a worried young couple quickly grabbed their croissants and left in a hurry, not wanting to hear anymore. "You urged me to go to my brother's cabin and not tell anyone, so I'd be there all alone so you could come, have your way with me and then murder me without anyone knowing."

I noticed Sandy raising her eyebrows in the background as she pretended not to listen. By now Matt had come in and was using a rag to "clean" an already clean table nearby so he too could listen in on the fun.

"Think about that, Jessie, why go through the trouble of getting you into a remote cabin—besides the fact that I have no idea where this cabin is—to kill you when I could have easily done it after we slept together in your bedroom?"

Now Matt was raising his eyebrows, sharing a smile with his wife as they watched the soap opera unfold.

Jessie stood there, thinking, then finally sat down next to me on another stool. "So you *didn't* want to spend a week with me in my brother's cabin in Big Bear?"

I hadn't thought of it that way, and looking at this hot little brunette, a weekend in a cabin with her certainly intrigued me. But then I got rid of those thoughts and shot to the matter at hand. "It sounds fun, but no, I was trying to save your life at the time."

She reached over and started picking at my croissant, putting bits into her mouth. "Oh, yeah, from the saccharine-something-or-other"

"*The Sicario.* A cartel assassin."

"Oh," she said half-heartedly, as she devoured more of my breakfast. "But why would some 'cartel assassin' want to kill me?" She said, pouting her soft lips.

"He wasn't after you, but you were in danger because he was trying to find and kill *me.*"

"Well, I could certainly see someone wanting to murder *you,*" she said with a smile.

"Tell me about it." I said knowingly.

"You don't all seem that concerned now."

"That's because I took care of the problem."

"Did you... Did you shoot this Sicario-person with your fake gun?" Jessie's face turned serious.

"It's not fake!" Then I took a breath. "Look, Jessie, it's a long story, I'm hungry and I'm tired of talking and you've just eaten my breakfast."

Sandy must have been listening to every word, because it wasn't five seconds later that she had another croissant set in front of me.

Sandy looked at Jessie and winked. "Monsieur Baker is, how do you say, 'irascible,' but I know Monsieur Baker, and he is a good man,"

That seemed to set Jessie at ease, because she was now drinking my coffee too. Sandra then winked at me, like she'd just set us up on a blind date, and went back to setting some brioches on the counter. Matt whispered something in her ear. They both laughed.

Jessie took another sip and looked over at the Parisian couple. "This coffee is excellent, by the way!"

"Merci!" Sandra bellowed, as she quickly poured another cup for us.

I shook my head. Was I having nightmare?

Jessie drank the rest of my black swill and put her arm around me, tickling my neck. "Well, Harry-Haim, I forgive you for wanting to murder me, and I do appreciate that you were concerned enough to invite me to Big Bear."

I automatically reached into my pocket looking for my Oxy, forgetting that Ratso had probably sold it all by now. I really needed something for my head because this chick was driving me crazy. Then I remembered one of my old haunts, the Basement Tavern—it was only few doors down...

CHAPTER FOURTEEN

I slowly opened my eyes. They were blurry and my head was pounding from one of my famous hangovers. How much did I drink yesterday? I vaguely remembered slamming some old-fashioneds at The Basement before moving onto tequila shots. There may have been a bottle or two of Macallen 18 in there as well—as I remember spending the Sicario's money pretty freely last night. I vaguely remembered some cute girl with some sort of flower necklace...

I squinted, and figured it was the next morning because the bright AM sunlight was streaming onto my face. But then I looked up, focused my eyes, and that's when I saw them, clear as day.

"Oh God, no."

Little smiling angel and flower frescos on the yellow domed ceiling were staring down, mocking me. And as if to taunt me, my knowing eyes automatically tilted down to that stern face of Jesus with his disapproving look.

"No, no, no, not this..."

"Happy, you're awake!"

I turned and saw Jessie leaning over me, wearing nothing but a sheer nightie, her pert little breasts tantalizingly close. Then I came to my senses.

"I'm not happy."

Yes, that's what I decided to call you. 'Happy.' You can be Harry with some people, Haim with others, but with me you're 'Happy.'" She must have waited all morning to say that.

"NO. Besides, the fact that I do not look like a 'Happy,' I'm rarely happy. I'm actually quite dour."

"Well, I'm calling you 'Happy,'" she said, as she slid on top of me.

I realized right then I was completely nude and had my morning stiffy going on. It was actually growing ever stronger, thanks to the sight of Jessie's braless bouncy-bettys. I couldn't help but eye them hungrily, and was soon unable to stop myself from caressing them. That's when I noticed a slight scar on the right one. I gently rubbed my thumb over the rough spot.

"Hey. What's that from? Pole dancing accident?" I laughed.

"I had a lump removed last year," she said, as if that kind of thing happened every day. "No big deal."

I sat up, instantly concerned. I was no fan of hospitals and surgeons and especially cancer. "Was it..."

I couldn't even say the *C* word. That horrid disease had killed my mom. I had watched her waste away from the disease and the chemo ravaging her body. Out of all the things I've seen and done—including murdering, maiming and worse—watching my mom go from a combo of cancer and chemo was something I couldn't endure again.

She held my mouth and kissed me hard on the lips. "No, silly. It was fine."

I took her word for it, but I didn't like the tone of her voice. A small quiver under her bouncy exterior. Being a dick has taught me about those little clues to the little lies we tell ourselves and others. But I didn't want to think about that. Besides, her warm, wet tongue was in my mouth and I was in her and before I knew it we'd both consummated our relationship—again. A relationship I wasn't looking for, never wanted, and was unprepared for, but was somehow being coerced or shanghaied onto me.

By the time she rolled off, I'd forgotten all about her right breast as I swung onto my feet and hopped off the bed. Her mattress was one of those super tall Sertas, perched atop of a giant boxspring set on a yellow, quilted bed frame, lifting me and my naked body over four feet from from the floor. I found my fedora on the skyscraper bedpost. I reached up and slipped it on.

"Where are my clothes?"

"Oh, they stunk, so I washed them. Did you know you spilt coffee all over your collar? How'd you do that?"

"You don't want to know. Just get me my clothes. Please," I begged.

"Can't—in the dryer right now with a handful of Downy sheets, so at least *they'll* smell pleasant," she told me as she made a face, crinkling her long nose with a prominent sense of humor. "And you can use my deodorant—it's Tom's so there's no girly scent. I've left it out for you in the bathroom. Just in case, you know, you wanna take a shower at some point." She said, as she skipped into the kitchen to toast some sourdough. "And don't worry, I didn't wash your bougie German sport coat—but it is airing out outside the window." She crinkled her nose again.

"So what am I supposed to wear?" said the nude man wearing nothing but a fedora and a tired penis.

Jessie stepped into her closet and tossed me a baby blue bathrobe printed with yellow flowers. I unceremoniously slipped it on, the arms coming to my elbows, the bottom barely covering my hairy thighs. I felt ridiculous.

"You look sooo cute!" Jessie bounced up to me and gave me another kiss. "Oh, and thank you sooooo much for my necklace. It's beautiful! I love it! LUV it!" She clipped a delicate rose gold chain with a big gold and ruby rose flower pendant around her neck. It hung perfectly between Jesse's breasts. Must have cost a cool grand. At least.

"I bought you *that?*" I couldn't believe what I'd done. Neither could she, apparently.

"I know! We saw it in that jewelry store window and you just went right in and paid cash! I'm always gonna wear it. It's so beautiful!" She said again as she hugged me tight. "You make me so happy, Happy." Her eyes literally started to water.

As I held her, I made the mistake of glancing in the full-length mirror on her closet door, aghast at the image I saw—a sad-looking man with a bewildered face wearing a fedora and a small woman's bathrobe being hugged by an ecstatic girl in tears who seemed to be in a relationship with this perplexed man who had no idea how this had all happened. "I need to stay away from alcohol," I murmured.

As the cool Pacific Ocean breeze billowed through the sunny window sheers, I sat at the little flower-print Pottery Barn table, wearing the silk flower-print bathrobe (it actually felt pretty nice on my skin), and ate a plate of warm scrambled eggs and sourdough toast Jessie made for me. Jessie even brewed some pretty good coffee with one of those pod coffee machine things. I was impressed, and didn't realize how hungry I was. She then cut up some green apples into little thin spirals like some sort of art project apple flower thing, and I ate those too as I looked around her kitchen, admiring all the little drawings and paintings of flowers and angels and landscapes she had framed and festooned on her wall.

"Those all your art pieces?" I said, impressed.

"Yeah. I was gonna go to art school, but my dad told me he wouldn't cover the cost unless I chose something more practical." She shrugged her shoulders. "I figured I'd at least get to do some drawings as an architect, but mostly I'm just using CAD, Sketchup and Revit; sometimes I get to use V-Ray," she said, mildly excited.

I had no idea what she was talking about, so I nodded along as I ate some toast.

"But, you know, at least it's a job and I don't have student loans." Then she said wistfully, "I draw for fun when I can. I love drawing."

She didn't eat, but she did sip some coffee, telling me she liked to do that intermittent fasting thing. Then she worked out her morning exercise routine on the stripper pole. She was flexible and sultry—probably more than usual since I was a captive audience, and the whole thing made me hungry again for her—plus it gave me an excuse to quickly strip off the silly robe.

After another romp in the bed (on the sofa, actually), I finally took a shower (I didn't realize how bad I stunk). But even standing under the spray of hot water, my head wouldn't stop pounding. I thought the food, the coffee, the sex and the shower would have freed me from my migraine, but it was only getting worse. I was fooling myself. I knew what it was. It had been over twenty-four hours since Ratso had clipped my Oxy, and my head was screaming from a lack of dopamine, something I should have gotten from my brain at least after the rambunctiously fun fornication. But now that I rely on a synthetic form of feel-good in the guise of those white pills, my body was screaming for endorphins that it couldn't produce anymore on its own.

I peeked out the shower curtain and stared at myself in the fogged-up mirror. I saw a man who was no better than Eddie Schwarma, taking synthetic drugs to be the person I wanted to become. Okay, maybe I just wanted to be the guy who wasn't depressed and filled with anxiety, but of course using those pills just made anxiety and depression worse when they weren't around. I was a fucking addict, but I couldn't admit it.

I called out from the shower. "Hey Jessie, you got anything for a headache? I've got a whopper of a migraine."

She quickly walked into the bathroom partially dressed, wearing a flower skirt, a black bra and a pouty, concerned look on her pretty face. "I'm sorry. Should be something in the cabinet there," she said, setting my folded clothes on the counter. "Gosh, I hope you feel better," she said. Then she smelled my clean, softened, shirt, and smiled. "At least you'll smell nice, Happy."

She slipped her face past the shower curtain and gave me a quick kiss before retreating back to the bedroom. I realized that everything she did this morning was something your girlfriend would do.

"Girlfriend"? Did I have a girlfriend?

"Thanks," I said as I stepped out, dried off and opened the medicine cabinet above the sink. I quickly located a bottle of ibuprofen. I would need about four of those oblong things to make even a tiny dent in the pain. But as I shook the orange pills into my hand, I noticed a slender prescription bottle near the back of the cabinet, next to some PMS medicine.

I had the the bottle in my hand in an instant. I couldn't believe my luck—it was Norco. A form of Vicodin. My old favorite.

I quickly checked on Jessie, then closed the bathroom door. I had glimpsed Jessie humming some Taylor Swift song while buttoning up her complicated blouse, so I had a bit of time.

I searched the label. The drugs were prescribed almost a year ago and still hadn't expired. Must have come with Jessie's surgery. But I didn't have time to think about that, because I had ten of them down my throat before I realized my mouth was already under the sink, drinking a gulp of warm water to get the bitter pills into my gut and the feel-good stuff up into my head as soon as possible.

I closed the mirrored cabinet door and stared at my face—the image still mottled from the steam. Opaque. Distant. Shrouded. For some reason I thought, since I couldn't see my eyes in my reflection, just a blur of darkness under my eyebrows, that somehow this gave me permission to do what I knew I was going to do. I would do what I wanted. What I needed. What might be wrong, but was easily justified. Jessie didn't tell me specifically to take the ibuprofen, right? She could have meant the Norco? Besides, Jessie said her surgery was fine, and it was in the past, right? She didn't need the pills. It's all good, I convinced myself.

I opened the mirror again and quickly palmed the slim bottle, carefully sliding the ibuprofen to cover the missing space. I reasoned that Jessie wouldn't miss Norco. She wasn't going to use them. Besides it looked like she had only taken maybe a couple of them, and that out of the 30, there were now 27 left. I counted them all as if they were priceless diamonds. I would ration them, I promised myself.

I quickly dressed in my freshly laundered clothes, remembering to slide on some of Jessie's deodorant over my hairy pits. I began to smile. I couldn't believe the fact that someone actually cared enough for me to wash my dirty clothes, someone really cared how I smelled and was concerned about how I felt. Someone actually cared about me. *Somebody cared.* Something that hadn't happened in so many years, I'd forgotten how great it felt, how much I needed to feel it.

But then a dark part of me laughed at such a thought. No, it didn't matter that Jessie cared about me. No, I didn't need her or anyone else. Jessie didn't matter a whit. All that mattered, I knew for certain, was the Hydrocodone. That beautiful chemical, which was finally hitting my system, satiating my brain with its warm bath, that was my real girlfriend, my lover, and my savior all rolled into a tiny white piece of heaven. By now I didn't care how many or how few pills I had. I didn't care. My tired and abused body had a second life thanks to the medicine. I was currently feeding off Pharma superpower—a power I could swallow anytime I wished. I was chemically charged with the false bravado of control and fortitude. I didn't need fresh clothes from a silly girl and her washer/dryer and her scented sheets. In fact I didn't need anyone, I convinced myself. I just needed a handful of white pills. My white mistress.

CHAPTER FIFTEEN

I told Jessie I needed to go because "I had plans." I needed to get back to Santa Monica and pick up my Saab. Since I was going to be busy, she decided she might as well go to work, even though she had the day off. Something about working on red lines or some architect jargon. She told me she might stop off at Mass first and wondered if I wanted to join her. I politely declined. I was in no mood to kneel before God. I didn't need God. But I did need a place to stay, and before I could ask, Jessie handed me her spare house keys. I told her I was only going to be in LA about five more days or so, and after that, well, I would probably be going somewhere else—intimating that our relationship was not likely to last more than a week. She took it all in with a smile, as if she only cared about the present. She evidently wasn't someone who lived for the future. "That's something we can't control," she told me. "But we still have a week together." She said. "Isn't that beautiful?" She hugged me.

I was amazed. I had all but broken up with this girl, and she was as joyful as ever. Why couldn't all women be like this? But then I quickly wondered to myself, "Why was I breaking up with her?" I actually felt pretty wonderful when I was around Jessie, and deep down inside I was excited that I got to live with this hot, sweet woman for the next few days. I was getting used to all the flower and yellow insanity that seemed to surround her, and I found myself liking the way she smelled and the way she smiled and the way she scrunched up her sweet long nose sometimes when she pretended to be mad at me... Hell, I realized I was thinking more about having fun with Jessie than finding Mr. Dorado. I was thinking about Jessie all the time. Because of her, maybe I was actually starting to like LA.

But then I forced myself to lose my smile as I pulled away from her embrace. My sensible self took over and stuffed down and kicked away this emotional nonsense. Jessie was no more than a crutch, a temporary distraction. A silly yellow flowered place to lay my head, to exercise my johnson, and to temporarily stave off the inevitable loneliness of my life. I knew she was nothing more. She couldn't be anything more than that, because I wasn't going to let her get close to me, because those close to me always leave... or they die. Much better if I run away first. Because that's what I do. Fuck her and fuck my feelings. I had a job to do, a case to solve.

"Let's go," I told the girl in the flowered skirt.

As we were about to walk out the door, I noticed something tacked to the wall by the entry-way, something she obviously wanted me to see. It was a small pencil drawing—a portrait. I was stunned.

Hell if it wasn't a picture of me—my sardonic face, my fedora tilted just so, and a perfect rendering of my patented wry smile. Underneath my visage she'd written the word "Happy." She removed the tack and handed it to me.

"I drew that while you were sleeping this morning," she said as she admired her work. "Take it. I can always make another one."

I couldn't stop staring at the drawing. Like I was looking at a stranger, yet at myself at the same time. It was uncanny. She seemed to like that it moved me somehow as I drifted out the door, mesmerized by the image.

"You can think about me when you look at yourself." She winked, locked the door, gave me a kiss, then trotted down the steps to the parking garage. I pulled my eyes away from my smiling face, slipped it into my pocket, then followed her down to her car.

I slid into the smallish passenger seat of Jessie's little yellow Miata. She dropped the top and I held onto my fedora as I enjoyed the fresh ocean air as we drove the two miles down to Ocean Park. My battered Saab with its fake handicap tag was miraculously continuing to sit in the expired meter on Main Street, somehow avoiding the ever-present tow trucks. Sandy looked over from her cafe, seeing me with Jessie in the little yellow sports car, and gave me a knowing wave, as if approving of my latest rendezvous.

I kissed Jessie goodbye, watched her drive away off to work, then sat in the Saab, wondering what the hell to do next.

I didn't have to wait long, because an unmarked Dodge quickly pulled in behind me and the hidden blue flashing lights gave a warning not to do anything but put my hands on the dashboard. I knew right away Detective Hazard had been staking out my car, waiting for my return, sitting silent in the little parking lot next door at the former pizza place that's always under construction. I'd noticed a car parked there but didn't think much of it. The way Hazard looked as he walked up to the driver's side, I could tell he'd been there all night, waiting and waiting and waiting.

I slowly rolled down the window as he glared at me with heavy bags under his unslept eyes and breathed out some stale coffee breath.

"Alright, Baker, exit your vehicle and come with me."

"Detective Haggard, so nice to see you again."

"Funny. Now get out," he said in his usual to-the-point manner.

Hazard opened the rear door of his unmarked Charger and guided me in. I assumed he was going to have something to say about the shootout at the Wilshire Motel.

I didn't have to wait long, because before he'd jumped into the driver's seat, he started going off. Hazard wasn't happy.

"Fuck, Baker, do you fucking know what kind of shitstorm you stirred up?!"

"Well, Detective, if you knew me a little better, you'd know that's par for the course." I tried to make myself comfortable on the hard rear seats.

"I don't want to know you. I don't want you here. I want you to get out of LA," he growled.

"That seems to be the consensus of the local denizens." I thought about Eddie Schwarma. "Guess I'm causing problems for both the robbers and the cops now." It was then I finally noticed his partner wasn't with him. "Where's your sidekick, by the way?"

A serious look washed over Hazard's serious, unshaven face. "This is between you and me." He rubbed his forehead.

"That make us pals?" I chortled.

"Tell me what happened at the Wilshire," he ordered, ignoring my comment. "Start from the beginning."

"Oh yeah, I'd heard about something happening at that motel," I said, being coy.

"Don't play stupid with me, Baker." He glared with his red eyes. "I need to know exactly what occurred." Hazard seemed genuinely interested.

"You know you have no proof I was at the Wilshire Motel," I pointed out.

"I have several witnesses that put you at the location. That saw you drive away from the crime scene," he countered.

I shot back at him. "Go ahead and put me in a lineup. It was dark and late at night. And in that situation, no way could anyone positively ID me in court."

"Look, if I wanted you in jail, Baker, we'd be at the station right now. There's a whole host of charges I could lay down to lock you away in Santa Monica for the foreseeable future." Hazard rubbed his temples again. "But, like I said, I don't want you here. I don't want you within a hundred miles of here. So please just tell me what happened."

"Off the record?" I asked.

"Like I said, this is between you and me."

I could tell from his eyes and demeanor that Hazard wasn't trying to frame me. Besides, he wasn't recording and I would deny anything I said anyway and he knew it. No, he was probably telling me the truth. Plus the fact that Sanchez was missing told me he didn't trust her anymore than I did. Maybe Hazard was on the up and up after all.

I recounted finding Kerry's body, then how the Sicario had upended Jessie's condo, then detailed the dustup at the motel, leaving out the part of me executing the Sicario at point blank range on the sidewalk. I made it sound like I was simply defending myself from a dangerous illegal alien bent on murdering me. I didn't bring up the nonsense with Eddie Schwarma, but I did tell him of my suspicions about Sanchez being dirty. That she was probably on El Dorado's payroll and that she no doubt set me up for assassination, with the death of the motel night clerk on her as collateral damage.

Hazard took it all in, barely nodding. "Detective Sanchez's son is in a wheelchair," he said, as if trying to justify his partner's possible actions that could have very much gotten me killed. Then, as if knowing my thoughts from the cynical look I was giving him, Hazard lowered his voice. "Detective

Sanchez has only been my partner for a few months. She's still on probation, as far as I'm concerned."

"What happened to her son?" I asked.

"Her kid was jumped on the street. Ended up in the hospital."

I knew that sometimes, when a cartel or a crime family wanted a reluctant or clean good-guy on their dirty payroll, they'd make it a deal you couldn't refuse. Maybe Sanchez was offered a bucket of cash to work for El Dorado. Maybe she turned it down. Maybe then they sent some bad guys to give her son a beating to send Sanchez a message: next time the boy doesn't make it out of the hospital. Besides, with enough damage, she'd have no choice but to take the money to pay the medical expenses. I actually felt sorry for her. Then I thought about the man who tried to kill me.

"You ID the Sicario?"

Hazard thought some more, then revealed that, judging from the tats, the dead Sicario was a member of the notorious Jackal Muerte cartel, known for migrant and drug smuggling, specializing in human trafficking and assassination on both sides of the border, especially now that the border was wide open and essentially run by the Mexican cartels themselves.

Then Hazard told me that he'd sent a fresh forensics team over to Kerry's house and they did in fact find traces of Kerry's blood in the bedroom, as well as some 12 gauge buckshot, with Kerry's DNA on the bullets buried in the bedroom wall behind fresh plaster and paint. The buckshot matched the gun left behind at the Wilshire Motel.

Then Hazard did something I hadn't expected. He reached into his glove compartment and pulled out a paper bag. He turned and handed it to me. I checked inside—it was my Heckler & Kotch Mark 23, still loaded with the Fort Scott .45 tumbler-killers.

"You might need this." Was all he said.

I thanked him. He nodded me out of his car. As soon as I was standing on the sidewalk in front of Buffalo Exchange, Detective Hazard drove away without looking back.

I checked the chamber, racked the slide, set the safety and stuffed it in my formerly empty holster beneath my left shoulder under my sweet-smelling Hugo Boss wool blend. I was back in business.

CHAPTER SIXTEEN

I again sat in my Saab without a clue as to what to do next. The only lead was Sanchez, but I couldn't go after her. Unlike Hazard, she'd have no hesitation about locking me up—setting your's truly up no doubt to be "Epsteined" by a bad guy paid handsomely to make sure I didn't leave the cell alive.

At least I had my gun. I decided to check the glove compartment to see how many .45 rounds I had left, but as soon as I did, I noticed the papers on the floor of the passenger seat—the flyers from my windshield the other night on Hollywood Boulevard. Then I saw Willis's star map.

That didn't make sense. Why the hell would he put a star map on my windshield?

Unless he was trying to send me a message!

I quickly picked it up. Nothing on the front other than the usual fake Hollywood movie star addresses. I turned it over. On the back, Willis had hastily pencil-scribbled a name, along with a phone number. *Tyler Hintzman.*

I whipped out my phone and duck-duck-goed Tyler's name. Turns out Mr. Hintzman was a mid-level talent agent at Annotated Agency, one of the big four or five talent agencies in Hollywood. AA was also affiliated with Golden Studios and Management—all of it run by uber-agent/producer/film-mogul/billionaire Nash Gold. Nash was responsible for some of the most iconic and classic movies in Hollywood—movies you've all seen and loved—all those action and cop flicks, the wild pre-Marvel sci-fi stuff, even some first rate dramas and biopics. Gold's collection of Oscars is legendary. When you think of George Lucas, Spielberg, Scorsese, Jerry Bruckheimer, and the top of the cream in Hollywood, you think of Nash Gold. With his storied career he'd definitely earned his nickname *"Solid Gold."*

I knew Gold could be the key to lead me to El Dorado. But you don't just call up Nash Gold and ask him a question. As usual with powerful billionaire types, there are layers and layers of buffer protection to keep gawkers, fans, wannabes, and the prying eyes of private dicks far away.

But Tyler Hintzman? Who the hell was he on the totem pole? What did a talent agent with no real juice or power have to do with anything but keeping the hopeful and unlikely dreams alive of the wannabe actors, writers, directors, and film school grads who start practicing their Oscar speeches once they coax their internet browser to conjure up Tyler's direct phone number? I doubted Nash Gold even knew this guy's name.

The more I thought about it, the more I was skeptical. Obviously Willis's fascination and obsession with Hollywood and his fantasy of someday being a movie star had finally gotten the better of him. All Willis fantasized about was Hollywood, living in a delusional dream of someday having Willis's address (once he actually *gets* an address) printed on one of his star maps, so of course he'd have a talent agent's name in his rolodex. Maybe Willis finally had gone off the deep end. At least his chosen insanity was trying to be an actor and not killing kittens or something awful like that.

I wasn't sure how to move forward. I figured no talent agent was going to be connected with the cartels. But then I started thinking. Both Ratso and Frenchie had transitioned from mob work to doing jobs for Hollywood types. Maybe there's not all that much of a difference? Maybe Tyler was connected with the underworld? Well, what the hell did I know?

All I did figure was that Tyler was now the only lead I had so I dialed up his number and got his secretary—or "assistant" as they call it nowadays. I told the teenage-sounding young man my name and that I was a private investigator needing to set up a meeting with Hintzman ASAP. I did my best to sound official and no-nonsense. The guy got very nervous and seemed unsure what to do. He put me on hold—probably so he could ask his boss what to do—then came back and quickly set me up for a ten-minute block at three o'clock. I figured the "investigator" angle would get me a better chance of a meetup than the usual schmuck story like I wanted to pitch an idea or a script or something. I was surprised it worked so well.

I drove down Wilshire, past the Wilshire Motel, replete with yellow police tape still sealing the door of the green bungalow, then through Westwood, past UCLA, and down across Santa Monica Boulevard into the heart of the ritzy Beverly Hills business district.

The Annotated Agency sits across the street from its corporate nemesis William Morris Endeavor—a purposeful testament to the legendary rivalry between Nash Gold and Ari Emanuel, the storied leader of WME. When Nash decided to move Annotated away from Santa Monica because he hated the local politics and high taxes, and the fact that the building commission wouldn't allow him to construct a needed addition to the skyscraper he owned off 7th Street, of course he chose a new site for his super agency right next to Ari and WME in Beverly Hills. The expensive purchase and renovation of Nash's new gleaming skyscraper on Wilshire Avenue made good fodder for the local industry rags, but it also made it easier for talent to set up meetings at both agencies without having to punch their valet ticket twice. It probably also meant both moguls could keep a keen eye on one another at the same time.

I pulled up in front of the sleek steel and glass joint, took a breath, and decided to pop some Norco to give me courage. As I opened the car door, a Mexican valet quickly ran over to me. He tried his best to hide his disdain of my vehicle as he handed me my ticket and I handed him the keys to the old Saab. I watched him maneuver the 96 past a gaggle of Teslas, some Porsches, several Ferraris, an AMG, a Lamborghini, a rare Pagani, and an even rarer Koenigsegg—a veritable Pebble Beach of beautiful supercars. My ugly brown beater trying to thread its way though five million bucks worth of steel and carbon fiber made me laugh.

As I entered the huge revolving door, I was met by two large security guards. They immediately asked me to hand over my firearm. I told them I was a detective and showed them my official CCW license, but they weren't about to let me go into the lobby carrying heat. The door must have had a metal detector with a silent alarm. Both guards wore earpieces, and with the closed circuit cameras everywhere, they probably already had me on facial recognition software because they already seemed to know my name. I was escorted to a desk, where another guard opened a sort of mobile gun safe, and the larger guy told me to deposit my .45 inside the box. I did so. He closed the lid and it locked electronically. He told me I could retrieve it after my meeting. The younger guard scanned me again with a mobile metal detector, and when he was satisfied I had no more weapons, I was given a lanyard with my picture and name and meeting time boldly printed on it, along with "Floor 5". I guessed that any deviation from my schedule would result in my getting jettisoned from the premises. The lanyard also had a QR code, which I was to use, he explained, in the elevator to get me to the proper floor for my proper meeting. Highly secure and highly efficient, this place was. I'd hate to have to break in.

The elevator took me to floor 5, and the floor secretary had me wait in the lobby with a big bay window that looked out over Wilshire Boulevard, until a thin kid who looked about 20, sporting a Jewfro and wearing a grey Men's Wearhouse suit, introduced himself as "Jason, Tyler's Assistant." Jason escorted me past his little cubicle (with a desk badge that said "Jason Greenblatt") and into Tyler Hintzman's corner office.

Tyler leapt up from his glass desk to greet me. He was about 30, with a zero-fat CrossFit body wearing one of those smooth botox faces sporting a neatly cut beard, coiffed eyebrows, and a perfect haircut that sort of faded on the sides and back. It also looked like Tyler wore mascara or something, as his eyes seemed to have these dark, painted rings bordering the deck of the eyelids, and his eyelashes were unusually thick and long. He certainly had painted fingernails—dark blue to match his $2,000 Armani suit. I shook my head. These Hollywood types...

"You must be Haim," he said excitedly. "Please have a seat." He motioned to a thin modern leather and metal sofa across from his desk. He moved over and sat down next to me. "We don't get many private eyes in here." He beamed. "So evocative." Then he turned to Jason, who had a leather binder in his hands and was dutifully taking notes in a nearby chair. "Jay, could you please get us a glass of Gerolsteiner?" Then he turned to me and asked, "Haim do you prefer ice or no ice? Or would you prefer Pellegrino?" He was genuinely curious.

"Neither." I said.

Tyler turned back to Jason, who was now visibly nervous about getting this order right. "Get me a Gerolsteiner, no-ice, and bring Haim a Pellegrino, ice on the side, just in case."

Jason nodded and quickly exited the room.

"So, what can I do for you?" Tyler said with a pleasant tone, sort of like you'd hear from a game show host. I had no idea what to say next, so I just pursed my lips, stared into his mascara eyes and made it look like I had so many important thoughts, I didn't know which one to utter first.

Tyler just smiled at me silently, as if waiting to hear my movie pitch. But I had no pitch. Then he suddenly furrowed his brows and said, "Wait a minute..." Tyler rushed back behind his desk, did some quick tapping on his laptop keyboard and smiled broadly as he read the info on the screen, lighting up his eyes. "Yes... Yes! *Haim Baker.* Now I know where I'd heard your name," he exclaimed as he kept reading some text on his computer.

Just then, Jason came in with a small round tray carrying a can of Gerolsteiner, a can of orange flavored San Pellegrino, and three wine glasses, one containing all ice. Tyler glanced up, frowned, stopped typing, and raised his voice.

"What the fuck, Jay?"

"Didn't you ask for Gerolsteiner and Pellegrino?" Jason said with a nervous voice—like an oft-abused child who knew he was gonna get a beat down.

"Did I say get me *cans*? Where'd you get these, from the fucking vending machine? Glass bottles, dude. Get us some *glass bottles.* Please. And Jay?"

"Yeah?"

"Pellegrino sparkling water. Not the flavored shit. I don't remember talking about orange-flavored anything. Capiche?"

"Oh, okay. I'm, I'm sorry, Tyler. Sure. Be right back." Jason froze for a second, unsure whether to leave the tray and glasses and take the cans, or take the whole thing and start all over. He decided on the latter and took the tray and left, nearly dropping an ice-filled wine glass on the way out. Thank God he didn't. Probably would have suffered an early coronary.

I wanted to remind Tyler that I didn't want any water, flavored or not, but I knew he didn't care. This is how these H-wood executives train their subordinates. Berate them, punish them, make impossible demands on them to toughen them up for a dog-eat-dog industry—while thoroughly enjoying the power, lording over those that depend on their tinseltown demigods for a minimum wage paycheck and a potential career. I'd love to try to get Tyler fired, but he'd only land at some other agency or management company making even more money. Besides, Tyler also no doubt started at the bottom as a berated assistant just like Jason. Now he's come full circle to complete the cycle of abuse.

Tyler went back to reading his laptop as if the entire interaction with Jason had never happened. He finally looked up at me. "Yeah, I read about you in the Union Register. That thing in San Diego, over near El Cajon. You busted a sex slave ring or something." Then his eyes went wide as he read something else and seemed to get even more excited. "Wow! A shootout, half-naked girls running around a warehouse. Some billionaire was involved. That's one hell of a story!"

Just then Jason stepped in, balancing a new tray of tall thin glasses and two small bottles of unflavored sparkling water. He set them down on the table but then Tyler immediately waved him off.

"I don't need that shit, just take some fucking notes please?"

Jason quickly set down the tray, grabbed his notepad and started writing. Tyler told him to reference a story in the December 12th Union Register about a busted human trafficking ring. Then, when he was done scanning the article, Tyler quickly walked over and sat down next to me, looking at me anew as if I was solid gold.

"I'm seeing a fucking movie here, bro. Maybe a series."

"What?" I said, completely taken aback.

Tyler's eyes looked up to heaven, like he was thinking deep, creative thoughts, then suddenly came back down the Mt. Olympus of his mind.

"Yeah! This is like an American version of *Narcos* meets *Taken*. I love it!" Tyler looked over at Jason, busy scribbling, "Who do you see, Jay, like a Frank Grillo?"

"Grillo's great." Jason said, still writing, nodding his head. "Kicked ass in *The Purge.*"

"Nah," Tyler said, cancelling his own brilliant idea. "Grillo's too old. What's he like, like sixty now?"

Jason continued to nod. "I think he can play younger."

"Maybe, but I've got a better idea..."

Tyler paused for effect as he looked at both of us. Jason used Tyler's pregnant pause to stop writing, looking up at his boss with faux rapt attention. I was guessing Jason had become used to Tyler's theatrical, game-show-host style of conversation.

"Know what I'm thinking?" Tyler said as he kept looking back and forth expectantly between me and Jason, as if we could somehow read his amazing little mind. We both stared at Tyler, waiting for his revelation, then we looked at each other. Neither one of us had any idea what this maniac was going to say. Then Tyler suddenly slapped his desk, beaming loudly, as if he'd just discovered plutonium:

"Chris Pratt!"

Tyler looked over at me and somehow saw the A-list star of *Jurassic World* and *Guardians of the Galaxy* in my scruffy, skeptical exterior.

"Chris Pratt is perfect for this: a grizzled private detective taking on a billionaire who may or may not be trafficking sex slaves. A wild action thriller with mystery, fornication and plenty of action centered around a redemptive down-on-his-luck private eye. I love it!"

Where did he get this stuff? Did he just make this up?

Tyler stood, as if to burn off some of his newly acquired creative energy. "Jay, find out if Jason Heymen is still Chris's agent at UTA." He clapped his hands like he was giving orders to a rickshaw driver. "Chop-chop!"

Jason scrambled onto his iPhone, checking the IMDBpro database. "Chris is still with Jason," the overworked and over-harried assistant said. "And *Terminal List* hasn't been renewed, so Chris doesn't have a series right now."

"Perfect! When we're done, let's get Jason on the phone right away. This is fucking great. Timing is fuckin' everything, Jay."

Jason nodded again as Tyler suddenly reached out his hand to me. I had no idea what to do, so I stood up and shook it. The grip was wimpier than I expected.

"Haim, I'm excited. I love this." He started escorting me to the door. "I know I can sell it to Netflix as a series. But I'm thinking a movie too. We just need Chris on board, but that's my problem, not yours. However, I would like you to jot down some ideas. You know, nothing formal, just some things we might be able to use in our pitch and a treatment..."

What the hell had Willis gotten me into? Before I could tell this nutjob that I wasn't interested in writing anything down other than the location of El Dorado, he quickly tapped some keys on his Galaxy and suddenly my phone dinged with a text.

"Just sent you an address to a party tonight. I want you to come. Promise you'll have a great time." He put his arm around my neck, the way LA people do, as if we were long time pals or frat bros. "It'd be seriously good to let people meet you. You know, be a rough and tumble private detective. They'll eat it up and it'll help sell the project." Then he looked me over and smiled. "And make sure to wear that Fedora. I love it."

My life was now a "project." My Fedora was now a prop. It wasn't, was it? I wasn't so sure anymore. I wiggled out of his embrace before he could turn me even more into a caricature of myself.

"If I may?" I said as he opened his office door to finally let me go.

"Sure, what is it, Haim? Don't you like the idea? It's your story. In fact, you'll get story credit. It's great. You've lived it man. You're livin' it!" Tyler seemed to forget that I'd set up this meeting to interview him, not to pitch another overwrought action thriller cop show.

"I'm actually on a case right now."

"Really? That's so fucking cool! Promise me you'll take some notes. This could be our sequel."

I ignored his rote excitability, resenting the way he ordered me to do his bidding, as if I were just an older, grittier version of Jason Greenblatt.

"I'm fucking serious, Mister Hintzman." I tried to throw in as much New York swagger as I could. "I'm looking for a man they call *El Dorado*. I was wondering if you've ever heard of the guy." I searched Tyler's face for any clues as to how much he knew, but for some reason I could't read him at all—just that botox and makeup game show face of his.

"El Dorado? What, you mean, like the mythical city of gold? Like in Florida or Colombia or Venezuela or something?" Tyler furrowed his two perfect brows, as if trying to make sense of it, trying to draw a creative line from El Cajon to El Dorado—and coming up short.

"No. El Dorado is a person. Probably a man. A cartel leader," I said. "'El Dorado' is what he calls himself. El Dorado is here in LA and I need to find him. I will find him. And when I do…" I made it clear that shit was gonna go down.

"Wow!" Tyler said with extra enthusiasm. "We're not saving him for a sequel, let's put this Dorado guy in our show right now! Sounds like a fucking cool antagonist."

"He's not cool. Or an antagonist. He's evil. He's a killer and he's the biggest human trafficker this side of the planet."

"Even better!" Tyler said, as he gave me the thumbs up, and closed the door.

I stood there, dumbfounded. What the hell just happened?

I suddenly thought about the fact that, in the span of three days in LA, I'd already killed a guy, found out I had a girlfriend, and maybe was going to get a Hollywood movie deal. But I was no closer to finding El Dorado than Sir Walter Raleigh.

I saw the tray of cans and wine glasses sitting on the table outside of Jason's empty desk. The kid was no doubt being tasked or berated or something inside Tyler's office. So I popped open the orange San Pellegrino and washed down a handful of Norco, hoping it would give me the supernatural powers I desired to figure all this shit out. Mostly, unfortunately, it began to give me a stomachache, so I decided I needed something to eat as a remedy.

I made it down to the lobby and retrieved my gun from the guard station, exchanging it for my lanyard. They also validated my $40 valet ticket, thank God. The guards made sure to escort me out, now that I had my HK, making sure I didn't sneak back inside. I gave the ticket to the valet guys, along with a five buck tip. Within a few minutes I was in my Saab and driving up Wilshire back towards Santa Monica. It was rush hour, however, and I was barely getting above 7mph as I hit the endless snake of Beverly Hills traffic. The slow stop-and-go gave me time to think—and to notice the black Firebird that was following me two car lengths back...

CHAPTER SEVENTEEN

Good thing about LA traffic, it offers plenty of chances to block out a tail. I'd seen the Firebird pulling out across the street as I exited the driveway. By now we were just getting to Santa Monica Boulevard. At the last second I pulled right, onto the boulevard, forcing Firebird Man to do the same. But he didn't have an opening. As soon as he did, I threw a U-turn and then hit a hard right up Wilshire again, leaving the black car stuck going East. I made sure he couldn't see me as I quickly turned into the Beverly Hills Hotel, then drove through over to Santa Monica and jammed it West against traffic, moving the little Saab as fast as it could go. I looked back. I'd lost him.

I stayed on Santa Monica for a few miles, passing under the 405, driving by the old Nuart theater, where they still play Rocky Horror at midnight, then I crossed Sawtelle. I used to live in this neighborhood long ago, but except for the theater, everything seemed to be different. The old Vons supermarket was gone, replaced by "luxury apartments." In fact most of the blocks that had small businesses and car dealers and bodegas were all now full of "luxury apartments'."My stomach growled and my head spun and then I began to sweat from the heat and the desire for more pills to numb myself from the fact that the whole world seemed to be getting paved over with empty "luxury apartments" that no one could afford.

I wanted to eat something, anything that wasn't Starbucks or Panda Express or some other chain store. I finally saw place a few blocks down called the Naan Hut'—it was a Middle Eastern place I remember seeing back when I lived in the neighborhood and I was glad it was still here and decided to finally try it out. I found a space in front, and ordered a chicken kabab gyro thing with a bottle of Corona Extra, and sat at one of the tables outside on the sidewalk, next to a gym—hoping to get a view or two of some workout gals in their Lulus. Thanks to the very slow service, I sat there for a good twenty minutes and got to spy a few pretty birds on their way to pilates, but for some reason all I thought about was Jessie and her stripper pole. Why couldn't I get that damn woman out of my head?

I decided to watch the cars go by, a great pastime of mine. Out here in the upper-crustier parts of LA, you get to see all sorts of exotic automobiles, and sure enough I spied my share of ubiquitous red Ferraris, orange Lambos, and a rainbow of 911s, even one of those insane GT2RS's, the exhaust note nearly knocking off my hat. As it drove past, however, I saw another car sitting across the street by the 99 cent store. The dark tinted windows matched the black paint of the Firebird. Mutherfucker!

Thankfully the food was still apparently cooking, because I knocked over the empty round metal table when I jumped up and sprinted over to the black car, nearly getting clipped by the honking traffic in the process.

The Firebird started to pull away, but I stood in front and pulled open my jacket, making it clear to the driver that I had a big ass gun ready to go if he did anything stupid. He turned off the car and rolled down his window.

I walked up to the driver door and saw the guy was short and rotund, with a stupid looking mustache, balding hair and round prescription glasses with smudge marks on them. He stared at me like he was in awe.

"Haim Baker. It's really you. And you wear a fedora. Now that is classic." He ogled me like I was some sort of movie star. What is it with this place?

"You seem to be plenty acquainted with me, but I don't know you from Adam, asshole, so you'd better fucking tell me why you're tailing me or I'm gonna start putting .45 sized holes in your car, and maybe in your face," I said as stern as I could. "So what the fuck?"

"Oh yeah, oh yeah, oh yeah. Just like I imaged it. You're a bruiser, you are, Haim Baker! Quite the bruiser! I can't tell you how long I've waited to finally meet you," the fatman said.

I had no more patience, so I quickly pulled out my gun and pressed it hard on his cheek. "You better start talking pal, cuz I hate having assholes on my ass," I pressed the gun harder.

"Okay, okay, okay," he mumbled as he put up his hands, as if this guy was ever a threat. Then he offered his right hand to shake. I stared at his greasy fingers and then saw the entrails of a Subway sandwich next to him on the passenger seat that he must have devoured while driving, because there were also a few soda cans and used, bunched-up napkins on the floor all around him as well. His car had the off-putting scent of stale lemonade and his steering wheel had one of those $8.99 rubber covers over it that had smears from his fingers. No way was I ever gonna shake this guy's hand. He finally realized this and retracted it.

"Name's Candy. Andrew Candy. You can call me Andy. Andy Candy. I write a blog that I call "CandyEye," which is a play on the term "Eye Candy..."

"No shit." Like I would have never figured that one out. I prompted him to go on with a wave of my H&K.

"Yeah, I thought it was pretty clever," he said with a self-satisfied grin. "In fact, I own the URL 'CandyEye dot com,' I had to pay some online sex worker five hundred bucks for it, but I got it and registered it for five years on GoDaddy."

"Could you please just get on with it," I said, exasperated.

"Oh yeah. Sure. Anyway, so I'm from San Diego, actually Kearny Mesa. You see, I'm a journalist, a blogger, and I write about true crime. Well, the thing is, I've been covering Nobel Industries for years, but I couldn't get anyone to pay attention to what Patterson Nobel was doing to those kids. I knew that rich dude was importing the prostitutes who were flooding downtown, working the tourists, traveling the skin route to Oceanside for the Marine base, and even plying their trade in the SoCal shopping malls. And when I saw that you took out his operation in Santee, I thought, Wow! Never figured that would happen! So, it's a real honor to meet you, Baker." He put out his hand again, forgetting that I wasn't going to touch it. I made sure my hand was busy so I couldn't shake that five-fingered germ factory, so I holstered my gun, rubbed my face and nearly got clipped again by a Ford Mustang. As I simmered down I realized I was foolishly standing on the busy street, only inches away from angry, anxious California drivers trying to get onto the 405 at rush hour—not a good place to park my campers. I looked over at my table across the street and saw that it was sitting upright again, but now, finally, sitting pretty with a hot gyro perched upon it along and a cold Corona beckoning me back to my little metal chair.

Candy-man was still blabbing about something and I'd already figured he was a total waste of my time, so I gave him a glance good-bye, then turned away and trotted across traffic to my table.

I sat down and had barely got the round rim of the lovely cold Corona to my lips before the Mr. Blogo was pulling up a chair next to me.

"So, the question is, what is Haim Baker doing in Los Angeles?" Andy said, as he looked hungrily at my gyro. "My guess is that there's a connection here to Nobel Enterprises, and I wanna be the one who breaks the story. Can you tell me, on the record?"

Because of my brief experience with Candyman, I'd now completely lost my appetite, so I pushed the plate in front of him, ignoring his questions, hoping he'd simply eat and run.

"Go ahead and have some. I'm really not hungry."

"You sure?" He said, expectantly. "I love Gy-ros."

I'd already polished off most of the Corona by now, filling my mouth up with beer so I wouldn't have to talk. I nodded, absently. In seconds he had half of the kabob thing in his mouth. Of course this guy talked as he chewed.

"Come on Baker," he mumbled and swallowed, "gimme the scoop!"

I gulped the rest of the beer and longed for something stronger. I automatically reached for the Norco, but stopped myself—not wanting this guy to spill my Opiate addiction to the online world. So I stood, figuring I had a break while he still had half my gyro to chow down.

"Look, John Candy…"

"—John Candy was my cousin!" Andy exclaimed.

"That makes sense," I added.

"Of course you'd figure that out—you're a detective!"

"And this detective has to go. So, nice meeting you Candy Andy, see ya around."

And with that I was already up walking away and sliding into the seat of the Saab. But Andy had grabbed the remaining half of my gyro, bits falling out as he rushed towards me, still chewing the other half in his mouth as he yelled.

"Wait!" He yelled. I had the car started, but he'd somehow made it to my door. "I can help you! We can help each other." He finally swallowed some kabob, parts of which were still rolling around in his mouth as I began to pull away. Candy's turn to step in front of the car. He didn't have a gun, but he had greasy fingers and a greasy bomb of a half-eaten gyro nearly falling out of his hand. I didn't want either on the exterior of my Saab. He suddenly bent down, out of sight, then reappeared again in a flash. I was afraid I might have hit him but he smiled and gave me the OK sign.

I hit the clutch, then rolled down the window. "What!?"

"I haven't told you everything, Baker. I'm working on a big story in LA, and I think it's all tied together with San Diego. You wouldn't believe it! There are things you need to know."

"Sure," I lied. "We can talk some other time. Gotta go."

With that I shifted into first, floored it and sped West onto Santa Monica Boulevard, leaving Andy Candy to finish eating all by himself.

CHAPTER EIGHTEEN

As soon as I pulled away, I got a text from Jessie. "Be home for dinner???" She added a heart emoji, a face with hearts for eyes emoji, and a cat emoji. I texted as I drove, simply saying "Sorry. Onthe case. Behom late."

She replied with some sad emojis, and a "Luv U," but I didn't see them, because I'd already swiped up to the address to the party in the Hollywood Hills. Waze told me to take the 405, but I hate the 405. As the sun went down, I decided to cruise Sunset Boulevard, so I pulled right on Bundy, puttered up to Sunset, took a right, and did the winding drive past UCLA and the Brentwood and Bel Air mansions, up to Doheny Drive, then left, up to the famous Bird Streets with all those giant view homes that lord above LA, turning a chaotic, snarled city into a beautiful palate—an endless sea of pretty, colorful lights of the speckled worker bees doing their menial jobs to support the kings and queens that look down upon them with indifference.

Down here on the dirty tarmac, the ant-like traffic was a bitch, but about an hour later, I'd finally crawled up the steep hills and matched the address on my phone, discovering a vast, gated, 25 mil, 12,000 ft, seven-bedroom, twelve-bath mansion perched at the end of Swallow Drive.

It was dark when I arrived at the buzzing party. The road was narrow, but there were a handful of tuxedoed Valets frantically taking over the beautiful cars of the many beautiful party goers, and parking them godknowswhere.

I went through the usual give-the-key-take-a-ticket routine, and saw the usual sad face plastered on the unlucky foreign-born valet who drove my car away as I walked past the black guy, wearing all black, guarding the black metal gate. He nodded and let me pass, assuming I belonged here. Of course

I belonged here. These H-wood galas are strictly in-the-know affairs—only those invited have the info to the location (they're never at the same place twice in a row), and if you reveal that address to your friends, or online, or bring the wrong kind of guest or crash the party, you're never invited again and are essentially exiled from Hollywood. Keep in mind it's at these clandestine parties where all the wheeling and dealing actually occurs for the actors, writers, directors and producers of tinseltown, so these private affairs are the lifeblood of the movie-making machine. To be invited to one means you're either a player, a plaything, or an amusement. I figured I was the latter—a little Brooklyn color to add a bit of spice and fun to the otherwise beautiful, bland, Botox and Bulgari crowd. For me this was a fishing expedition—I'd find the characters linked to the underworld, then follow the trail to hopefully reel in El Dorado. It was my biggest lead so far.

As I walked behind the secure gate, I saw a lone, Nordic supercar sitting in the driveway—a white, seven-figure Koenigsegg. Same one from the Annotated Agency. Past it on the lawn were lots of fashionable, happening Hollywood hipsters hooking up, making deals, and milling about outside, cocktails and joints in hand. I looked up and saw two stories of giant floor-to-ceiling windows of glass and concrete that revealed the trendy house was filled to the brim with pretty, perfect party-goers. The place was lit up like a Christmas tree, inviting me in for the fun. And I was ready for some fun. But first I needed some nerve, some kick, and some warmth all rolled into one. I reached down to grab a fistful of Norco—but to my horror, the bottle was empty.

Shit. I'd promised myself I'd ration those pearls, but in less than a day I'd already gone back on my word.

I realized I was now sweating under my fedora from The Need, and I was beginning to tremble from the fear of what was happening to me, what I was becoming and what knew I faced without my pills. I was desperately missing the feel-good in my brain and body and I needed it, wanted it, required it, and *right now.*

A young female server holding a tray of exotic drinks sauntered over to welcome me in with a low-cut top that just barely covered her nips along with a choker bow tie strapped around her neck. The old Baker would have made some inappropriate comment with my trademark smile, and perhaps may have received either her name and number or a scowl and a slap. But now I hardly noticed the sparkly flesh and spry figure. Instead I immediately went right for the oddball margarita drinks on the tray she held—which should have been a warning. I had highball glasses in each hand and had both drinks down in less than a minute. But the sweating and trembling continued as she left me for another guest.

As I was contemplating what to do next, I felt a hand on my shoulder. It was Tyler. He was wearing a garish purple suit with matching purple nail polish.

"Haim, you made it! This is great. Remember, just be yourself."

"Who else am I supposed to be?"

Tyler ignored my comment and continued his speedy "every-word-I-say-is-so-fucking-important-while-I-pretend-to-be-casual" nonsense.

"Act like you're on a case or something and be, like, the cool-detective-guy."

"I am on a case, Tyler."

"Cool!" He said as he dropped the hand on my shoulder down to my back, and gently, but firmly steered me to my left. "Let's go inside. Someone I want you to meet."

He directed me into the open door of the house. I despised being controlled like this, and was really starting to hate this guy—so much so that I wanted to suddenly turn into him, grab his little CrossFit arm and throw him into a quick, painful shoulder lock—knowing it would only take seven pounds of pressure to dislocate Tyler's perfectly muscled shoulder socket. Or perhaps I'd dislocate his elbow, or better yet, both. Now that would have been fucking satisfying.

But in my current, endorphin-deficit state, all that my harried and jumbled brain could think about was the missing warmth of the beautiful pills and the hard, cold chill that was now creeping up my spine as I meekly let this guy push me around like a wet, sweating noodle. That chill reached a climax when I found my hairs standing up on my arms as Tyler edged me over to a group of party-goers in the giant living room, all surrounding a short, bald, well-dressed man. The way I saw the sycophants supplicating to this old guy, I knew he was King of the Party.

"Fucking *Nash Gold*, Haim," Tyler said in total reverence. "He's the man. And if Nash Gold likes you, we're fucking gold. But..." Tyler used one of his stupid pregnant pauses for effect. Then he put his lips to my ear with a loud whisper, as if Tyler Hinstzman was providing a plebe with a privileged secret. "If Nash Gold doesn't dig you, Haim, well, you're finished, man... No pressure or anything!" He laughed.

It wasn't lost on me how Tyler suggested that *we'd* be gold or *I'd* be finished—Tyler takes the win and I take the loss. That's no doubt how it works out here in dreamland. Who's fucking dreams are these anyway? No doubt it's the guys like Nash Gold who do most of the dreaming while the rest of us are simply asleep.

"C'mon, Haim, lemme introduce you." Tyler put his arm back up around my neck into frat-bro mode, but he dutifully withdrew it as we got close. I was guessing this was just in case Nash disapproved of the pretentious fedora-wearing gumshoe now standing before him. I knew, however, if I got on Mr. Gold's Christmas list, no doubt Tyler would immediately be all touchy-feely again.

Tyler modulated his excitable voice into something more reverential. "Mr. Gold, this is Haim Baker."

Nash Gold sported a very expensive custom, pinstriped grey suit, a shiny gold tie (I hear that's his trademark) and a huge diamond pinky ring. Gold's eyes widened just a bit when Tyler spoke my name, then gave me a quick once-over, as if he were sucking the soul out of me with his dark pupils. But I had no soul anymore, just The Need. All I had was Need.

Nash must have caught the slight addict-tremble in my hands, even though I was working hard to steady myself. It made him smile, ever so slightly.

Tyler cleared his throat, then offered, "Haim's a private detective with a hell of a story."

"Yes." Was all Nash Gold finally said, as if he already knew all about me, and wasn't all that impressed with my so-called story. Then he stuck out his right hand. On it he wore an uber-rare $500,000 Piaget Altiplano watch.

"Pleasure to meet you," Gold said softly.

I had no choice but to steady my nerves and shake his small, thick hand, which, though buttery soft and throughly manicured, had more calluses than

I would have expected. Nash must have felt the clammy coldness of my palm because his firm grasp didn't last. He stared at me for a few more seconds with questioning eyes, then nodded briefly before turning away to a beautiful, tall, dark woman in a black mini dress with dark tats on her dark thighs and arms and neck and thick, cornrowed hair styled up high that gave her even more of a heightened presence. I realized this woman had been watching me the entire time.

As soon as Nash Gold turned his back on me, I figured that was it. My brief career in showbiz was over, thank God.

I started to walk away, but Tyler already had his arm around my shoulder, squeezing it with his purple-nail-polished hand, like I was his date and not his bro, and then he suddenly gave me a quick kiss on my cheek (WTF?!), patted me on the back and beamed,

"We're fucking *in,* man. You did it, Haim. You fucking did it!" He steered me over to the wet bar as another hot female with a black choker bowtie waited patiently to serve me, especially when she heard Tyler open the special, VIP alcohol spigot:

"Get anything you want, Haim. The night is yours."

With that, Tyler finally left me to the small glass of amber liquid I'd already ordered when I saw the unique Lalique crystal decanter nestled in between the most expensive array of single-malts I'd ever seen.

I had the exquisite Macallan 72 slipping past my quivering lips in seconds, allowing the seven-decades-old scotch that felt like thick, warm, ultra-smooth nectar, to fill my mouth with its sweet, aromatic magic. I tried to savor the unique flavor, knowing I'd probably never again get to sample a $150,000 bottle of alcohol. It tasted like liquid 18karat gold lusciousness.

Before I knew it, I'd drained the tumbler in two gulps and wanted more. God did I want more. But bargirl shook her head. A strictly one drink maximum for this stuff, even for VIP guests. I didn't blame her. I would have easily drunk the entire bottle. In minutes.

I was pondering the choice of my next single malt, when a smoky, sultry voice whispered to me like a voice on the wind, a sound that wafted right into my head. *"Come with me."* Something about her words stirred my loins— maybe it was the breathy tone, or the wet heat in my ear canal, but I was hard as a rock when I turned to the tall, dark woman with the black cornrows and dark tats now standing next to me, her piercing eyes stabbing right through my sockets. "Let me show you around," she said.

She had her arm though mine and was leading me upstairs before I knew it. She was easily a foot taller than me, even with my Stetson on.

"I don't have the pleasure," I said as we stepped to the top of the stairs. She stopped, turned and smiled.

"I'm Clara. Clara Scattino." She purred.

"So just how do you fit into this menagerie?" I wondered.

"My brother Gato. This is his house. Isn't it lovely?"

I looked around and noticed the wood and steel furniture, the dark planked ceiling, the bits of East Asian art and artifacts. It looked like a rich resort hotel in Bali.

"It is." I agreed.

"I designed the interior." She started walking again, pulling me along. "Let me show you the bedroom."

"How can I resist?"

She smiled. "You can't, of course." She laughed, and opened the door.

CHAPTER NINETEEN

The bedroom was smaller than I would have thought, though the floor-to-ceiling glass door opened up to a spacious deck overlooking the infinity swimming pool down below, while also lording over the horizon of twinkling lights from the bottom-dwelling drones of downtown LA a few thousand feet below that. In the middle of the deck was a large bronze statue of a scanty clad Indian goddess, with voluptuous breasts, a necklace of skulls around her neck, four arms waving weapons, and two feet stomping on a man's chest.

Clara followed me out to the deck.

"That's Kali. Beautiful, isn't she?"

"I wouldn't kick her out of my bed." I remarked, mesmerized by Kali's plump breasts and her wild, wagging tongue.

"But what would she do to you?" Clara laughed again, and strolled back in to the room. I was about to follow her, when my phone dinged with a text. It was Jessie, wanting an ETA so she could save me some dinner. I replied I was still working and told her not to wait up. For some reason I felt a pang of guilt. But guilt for what? Ogling a statue? Talking to a tall, dark Valkyrie?

Before I knew it, I'd turned off my phone and was on the bed, kissing Clara. Her tongue swirled inside my mouth. She was hypnotic, this woman. Then she told me to close my eyes. She had a surprise. I obeyed. She knew what I needed, she told me in that mesmerizing voice.

I heard her open a drawer and flick a lighter. Then I felt a pinprick between the big toe of my right foot. I opened my eyes and sat up as Clara withdrew a syringe. I hated needles.

"What the fuck!?"

"Shhhhhhhhh." She put her finger to her lips and smiled.

Before I could gather the muster to swing my legs over the bed and maybe kick this dope fiend in the gut, a sweet warm river suddenly began to course through my entire body, and the endorphins that I was sorely missing suddenly burst into my head like a supernova, as fading eyes watched Clara undress and I slowly lay back, drifting into serenity...

It was all a dream. The orgasmic burst of dopamine, the powerful thrusting, the screams, the pleasure and the lovely painfulness of it all. When I awoke, it was the afternoon. I was naked and alone in a strange bed again. I looked desperately for the angels and flowers on the ceiling, but only saw brown wood high above, as if I were in some sort of dark fairytale forest cabin. I forced my cloudy head to think, and then I remembered. Yes, I remembered now. It was that woman. That Clara woman. I was in her bedroom. Or the bedroom she laid me in. Tyler, Nash, the party...

I stumbled onto my feet, but my right foot hurt immediately as I hit the bamboo flooring. I looked down at it and spied several, painful track marks between the toes. When I took another step with my left foot, I discovered my ass hurt, and then I felt aching pain in my very overused penis. It was still huge. There was some sort of rubber cock ring on it. I quickly pulled the thing off, finally giving me some relief as Mr. Johnson happily began to deflate. But then I saw that someone had written two small letters at the base of my cock with permanent ink: *C.C.* I knew it must have meant "Clara's Cock." Like she owned me. Yeah right. I tried rubbing it off, but couldn't get it all.

I suddenly felt vulnerable and wanted my gun, my clothes, my fedora. I wanted the hell out of there. I searched the sparse room in my groggy condition but was unable to find anything that belonged to me. Not my phone, not my gun, not even my Stetson. No clothes or anything of mine anywhere. There was a locked dresser I couldn't open, a wet bar with an array of alcohol, and a big walk-in closet. I searched the closet, but there were only Clara's exotic designer clothes and shoes, but nothing for me. I stumbled over to the glass door, yanking the shades away. Rays of bright LA sunlight burst into the dark room, blinding me. As I adjusted to the daylight, I saw Clara, wearing nothing but a black silk robe with some sort of Asian design on it. She was sitting in a leather lounge chair, smoking some sort of clove cigarette. The door was partially open. I walked out, best I could, to confront her.

She must have heard me, because she was up, cigarette in hand, to greet me with a smile and her open robe. "Mmmmmmmmm. My lover." She purred as she embraced me. I was mesmerized by her soft dark skin and her exotic, musky scent, and the strange tattoos that seemed to cover her entire legs, arms and torso: naked women, tigers, dragons, skulls, and all sorts of weird symbols. A dark tapestry of some sort of mythical Asian chronicle of life and death. "You're ready again."

She began kissing me, overwhelming me. I gathered the courage to pull away, even though I wanted more than anything to become lost in that dark embrace, to dream again.

"Where the hell are my clothes?" I said as sternly as I could muster.

She sauntered over to an ashtray and crushed out her clove. "Oh, they're safe, my darling."

"Can I have them back?"

"Is that what you really want right now?" she purred, her eyes twinkling as she moved inside, beckoning me. "Come."

I wanted out of here, out of this house, but I realized I wanted her more. So I followed Clara back to the bed. She was pouring some absinthe into a martini glass. "Here," she said, handing it to me as I sat on the mattress.

I stared at the green liquid. Figured it might stop my head from pounding, so I drank it. The taste of anise filled my mouth. I liked it.

"I need my phone. Where's my gun?" I ordered, as I drank the rest of the liqueur.

She began to slide out of the robe. "Is that what you need? Is that what you really need?"

I thought about it in my fractured state. Maybe she was right? What did I need? What did I want? Yes, this woman knew me. Knew all of me. My overused appendage was already stiff again, and I couldn't get her scent off my mind, and her curvy body was so inviting as she lay there waiting for me, for my embrace...

I couldn't concentrate, but then I didn't want to. I wanted to feel. I wanted to feel her, feel good, feel warm, feel pleasure.

I also wanted the pain. And as I got on top of her, I put her hand on my neck. She smiled broadly and began to squeeze. The harder she cut off my oxygen, the more I loved it, the more excited I became.

I kept thrusting, wanting this to never stop.

"Want more?" She whispered into my ear.

"Yes," I begged. "Yes. More. I need more."

Using the hand she had around my neck, she rose, lifted me with her amazing strength, and put me down in the bed until she was on top. She squeezed until I couldn't breath at all, and as I started to pass out, she slid off of me, slipped another ring onto me, and went to the locked dresser.

My head was in darkness from oxygen debt, and as my vision began to come back, I felt another pinprick in my left foot. But this time I smiled. I knew what it was and I never wanted it to stop. "More," I said.

I heard her sing-songy laugh as her voice billowed, "No, my love, we have to wait a bit. But I promise..."

She was soon lying down next to me. I was again in warm heaven. My eyes blurred from the pleasure and the serenity. Before I knew it, I was on top of her. It felt like I was there for hours, feeling her, part of her, but it wasn't enough. The warmth was nice, but not intoxicating like the first time. I wanted more. "More," I begged. She squeezed my neck. "I need more." The pain was intense as the drugs filled my head and she filled my body. She owned my body. And she knew it. Clara's Cock all right.

And then she smiled at something that wasn't me, and thrusted her hips higher, forcing me to bend over. Then I felt it. It wasn't like the impersonal, cold, hard, metal barrel of Patterson Nobel's gun. No, this was firm, but soft. It was warm and alive and piercing me, owning me, caressing me from the inside. It was pleasure. It was pain. And I wanted more. I thrust into her, I thrust back into the man behind me and the three of us developed a rhythm that exploded into ecstasy as she squeezed the air from me and he thrust deep into my prostate. It was unlike anything I'd ever experienced. Maybe I'd been waiting for this my entire life?

I was complete, and I finally expired into a "little death" as the French call it.

I had passed out.

I was lying on my side, and as I blinked my eyes open moments later, I saw a tall, dark, thin, bald man with a goatee with gold hoop earrings, kissing Clara passionately. He was next to me, on top of her, and they both screamed in pleasure as the bed thundered with their movement and I passed further into the dark abyss, having eaten the lotus and tasted the sin, the beautiful sin...

I awoke later. I was alone. The were no angels. Not even flowers. Only the bare, lonely darkness of the room. My ass hurt like hell. And both my feet were in pain from all the needle-pricks. I began to cough. I stumbled to the glass door, pulling back the shade. But it was dark outside. Was it that night? Another night? How many days and nights had I been here? I hadn't eaten, but I wasn't hungry. I was thirsty as hell, though. I stumbled into the bathroom and realized I had to pee. But I couldn't. I had one of those damn rings on again. I pulled it off and angrily tossed it into the trash as I pissed, mostly hitting the toilet as I stared at the faded "C.C."

I shoved my face under the sink faucet and poured water into my gullet. I couldn't stop drinking. I searched the wall until I found the light switch, turning on a few ornate standing lamps. Then I went back to the bathroom, turned on the light and stared at myself in the mirror. I had dark lines under my eyes, like I'd aged ten years. My skin was a pale yellow. But I didn't care. I wanted that feeling again. I turned off the light. Turned off all the lights and sat on the bed. What the hell was I doing? I began to clear the spiderweb of darkness in my mind, remembering why I was here. I had to get back to Jessie. I had to get out of this place.

That's when the door opened.

Clara stood, fully dressed in a see-through blouse and a sexy high cut skirt that slit to the top of her thigh. She had on no underwear, and I could just see a peek of the thick black hair between her legs.

"What do you want, my love?" She asked.

I tried to get my mind straight, and the old Baker began to take over this nonsense.

"I want my fucking gun."

I felt like a prisoner in this dark place and I knew feeling the handle of a pistol in my palm would gave me the sense of strength and power that I know I've always been missing in my life.

Clara closed the door. "Lie down," she ordered.

"Fuck you. I want my things. I need to go."

"Lie down if you want your gun," she said, forcefully.

Before I knew it, I was lying flat on the bed again. Clara went to the dresser, unlocked it, and slid out a drawer. Then she told me to close my eyes, but I'd had enough of her theatrics.

"Close your own fucking eyes," I said.

"My love," she said flatly, "If you want to see your gun again, that's what you have to do. Close your eyes." Her back was facing me. I knew she wouldn't turn around until I wasn't looking.

"Okay. Fine." I had no choice, so I complied and shut my eyelids.

I felt her climb on top of me, she opened my mouth with her fingers, then slipped in her warm tongue. We kissed as she owned my mouth with her lips—until I felt something hard and cold. I knew right away it was the barrel of my Mk.23, and it was now halfway down my throat. I began to choke and snapped my eyes open. Her finger was on the trigger and a dark smile was on her face. She pushed it harder and farther down into my mouth. I was panicking, having trouble breathing, trying to tell her to stop, but I couldn't talk with the metal in my mouth. I didn't dare do anything to stop her, as she only needed about four pounds of pressure to quickly and violently end my life.

"Show me what you want."

I began to relax.

"Show me..."

I began to taste the thing in my mouth. The bitterness of the steel, the hint of gun oil and cordite. She pulled it back just a bit as my tongue began to swirl around the barrel.

"Yes. That's it. Show me..."

I kissed the gun.

"What do you want?" She said again.

I then sucked as hard as I could, trying to pull the bullet from the barrel into my mouth and into my head. I longed for the burning flash of gunpowder in my mouth and the ultimate exploding ejaculation of lead that would be the last thing I ever experienced.

"Yes." She said.

She began pulling on the trigger slightly with her finger. One more millimeter and I would cease to exist. As she eased the gun out a bit so I could breathe, I reached up and pulled it back in, all the way into my throat, kissing it, caressing it. I closed my eyes as saliva filled my mouth and ran down my cheek. I licked and sucked the barrel, hoping she'd pull the trigger, willing her to pull the trigger, wanting her to pull it, until it was her tongue that I was kissing and sucking.

She swirled around my mouth as if she owned me, as I knew she did. I tried to suck her long, thick, soft tongue into my throat, into my soul. She was murdering me. And I loved it.

Finally she pushed me back and released me, taking gulps of fresh air. I'd nearly suffocated her with my need. She looked at me like I was a monster, a killer, a destroyer—all the things I knew I was. And then she suddenly burst out laughing. It wasn't a laugh at me. It was a laugh of victory.

"What do you want me to do now?" She said.

"Take me." I wanted her. I wanted her to hurt me, to use me, to own me. I wanted her. I needed her. To complete me. To mark me. "Own me," a voice said. I realized it was my voice.

And as I lay there naked, she smiled, lifted up her skirt, and slid her thick black hair over my face, my nose, my mouth. Her moist scent was everywhere. She continued down my chest, my torso, covering all of me with the wet musk that exploded and covered all my senses. When she was done, I felt another pinprick between my toes, and the world went warm and black...

When I awoke, I found my clothes tossed haphazardly on the bed next to me like they'd been there all along. I reached over and grabbed my fedora and my gun and my phone. Everything was there. Where they ever gone?

It was morning. I had no idea how long I'd been in this prison of pleasure and pain. It felt like years. My phone was dead, so I couldn't tell the date or the day. I was ravenously hungry, but all I could think about was her. Her scent was all over me. I needed to gather my senses, find myself again. Get out of my head and out of what my body had become. I had to get her off me. So I jumped in the shower and soaped off in the hottest water I could endure. After I dressed, I checked my gun—still loaded with a bullet in the chamber. I holstered it, slipped on my hat and ventured out of the bedroom. But as I stood in the empty hallway, my mind reeled. Part of me was missing. I needed something in that room.

I came right back inside and marched directly to the locked dresser. I searched around the underside and seconds later found a tiny brass key. I quickly opened all the drawers. Inside the top left was a sharpie. What Clara liked to use on the engorged members of her victims, I surmised. On the upper right side was a tattoo gun and a sealed bowl of ink. I guessed that was how Clara made your cock permanently hers, when she finally had your soul in her mouth. Below that in another drawer was a small black pocket gun—a Bersa Thunder—chambered in .380 with a notorious habit of jamming at the wrong time. I took it, thinking that, with my penchant for losing firearms, having a little more heat in my pocket might not be a bad thing. I opened another drawer and found a metal hammer, some long nails, some very sharp knives and a few surgical scalpels. I had no idea what these were all for and thanked heaven I didn't have to find out. Finally, in the bottom drawer I found three sealed syringes, with a lighter, a silver spoon, and a small bag of brown heroin. I grabbed everything from that drawer and stuffed it in my pockets.

Then I realized I was staring at the stained, dirty, unmade bed. The place where I'd spent the last 24, 48 or whoknowswhat hours being raped and drugged, just like the Romeos did to the innocent young women I saw being trafficked in El Cajon. Get them used to the sexual abuse and get them hooked on drugs until they break, until they're owned, until they'll do anything for the next fix. Until their bodies aren't theirs anymore, just tools for the cartel. Cash cows. Human cattle. Until they're finally used up and tossed away like a dirty napkin. Only difference was that I wanted this. I wanted to be used. To be owned. I loved it. Clara didn't break me. I was broken long ago. And I hated myself. I wanted to vomit.

But thankfully there was still a small part of me that longed for angels and flowers. And the driving force was also there—maybe just a glimmer, but it was there. That force that has always kept me going, kept me walking out of the shadows and into the light, that intangible voice that whispers to me through my tears with those words that say I'm loved, no matter what, no matter what sin I commit. Those patient words that pull me from out from perpetual night over and over again. The words that tell me I have a purpose.

That I have a job to do. That I have to protect those who don't want to be owned by pleasure and pain and darkness. Time to stop being owned. Time to stop being fucked.

Before I knew it, I had my Mk.23 in my hand, firing off a .45 round at the bronze, tongue-wagging head of Kali. Her ugly face blew up into bits of ripped bronze that flew all over the deck. I slipped the gun back into the holster and walked out of the room.

CHAPTER TWENTY

I wondered if anyone had heard the gunshot as I ventured down the stairs. I didn't have to guess much longer as I saw a young, handsome dude with too much hair, calmly cleaning the bamboo floor. He smiled at me and continued his work, as if nothing had happened. Maybe gunshots rang out in this house all the time? Either he didn't hear it or didn't care. Nor did anyone else. There was another young, buffed guy in a white wife-beater, cooking up some sort of exotic French toast. He looked up at me, like I was part of the household, like I'd been there forever. "Have some," he said.

I shook my head and walked out the door, seeing a few other young men swimming naked in the infinity pool. They barely glanced at me.

As I walked by, I noticed one dude had a big, permanent tattoo on his Johnson: *C.C.* It was high time for me to check out of Hotel California.

I didn't know how I was going to find my car, but that's when I saw the brown Saab sitting alone in the gated driveway, keys in the ignition. Waiting for me.

I jumped in, noticing it had been washed and detailed. I plugged my phone in the charger so Mr. Apple could get some juice, and turned the key. The trusty, rusty Saab started right up and the gate opened as I backed out and began to drive down Swallow Drive. But right away I saw a car parked on the tiny road in front of the neighbor's house. A black firebird. I pulled next to it. A disheveled Andy Candy poked his head out of his rolled-down window.

"Baker! I was starting to worry they'd offed you."

"What are you doing here?"

"I tracked you—"

"Tracked me?"

"Put an airtag on your car."

"Airtag? What's an Airtag?" I wondered with my best Boomerish, luddite scowl.

"Couldn't believe you spent two days at Gato Scattina's house," Andy continued. Then he just stared at me, like I had returned from the dead. "Wow."

"What's so special about Gato Scattina?

Andy leaned in closer, as if he didn't want anyone in the house to hear. "Scattina, he's who I wanted to talk to you about. Gato's acres above Patterson Nobel. Probably his boss. Original Hollywood mafia. From an old Sicilian family that've been here since the twenties. He supplies financing to production companies and films, and he uses that avenue to launder his cash. Also owns prop and costume houses and imports artwork, but really, he deals in people. Scattina provides the actors for all the porn shoots in the valley and models for most of the porn websites. He runs the biz and uses the skin trade as a portal into human trafficking. The pretty ones end up in movies. The others end up on the streets and in hotel rooms."

"El Dorado," I whispered.

And just like that, I surmised I'd finally found my target. I rubbed my head. And it wasn't lost on me that I'd just been fucked and abused by El Dorado's sister. I felt even more dirty. Now the whole Romeo thing began to make more sense.

"Did you talk to him? What's he like?" Andy wondered.

"Didn't see Scattina. But I sure got to know his sister."

My phone restarted and began ringing as soon as my *Steve McQueen Great Escape* screen saver flashed on with 7% of power. Andy, ever the curious "journalist" eyed it along with me. It was Tyler calling. I saw I also had a handful of worried texts and unanswered phone calls from Jessie. I ignored them and swiped open Tyler's call.

"Yeah," I said.

"Baker!" Tyler boomed in a voice loud enough for even Andy to hear. "Great news! Can we meet up so I can spill the magic?"

"I dunno. I'm in the hills here. Just got out of the party."

"Didn't I say you'd have a hell of a time!?"

"Hell of a time. No kidding."

"Hey, I'm heading out from a meeting right now and wanted to talk to you, so let's meet up at La La Latte on Sunset. Right by you. I'll see ya in a few!" Click.

He didn't even give me time to say no. Andy already had his Firebird fired up.

"Where are you going?" I asked.

"Let's see what he has to say." Then Andy smiled and nodded, as if he were having the time of his life. "It's getting deep, Baker. It's getting deep."

I thought of ditching the Firebird Fatman, but then remembered he'd somehow tagged my car, so he'd only find me again and start up another annoying conversation. So I followed him and his GPS to a small, trendy, pretentious, overpriced LA coffee joint. I luckily got a nearby meter, fed it out of habit, not wanting to push my luck with the fake handicapped sticker, and walked through the open front door, shuffling past a few beautiful people sitting outside at little round tables drinking their little lattes.

Andy was waiting for me near the counter. I was guessing he wanted me to pay, which is why he apparently hadn't ordered yet.

I walked up to the bored-looking barista. "Will" was on his name badge, along with his pronouns "He/They." He wore a Hawaiian shirt with a blue beret, silver star earrings, and rainbow-painted nails with little silver stars on them.

"What'll it be, cowboy?" Will's singsong voice asked.

"It's a fedora, not a cowboy hat," I answered.

Will just stared at me, then rolled his blue eyes. He also had some blue eye shadow.

"I'll have a large mocha." Andy piped in.

Will turned to the short man. "Nonfat?"

"No way. Whole milk. And whipped cream if you have it." Andy seemed excited at the prospect.

"Of course," Will said, sotto, then he tapped something on an iPad.

"And a cinnamon cookie," Andy said with aplomb, as he gazed at a giant cookie on display. "I love chocolate and cinnamon." Will grabbed some tongs and pulled out the big cookie, setting it on a big plate. Then he turned back to me, trying to pretend little big Andy didn't exist. "So what are you having, Fedora-guy?"

I noticed on the menu chalkboard there was nothing but lattes. But I figured they'd at least have some regular Joe.

"How about a coffee."

"Are you being funny?" Will said with plenty of sarcasm. "What kind of latte?"

"I don't want a latte. Just a regular coffee. Cup of black coffee."

"You mean drip coffee?"

"Yeah. Or French press. Pour-over. Whatever. "

"Well, I'm sorry, we don't have drip coffee. Or French press. Or pour-over. Or 'whatever.'" Will probably would have rolled his eyes if he hadn't already just done so.

"You work in a coffee place. And you don't have coffee?" I was getting insolent. Will apparently didn't care. He kept going. Now tapping his star nails on the counter along with the syllables of his words.

"This is La La Latte—we have *Lattes*. Get it? That's espresso and streamed milk and flavor. Organic. Non-GMO and sustainable.

"What if I don't want a sustainable latte?"

"You wouldn't be here if you didn't want a latte. Unless you're a tourist."

"Do I look like a tourist?"

You look like you might enjoy our rose latte. Or golden turmeric? It's our most popular."

"How about a coffee without any milk or any flavoring?"

Will looked at me with even less respect. Then he faked a smile and asked, "What's your name?" Before I could answer with something impertinent, he beat me to the punch: "Oh, I know what your name is: 'Boring.'"

"Look, *Willy*," I said, getting pissed.

"That's not my name. Do you see a *Y* here?" He motioned to his badge.

"What I don't see is a Y chromosome." I retorted.

Andy laughed, watching the exchange as he ate his cookie while he stood there, crumbs dropping on his plate, belly and the floor.

Willy sighed loudly, then tapped something on his iPad.

"Look, if you can't decide on a latte, I guess I can make a two-shot espresso, sans flavor. It's not on the menu but I'll do it. Is that good enough for you?"

"I guess." I said, figuring my options weren't gonna get any better.

"Twenty three dollars."

"Twenty three!?"

Will ignored my astonishment as he flipped the iPad towards me for my card. I pulled out my roll of cash. But then he rolled his eyes again.

"Cards only, cowboy. Unless you expect to be declined, then you're just gonna have to go to Starbucks. They take paper."

He smiled, no doubt hoping for "insufficient funds" to flash on his screen. I wanted to pull that cockeyed beret down over Will's smug face, but instead I took a deep breath, dug out my wallet, and inserted my worn card into the device. Choose your battles, Haim, choose your battles...

The iPad asked for a tip. I put down .05¢ and happily signed the screen. Thank God the card went through or Willy would have had a field day. He ignored my diminutive tip, faked a smile again, and spoke to us like we were sitting in his own personal Barbie playhouse.

"Have a seat, boys, I'll bring your drinks out," Willy said with rehearsed, artificial vivacity.

I found a small table in the corner, and just as Andy and I sat down, Tyler strolled in, slapping me on the back.

"Haim! Guess what?"

Another pregnant pause. My turn to roll my eyes. Finally Tyler let us have it:

"Tom Kapinos!"

"This name dropping, it's is an LA thing, isn't it?" I asked rhetorically.

"Californiacation!" Andy exhaled after downing the last of his cookie.

"Californiawhat?" I looked at Andy quizzically.

"Yes!" Tyler's eyes lit up. Andy Candy's sudden outburst of simpatico now spurred Tyler onward, forging ahead with his freight train of exuberance, gazing at the captured audience of myself and the big blogger, who joyfully nodded along with Tyler's effervescent delivery, indeed enthralled with this rare insider experience brought forth by the one and only Tyler Hinzman.

Tyler turned, and now was exclusively focused on me, since I seemed to be the only one not getting the joke. "Tom created *Californication*. You remember that show. It was great. On Showtime.

"If it was any time in the last ten years or so, my memory would be a big black hole thanks to the booze and drugs."

Tyler laughed, as if I were making a joke. "Tom's perfect to write the story of Haim Baker. I mean, I see a little bit of Hank Moody in you, Haim!"

"Hank-who?" I was lost, even more than usual. Then I figured this was a character from the California-thing.

"Haim's Hank Moody with a gun!" Andy exclaimed.

"Absolutely what I was thinking! And you know what, Mr. Haim-Baker-Moody?" Tyler queried to me.

I shrugged. Tyler then did the bro thing, sliding his arm around my neck as I waited for him to finish his thought so I could nod, drink my damn espresso (whenever the hell Willy was going to bring it), and tell him I had to go. I planned on zipping to Montana Avenue so I could see Jessie. I realized I really needed to see Jessie, and I quickly looked at my phone to try to scroll through her text messages when Tyler squeezed my neck to grab back my attention.

"And guess what guess what guess what!!??"

"What?" I said, trying to mimic the perfect fake exuberance of Willy the barista.

"I just pitched your story to Tom and he absolutely loved it! Sooooooo... Tom Kapinos is now, today, attached to write your script!"

"Far out!" Andy slapped the table.

"And better yet, he'll do it on spec!"

"Okay?" I wondered. "What the hell does that mean?"

"This is huge, bro," Tyler beamed, sensing my lack of Hollywood comprehension. "Chris won't sign on until he sees a script, and now with Tom onboard, we're gold!" Then he pulled out his phone, checking his calendar. "All I need from you, Haim, are those notes and anecdotes, you know, a story outline, so Tom has something to work from. Right now all we have is that newspaper article."

Finally I had a chance to tell this guy I wasn't interested in any of this Hollywood shit. I wanted to take out El Scattina, take out Nobel, and then maybe see what happens with me and Jessie. I backed away from Tyler's eager face, pulling away from his personal space.

"Nope."

"What d'you mean, Haim?"

Tyler suddenly lost the wind from his billowing sails, looking at me as if he might have to renegotiate a deal or something.

"I mean I'm not writing anything."

I was about to tell him to cancel all this entire nonsense, that he was wasting my time and his and Chris Pratt's time and the spec time of Tom Kap-whateverhisname. I wasn't interested in Hank Moody or California fornication, or the dull, fucked-up story of one Haim Baker.

That is until Andy leaned forward and cut me off. "That's because *I'm* writing it." Andy Candy said with aplomb.

"Yeah?" Tyler questioned. "You're a writer?"

"I'm Andy Candy. I'm a journalist and I've been following Haim's exploits in San Diego. I write a blog that has plenty of info on this, and I'll gladly write an outline for you. I'm the expert on the Santee/El Cajon underworld."

Tyler jumped up, his business concluded.

"Perfect!" We'll get you on the team. Maybe in the writer's room," he promised.

"Oh, that'd be cool!" Andy was so beside himself, he nearly fell off the stool when he jumped up and shook Tyler's weak grip hand.

Tyler gave him his business card. "Send me a link to that blog, Andy. And give me that outline ASAP." Then Tyler winked at me and hustled out to whatever the next meeting was for this go-getter, just as Willy finally showed up with a tray of cups.

"Oh my God! Was that Tyler Hinzman!?"

I picked up my tepid espresso, wishing I was somewhere else. Wishing I was in Jessie's bed.

"You know him?" These Hollywood people tend to know everybody in the business.

"Oh, I wish." Willy said. "Saw an article about Tyler on *Deadline.* Do you know he does three hundred sit-ups every day?"

"I'm lucky to get up every day," I said, trying to swallow the muddy espresso. Now I see why they put syrup in it.

Willy suddenly turned on the charm, smiling like I was now his best pal. "Can you do me a huge favor? Can you please give him my headshot?" Willy handed me an 8x10. He must have had a stack of them behind the counter. It had several versions of his "look": Willy as a charming guy, a thoughtful guy, and the funniest one, Willy as a tough guy.

"This could be a huuuuge break for me." He said with confidence, then put his hands up in a sort of prayer, namaste thing, like this sardonic barista's life was now in my sordid sarcastic hands. "I so appreciate this." Then, as if to seal the deal, he bent down and whispered, "Next time, the espresso is on me."

Willy's overt desperation mixed with his unabashed commercial ambition was impressive in an LA sort of way. But before I could say, "Sorry," he had patted me on the back, like we were long time besties, and left the table. I turned around to see him back at the counter taking rose and golden latte orders. I had to hand it to Willy, he certainly knew when to drop the mic.

I looked over to Andy, who had already sucked down his giant mocha, with the remnants of whipped cream and chocolate on the edges of his mouth and mustache. I handed him a needed napkin. Thank goodness he obliged. But then he handed it back, properly soiled. "Keep it." I said.

Andy suddenly looked over his shoulder, just to make sure no one was listening, then in a low voice said, "So, what's our next move?"

"*My* next move is to go sleep with my girlfriend. *You* need to get onto the 405 and start the long, fun drive back to San Diego."

Did I just call Jessie my girlfriend?

"C'mon Baker, we're close to tying up Nobel and Scattina and blowing this whole conspiracy wide open."

"Andy, you don't need to be here. Just go write your blog, do an exposé, whatever. It'll be safer for you that way. And don't forget the silly outline that Tyler wants. I mean, I don't give a damn about making a movie or a TV series, but you might make a little cash so you can detail your Firebird. Maybe get your clothes dry-cleaned."

He laughed, then sighed. "I need concrete proof that Scattina is involved with human trafficking, and proof that he's connected to Nobel Enterprises. I'm a journalist, Baker, I have standards to follow."

Was this guy serious? Writing his conspiracy thoughts down on his Myspace or Facebook or whatever didn't make him a journalist. Did it?

I figured I was wasting my time and wanted to fill my mind on something important, so I pulled out my phone and searched through Jessie's plethora of worried texts. Her last text was yesterday, where she wondered if she should call 911, but then didn't know where I was so she decided to pray and wait for my phone call. I smiled at the thought of someone praying for me, then I looked up at Andy.

He was picking up the last of crumbs from his cookie plate, mushing them on to his forefinger, and sucking them into his mouth. He must have been doing this the entire time I was on on my phone.

"Besides, if my hunch is right, Baker, you're gonna do a little more than try to send Scattina down the river. And I want to be there to see some real justice done." Then he did a little finger-bang in the air with his saliva finger. *"Hank Moody with a gun."*

"Look," I said. But Andy cut me off.

"—No, you look," he said, "I happen to know where Scattina's warehouse is located in Long Beach. Where all his "imports" come into the country. Now I'm guessing it might be more than artworks and artifacts from East Asia in there. Maybe some live, two-legged artworks? He gets a shipment in every Tuesday night. Today's Tuesday. What do you think?"

I thought about it. Andy might have something here.

"Okay. Maybe we check it out." Then I remembered the last time I stormed into a warehouse filled with imported human victims. "But this place is going to be well-guarded, so we'll need a distraction."

Then Andy and I both looked down at Will's headshot at the same time. This little fatman was starting to grow on me. I gave him a nod. He nodded back. Game on.

CHAPTER TWENTY-ONE

As soon as the customers had petered out, I approached Willy, who was fiddling on his phone, checking social media.

"Willy!" I tried to belt out his name with a bit of forced exuberance.

"*Will,*" he said without looking at me, engrossed in an Instagram post.

I produced his headshot, thumping on it with my finger for emphasis. "This, oh boy, this is great stuff. Great pictures. Great look." I tried to gush.

He glanced up at me from the counter, supporting his chin with his hand as he flashed his blue-tinted eyelashes. "I work hard at it, cowboy. You asking me out? You're kinda old..."

"NO. I, I'm a producer. And I'm impressed with your experience."

"You are?" Willy was now giving me 100% of his limited attention. Uncertain if I was pulling his leg or not, but hoping I wasn't. He adjusted his blue beret, projecting a serious look of enthrallment. "Really?"

"Yeah. Yes. I mean, you've been in three Youtube videos - Youtube! And, wow, you, you took two classes at the Santa Monica Improv Club." I worried that Willy might be sensing my overwrought vivacity, so I looked back down at his headshot, trying my best to seem impressed and not sarcastic. "And that semester of Meisner and Stanislovky methods at LA City College - great training, bro."

I shouldn't have worried. Blue-Beret Willy was buying it all, and now getting quite excited, ignoring the latte line beginning to form behind me. "You know, Mark Hamill is an alumni. That's why I went there. I adore Mark Hamill."

"You could be Mark Hamill!"

"I wanna be Mark Hamill!"

I leaned in close, like what I was saying was important and secret. He leaned in too, giving me his enthusiastic ear. I could smell the aroma of the many Sephora products wafting from his skin, eyebrows and hair. "I'm producing a TV series about a private detective and I think you would be perfect in it."

Willy practically fell off his stool, glowing like glitter.

"Can I audition? I'll audition right now. You have a script?"

"I have a better idea - let's see you put that Stanislovky method to use in real life."

"Great idea." He gushed. "How do you do that?" He wondered.

"We're gonna have you break into a warehouse in Long Beach!"

"When?"

"Tonight!"

"Awesome!"

"And we'll be secretly filming the whole thing."

"Yes!"

Willy clapped his hands. He literally clapped his hands.

"I'll text you the details."

"Oh, thank you sooooo much!... What's your name, by the way?

"The name's Baker."

"Thanks Mr. Baker, this means a lot to me."

Then, before I turned away I pointed my finger at him.

"Mark Hamill!"

"Mark Hamill!"

When I left the cafe, Willy was fanning himself like he had the vapors and I was skipping to my car, ready to spend the rest of the day with my girlfriend.

I called Jessie as soon as I got into the Saab. Finally I had some privacy, sitting on the metered sidelines of the Sunset Strip. She was overjoyed to hear from me and agreed to leave work right away for a "long lunch" at her place.

I was looking forward to seeing her so much I was shaking. Trembling with anticipation. Sweating with excitement. But then I suddenly wasn't excited, I was becoming morose. Feeling a dark cloud wafting over my head, I needed to be happy, to be warm, to be content. I thought the anticipation of being with Jessie would give me that feel-good, but then I'd forgotten that I hadn't had any pills or injections since yesterday, and my body was crying out for the serotonin or dopamine or whatever it was that my brain couldn't produce on its own anymore. I was crashing.

Thank God I had the Answer in my pocket.

I briefly considered driving to an alleyway or an empty parking lot or somewhere more private to shoot up the brown goo, but the need was stronger than my tact. So right there on Sunset Boulevard, sitting in the front seat of my Saab in the middle of the day, with shoppers and lunchers and latte drinkers walking past, with my shaky hand I pulled off some of the brown drug, dropped it into the silver spoon, heated it up with a lighter until it was liquid, then sucked it into one of the syringes I'd pulled from my jacket. As people stared while they strolled past, and as La La Latte drinkers sat and watched in quiet dismay, I quickly injected the heroin into the first vein I could see—which happened to be on my left hand. I hate needles, of course, but the need was greater than my trepidation. I missed the vein, and blood shot out as I shot the heroin. I tried again and finally hit the vein, ignoring the pain of my feeble phlebotomy. I didn't know what I was doing but it must have worked, because within seconds it was all I could do to remove the needle before I sat back and fell into a warm vacuum of momentary bliss. The Saab's fabric seat held me, or I would have gladly fallen through the car, past the asphalt, and into Middle Earth itself. I was a Hobbit who was drifting in serenity and in my serene circumstance. I vaguely realized I'd probably injected more of the drug than I should have. But how much is too much? Why was this bad if I was happy? And I was happy. Oh so happy. Wasn't I? Who cares. It felt good. That's all that matters.

I opened an eye and looked out the window. La La La La La Latte. What a funny name. What a funny city. What a perfect day. What a fun day. What a funny sound. Sound? The ringing in my head. In my head? The buzzing in my pocket. The ringing. Wait, is that an alarm? Alarm. My arm. My arm is holding this buzzing bug that was in my pocket. This big bug, this squarish screen that my blurry eyes see has a name on it. *Jessie.* Oh yes, Jessie. I like Jessie. Jessie in my hand. Buzzing. Ringing.

Shit. I sat up, forcing my eyes wide open and willing myself awake. How long had I been sitting here? Several people walked past, pretending not to notice the blood on my hand and the bloody needle on my lap. Big city dwellers have learned to ignore such sights. I'd now become a Sight. A bad Sight. But I didn't have time to think about that. Jessie was calling me. I swiped the phone.

"Hello?"

"Where are you?"

I saw the time on the top of the phone. The digital numbers told me I'd been sitting in my hot car, with the windows rolled up, sweating and sleeping and drifting, for almost an hour. Shit. "I don't feel well. I, I got sick. Something I ate," I blurted out.

"Why did you eat? I thought we were having lunch? I made us some paninis."

"—I love paninis."

There was a pause. "Happy, are you okay? Are you drunk?"

I must have been slurring my words. I started to panic."Listen, I'll be right there. I'll be there in half an hour. I can't wait to see you." I hung up quick. I was trapped. Trapped in my lies, trapped in my drugs. Okay, I made a little mistake. Took a little too much. I can do this. I can fix this. I needed to figure this out. I needed to take charge. I can do this. I can control this. I'm in command. I can do anything. And I was already driving West down Sunset Boulevard. No problem. I had a song in my head, and the LA soundtrack played on as I drove down this LA boulevard in LA. It was all interrelated, man. I was going the right way. I was going.

L.A. Woman, L.A. Woman, L.A. Woman... something, something... *Into your blues, into your blues, yeah!*

I realized the tune was actually on the radio and not in my head, so I turned it up. How appropriate. This music. At the right time. It was meant to be! The drugs. The fun. I was having fun, wasn't I? I passed the Beverly Hills mansions with their hedges and high fences. Keeping me out. High hedges. High fences. I was high. Yeah I was high. That's what it meant. Kismet! What does she call me? "Happy!" I was happy. I knew I was so happy. So fucking happy. Turn it up!

Driving down your freeways. Midnight alleys roam. Cops in cars... Topless bars. Never saw a woman... So alone. So alone... So alone...

I'm so alone.

I'm so fucking alone.

CHAPTER TWENTY-TWO

I drove as fast as I could, considering my wispy condition and sad, contemplative nature. I managed to find a parking spot on the busy street, in a red zone, thanking again whoever made the fake handicapped sticker hanging from my rearview.

I looked in the mirror, tried to spruce myself up as much as I could, then found some old napkins in the glove compartment lying under a box of ammo. I spit on napkin and cleaned as much of the dried blood on my hand as I could. I then deposited the drugs and spoon and lighter and syringes into the glovebox, shut it, locked it, and ran up to Jessie's condo.

I used the key Jessie gave me to get into the building, then ran up the stairway to her front door. I didn't know if I should just open the door or knock. I must have stood there, in my confused state, trying to decide what to do, when the door opened. Jessie's worried face stared back at me.

"I heard you out here. Why didn't you come in?" Jessie said in a concerned tone.

"I dunno. Having a bad day, I guess." I lied. I think.

Jessie was wearing a printed cotton skirt and a knit top. She looked great, but she gazed at me warily, obviously not happy with the man she saw in front of her. Finally she let me inside. I was expecting a hug. But I was unsure. So was she. Where did our relationship stand at this point? Did we *have* a relationship? At least as far as I knew, she didn't know or suspect that I'd spent two days fucking and being fucked by a tall, dark woman (and a man), and had what seemed like liters of liquid heroin pushed through my body.

Jessie stared at my eyes, which I knew were dilated. I tried not to look at her. Instead I focused on the two, cold paninis sitting on two green plates on her yellow round table. I went over, sat down and put one in my mouth.

"I thought you were sick?" She said as she watched me eat.

"I'm better now that I'm here," I mumbled through bites of salami, dried, melted cheese, wilted arugula, and some type of garlic aioli and mustard thing. It was good. Probably would have been great if it were warm.

She sat down across from me, trying to figure out what had transpired with me, between us. I wasn't the same Happy she was used to. She asked me what happened to me, or what's happened to me—I'm not sure which phrase she used. So I told her the best half-truth I could muster. Half-truths were part of my long-lived repertoire, so I quickly blurted out what I'd partially rehearsed on the drive over.

"Listen, Jessie, this is what happened..."

I told her that I'd gone to a party to investigate a man called Scattina, the man I'd been searching for. The human trafficker I needed to stop. But then I'd been held captive for two days as they drugged me until I escaped. I told them they shot me up with heroin and that I didn't remember much of what went on. Again she wanted to call the police, but I told her this man was too powerful, that I needed to get some solid proof—which I planned on doing tonight. That seemed to assuage her, and she came over to my side of the table and put her arms around me. She smelled wonderful—like citrus and flowers and sunny days. I quickly stood, draping my arms around her tight, short, thin body. Relishing the feeling of being close to her again. But then she pulled away, crinkling her nose.

"You smell weird."

"Weird like how?"

"I dunno. I don't like it."

She moved away, opening a window, as if that might cleanse the darkness from me. I figured I'd simply use my sexual prowess to distract her, to engross her, to take her mind off the last few days. I began removing my clothes.

"How did this man capture you? You have a gun, don't you?" Jessie wasn't buying any half-truths, especially when she saw me take off my holster.

"I told you, they drugged me." I said as I stripped down to my underwear. This was the truth, of course. Sort of. It seemed to set her at ease, at least. But her guards were up—until I played on her compassion. I knew how to exploit people, and this flower filled emoji girl could be twisted as long as I played the victim. Part of me felt awful for manipulating her, but I convinced myself that I needed her, I wanted her, and I was going to have her. Because I knew she was my antidote. My lifeline. She was my salvation. She saw the tears in my eyes and gave herself to me as I pulled off my speedos, leaving me bare and vulnerable.

But as I began to remove her clothes, she again smelled something on me. Smelled the sin. The Mark on me. She still had on her bra and g-string, but stopped me as I got on top of her.

"I, I don't want to do this." She said. "I'm sorry."

"I want you, Jessie. I need you, Jessie." I gave her all my attention, and all the gravel of my sordid life was now a solid rock of desire, ready to smash her doubts. But then I saw the look in her eyes.

"What is that?" She said, staring at the shaft on my nude body. I followed her eyes to see the faint, twitching letters *C.C.* staring back at her.

"You...You slept with someone else?" She had tears in her eyes. Tears of pain, tears of desolation.

"I don't remember. I told you. I was drugged." Another half-truth. She saw right through me.

"I'm sorry, Haim. But you're always drugged, aren't you?" She said, preceptively.

Jessie slid off the bed, as if to get a clearer picture of me. Of my cheating, sordid character. Of my transgression. She couldn't stop crying.

"Who was she?"

For some reason I couldn't lie to her anymore. Or maybe I didn't want to. For some reason it felt very wrong that she didn't call me "Happy."

"Hey..." I said gently, trying to soften the horrible truth of myself. I reached out to her, but she stepped back, shaking her head. I knew she now saw that I wasn't the man she'd hoped I was. Her large, thin nose could smell my true nature. She could smell my sins.

She could smell her. "Clara. She's the sister of Gato Scattina."

Jessie, looking sad and defeated, slumped down on the bed, pulling the quilted blanket around her. She was still crying.

"Jessie..." I didn't know what else to say. I was finally out of words.

She finally looked up at me, with sad eyes, like you'd get from a dog you'd just kicked as hard as you can.

"You need to go."

"But Jessie..."

"Please go... please?" She pulled the blanket higher. I wanted to do anything but leave her. I tried to reach out again, but Jessie hid behind her blanket. "My turn not to feel so good, Haim." Jessie said, wiping her tears with the quilt. "Sorry. I feel sick. You really need to go." She wouldn't look at me anymore.

Before I knew it, I had my clothes on and was walking towards the door, looking back at the sad, innocent young woman whom I realized had made me so happy. I hoped the angels and flowers and the picture of Jesus might help her pain to stop—the pain I'd caused. The pain I always cause. The people I always fuck. The things I always fuck up.

"Sorry," I said as I walked out and closed the door. I realized I was crying too.

CHAPTER TWENTY-THREE

I was in a daze and found myself under the track lights of R&D bar and grill on Montana Ave. I didn't remember driving there, but I must have, because I saw the Saab across the street, sitting in a bus zone. I was working on my fourth glass of Redbreast Irish whiskey when I found myself leaving the establishment with an older, divorced Latina named Cheyanne. She was pretty and plump around the edges and had an infectious laugh. Her kids were all grown and now she was just trying to have fun. I was totally sympatico.

I followed Cheyanne to her rent-controlled apartment on Delaware Avenue, off Pico Boulevard. It was near the cemetery, where she said most of her family was buried. It wasn't long before she and I were buried in a bottle of Jack Daniels and I was soon buried in between her large breasts.

I closed my eyes and tried to picture Jessie, but there were no angels here. And the only flowers were some dusty, artificial ones in a blue glass vase on a large table in her little living room.

We started up on the sofa. She was one of those vivacious divorcees who enjoyed every moment of available passion, because one never knew when the passion might dry up, when men might stop following her home.

I, however, was less excitable. In fact, to my dismay, I wasn't excited at all. Cheyanne was generous, however, and brought me to full strength with her ruby lips. I made sure she was happy, and her vocal moans and sharp fingernails directed me home.

But no matter how hard I tried, I couldn't finish on my own, even when we switched to the bed and to a bottle of Johnny Walker. I just couldn't find joy, no matter how hard I tried, no matter what she did, no matter what mental gymnastics I attempted; I wasn't going to fool myself into pretending this woman was Jessie.

Fortunately, the day had wound down, and thankfully I had an excuse to leave. I told Cheyanne I needed to drive to Long Beach, now that the traffic had eased. She appeared to understand, or did an admirable job at pretending, although I saw a bit of sadness behind her big, brown eyes. She quickly cheered herself up with another tumbler of Johnnie Walker, flashing her long, black eyelashes as if she'd had these "I gotta go" conversations many times before. She was a nice person and I realized I was again experiencing those achingly familiar pangs of guilt. Guilt for being with this woman and not the woman I really cared for. Guilt for pretending that this lady mattered any more than for a bit of excitement. Guilt for wanting this mother of two grown children, who was probably a great cook and who no doubt went to church every Easter and Christmas and knew how to make you feel better when you had a sore throat and was great at making your friends laugh—guilt for wishing Cheyanne was someone else, someone she could never be, this bubbly woman who was always going to be someone else and not herself for people like me. How many times had she woken up alone? How many times had she said "I'll see you"? I saw the broken expectations and knew it was myself staring back with that look or resigned inevitability.

As I dressed and walked to the door, I honestly hoped that Cheyanne got something out of our brief time together. She did seem thankful enough for the experience, that feeling of desire, of being desired—a tiny bit of physical love in a small, lonely, vintage, one-bedroom apartment next to the cemetery.

Cheyanne thankfully ended our lonely ceremony by toasting me with another drink before I left. We kissed dispassionately one last time, and before I knew it, I was back in the Saab. I pulled the drugs and paraphernalia and quickly lit up the spoon with a smaller chunk of the brown heroin. I injected it into my arm and sat back for a moment, enjoying the bliss.

Somehow I wound up on the 405 heading south to Long Beach and hopefully to the conclusion of my haphazard week in La la land.

CHAPTER TWENTY-FOUR

Before I met up with Andy and Willy, I gave a call to Detective Hazard, telling him I was about to nail Gato Scattina and expose him for smuggling, kidnapping, and human trafficking, that the proof was in his warehouse, and that it might be a good idea for Hazard to be there to see for himself. Hazard gave me the usual crap about letting the cops do cop work, that what I was doing was illegal, that Scattina was an upstanding citizen, yada yada yada. But in the end the grumpy copper grudgingly agreed to show, if only to make sure I didn't do anything stupid (as if I ever did anything that wasn't stupid!).

Scattina's warehouse was located on the docks in Long Beach, where the huge container vessels would unload the shipping containers right at the sleek industrial building, allowing the items to be off-loaded directly into Scattina's storage facility. This allowed for huge cost savings, plus, with Cali's new emission rules, Scattina's operation wouldn't have to pay the new carbon tax (Scattina donated heavily to push the new rules as well, knowing it would tax his competitors, putting them at a disadvantage).

You had to have a lot of clout and a lot of money to park your warehouse on the dock, and knowing that most of the dock workers were controlled by the union, which itself is controlled by the mob—well, Scattina *was* the mob—and that meant people looked the other way when those container doors were opened, and inspections were few and far between and telegraphed far ahead of time when they were scheduled. It was a sweet deal and a smooth operation. Andy had been tracking the operation for about a year and was certain we were going to hit jackpot.

Willy had shown up in "costume." Stepping out of his Prius, I saw him wearing a fake mustache and a flannel shirt. He'd also created some sort of badge on his computer, which he printed out and now wore around his neck on a Taylor Swift lanyard (it was the only one he had). The badge labeled him as a union steward from the International Longshoreman's Union—the East Coast version of the West Coast International Longshore and Warehouse Union. Willy came up with the idea of being a rep from New York, gathering data from the ILWU for a possible merger of the two unions. I had to say, it was a clever ruse, and it got our cars past the parking lot guard who sat in his kiosk and waved us through.

We drove in and parked near Scattina's warehouse and watched a giant crane unload the last of three containers from a huge ship called the *Red Swan*, flying a Bermuda flag. Andy checked on his tablet and found that the Red Swan was registered to a shell company in Bermuda, owned by White Swallow enterprises, which was itself owned by Scattina International, a subsidiary of ScattCo, the umbrella company that oversaw all of Gato's operations. Andy couldn't get any info on ScattCo, other than it was privately held.

I noticed the warehouse was strangely lacking in security. There was one bored guard stationed outside the front door, an older white guy who looked ex-Army, but that's about all I could see. I figured no one would be stupid enough to break into El Dorado's illicit holding pen—that is anyone but me and my motley crew of misfits. Hazard still hadn't shown but I didn't want to wait any longer, as it seemed like they were just about finished with the containers. I told Willy to do his thing and work the guard, taking along Andy, who actually looked like a union guy, for backup.

"Make sure you stir up a stink if they don't let you in. I need a distraction," I ordered.

Willy enthusiastically agreed and I heard his bombastic dialogue beginning as he confronted the wary guard while I snuck around back to see what I could do in the shadows.

I couldn't find any doors, and the windows were too high to get to. Around back the rollup door was open as three workers were moving in crates from the container box. I couldn't slip past without them seeing me. So I sauntered in like I belonged there.

"Hey! Who the fuck are you?" One of the bearded guys said as he stopped his forklift. I peeked inside—crates of all sizes were stacked inside the container. By now the other two guys inside the container had stopped and were looking at me too.

I stared them all down, and in my best Brooklyn mobster guise, I bellowed, "I work for Scattina. You guys are behind schedule and have been fucking up far too much, so I'm here to give you a little motivation." I stepped inside the container. If it held any sort of human cargo, especially from East Asia, the stench would give it away, but the only smell I got was wet wood and chai tea.

"Where is it?" I commanded.

The guys looked at each other, then back at me. The forklift guy seemed to be the senior dude. He stepped off, folded his arms skeptically, and looked me over.

"Where's what?" He said.

"Exactly," I said. Then I opened my jacket so Forklift Guy could see my Mk23. "Product's been missing. You got something to do with that?"

Forklift then pulled out his own gun, a Glock, slipping it back into his waistband. So did the other two guys. "You accusing us of something, asshole?"

I moved towards Mr. Forklift as the two others closed in behind me. "We're missing some girls." I guessed.

"Fuck you. They're all there. Everything on the manifest. We don't do that shit." He spat. "Aldo always counts. He's never said nothing."

I almost smiled, knowing I was about to blow up this human smuggling operation—an operation that the dude just confirmed. "Show me the ladies." I ordered. My head was buzzing with adrenaline. I knew they were here. I could feel it.

Forklift guy stared at me, but I stared back, determined. Like I was deadly serious. Finally he relented, keeping a hand on his gun.

"Frankie, Joe, let this fucker see the ladies." He then turned to me, pulling out some folded papers from his pocket. "Here's the manifest, asshole."

I scanned it. 160 "ladies" stood out amongst categories of furniture, beds, lamps, artwork and tapestry.

Joe, a black guy, led me into the poorly lit warehouse, with Frankie, wearing a headband, uncomfortably close behind. The area was surprisingly open, with several offices and doors along the sides. I figured that must be where they kept the women. But then Joe stopped in the center, where a bunch of big wooden crates were stacked. He pointed to them. "You wanna uncrate them yourself?" Joe said.

"You do it." I stepped back.

Joe sighed, then walked to the side wall, where a rack of metal crowbars hung. He pulled one, strolled over to the first crate—which was about four feet tall and six feet long. He stuck the crowbar into the wood slot and pulled off a corner of the crate. He casually walked to the other side, and pulled off that corner, then knocked the cover to the floor.

I had backed up enough so I could keep both men in view while watching the crate. I figured when I caught sight of the girls, I'd have to quickly take out Freddie, while keeping Joe at a distance so he couldn't brain me with that heavy crowbar.

Dust and straw spilled out of the wooden box. I wondered how anyone could be alive inside that horror. I figured they must have drugged the girls or something. But then Joe reached in, pushed away some straw, and lifted out—not a woman—but a three-foot wooden statue of Kali.

Joe looked back at me like I'd just made him do work for nothing. "There's twenty in each crate. See for your fucking self."

Statues. Fuck.

I didn't have time to contemplate my mistake. Just then, the front door flew open and the guard tossed a disheveled Andy and Willy onto the floor. Willy's mustache was askew and Andy looked like he'd been slapped. The guard held his gun on my two friends as they cowered on the ground.

"These two assholes just tried to break in, pretending to be union reps. I already called it in."

That was my chance. As Joe was staring at Andy and Will, figuring out that he was being played, I quickly moved to him, twisting the crowbar out of his hand before he realized what I was doing. "Force of action, Haim, force of action," I said to myself.

I quickly swung and cracked Joe hard on the side of the head with the metal bar, then, as he dropped like a marionette without a string, I threw the heavy tool as hard as I could at Frankie, who was attempting to draw his gun. The crowbar hit him on the arm, spinning him back as I charged. I heard gunshots, as the rounds blasting from behind me began cracking the air next to my head and ear, hitting the crates and the wooden Kali—right where I was standing only seconds before.

Suddenly a scent wafted into my nostrils. It wasn't gunsmoke. It was a scent that stirred my head, that almost took me out of my focus. But years of training and fighting and surviving took over and I got back on task.

I figured the guard and his gunfire was the immediate danger, but he was at least twenty yards back, and I also knew how hard it was to hit a target at that distance with a handgun, especially a moving target. I had to take out Frankie because he was the real danger as the closer combatant. I had to erase that threat before Headband Frankie could reorient himself and aim his 9mm at me.

Using momentum, I quickly jumped on Mr. Headband, knocking him to the ground. He dropped his gun but quickly tried to reach for it. I grabbed his arm, twisted it, then pulled back his forearm as I pressed on his triceps with my other hand, snapping his elbow joint. Then with a hard elbow to his temple, with all of my weight behind the blow, I finished him off. Hopefully he'd just be knocked out, but my adrenaline was pumping so hard, I wasn't pulling any punches. No time to worry about fucked Frankie. I had to save my friends.

I rolled and then jumped up, turning to the guard, when I suddenly felt a gun to the back of my head. Shit. I'd been so wrapped up in the fight, I'd forgot about Forklift Guy.

Thankfully Mr. Forklift was trying to make a point and instead made the mistake of using intimidation in lieu of tactic. He must have seen one too many gangster flicks.

With the gun barrel pressing hard into the back of my head, my two arms gently rose in mock surrender. But with my hands now less than six inches away from the barrel of Forklift's Glock, it took only a millisecond to quickly turn and move my head out of the line of the gun, while my left hand pushed the Glock away just as he pulled the trigger.

One round exploded, missing me completely. However, the sound was deafening, since it was only inches from my left ear. All I could hear now was the loud ringing aftermath of the gunshot as I continued my spin, using my other hand to twist the Glock out of Forklift's hand, and two seconds later I had it trained on his face, my finger on the trigger, itching to fire.

But instead of challenging me, Forklift backed away, nodding, his hands on his head, looking past me at the guard. Then he knelt down, like you do as instructed by a cop.

Then the ringing in my ear got louder. But it wasn't ringing anymore. The sound had formed into words that were beginning to seep into my brain. "...the gun!"

What gun? My gun? What? The guard wanted my gun? After trying to kill me? Yeah right. Fuck him! Then my hearing came back and I could make out someone yelling.

"Drop the fucking gun, Baker!!"

How did the guard know my name? Andy and Willy must have spilled the beans no doubt.

But now I felt stupid because, as I was thinking all this, I realized what an easy target I was, just standing there acting like an idiot. So I suddenly lowered my body, dropping my weight, bending my knees. I spun, turning with the gun, aiming with both hands, ready to fire a twenty yard shot at Mr. Security while expecting to see more rounds blasting towards me (and hopefully past me).

But I needed't have worried.

I didn't see the guard aiming his gun.

Instead, I saw the guard on his knees, handcuffed. Andy and Willy also sat against the wall, with their hands on their heads. And right in the middle of the room I saw Detective Hazard, his Beretta doublefisted, aiming his gunsights directly at me. I looked at him, dumbfounded. Then I saw Hazard place his finger on the trigger. He wasn't fucking around.

"Didn't you fucking hear me, Baker??!! Drop it!"

I then realized I was pointing the Glock at Hazard with both hands, mimicking Hazard's triangle pose pointing back. We were mirror images of each other.

I eased up and quickly dropped the mag, ejected the round in the chamber, tossed the gun down and kicked it over to him. Hazard marched over to me, pissed.

"What the fuck?" Hazard glared at me as he moved right past, checking on Joe, who was finally stirring, moaning from the hard impact on his head.

"What the fuck have you done, Baker?"

Hazard then checked the pulse on Frankie, who was pretty fucked up with a cockeyed arm, a swollen mound on his temple, and unconscious eyes. "You're lucky this guy's alive. You're so fucking lucky," Hazard growled as he got right in my face, like a Marine drill instructor.

"This is what you made me drive all the way down here for?! This is a shitshow!"

Then he pulled out another pair of handcuffs. "You're under arrest, Haim-fucking-Baker!"

Suddenly a soft voice came from the doorway.

"Go easy on him, detective. Haim was just doing his job."

Hazard grabbed my arm and had the cuffs on me as I turned and saw the tall, dark, bald man with two gold earrings. The man I saw, the man I felt in that horrible bedroom, was now striding towards me with a gait that was light as a feather.

Hazard was seething. "I'm throwing the book at you, Baker, and throwing away the key!"

The Man countered, "I'm serious, detective. Please release my friend." The Man smiled as he casually walked up to us. "It's okay."

"You know this sonofabitch?" Hazard said to him. "He just fucked up two of your employees and would have probably killed another had I not got here when I did."

The Man stepped closer. Smiling at me. "It was just a misunderstanding, I'm sure."

He looked over at his three guys, who seemed to cower in his presence. "I imagine Haim was only defending himself. It looks like they drew their guns first, am I not right?"

I nodded to Hazard. "He has a point."

Hazard grunted, then unceremoniously undid the cuffs. "Fuck," Hazard said to himself. He said a few more words but I couldn't make them out as he grunted in anger.

The Man continued. "This was all a big misunderstanding on everyone's part. And unless Haim wishes to file charges against my security guard for attempted murder, then please release him as well, if you don't mind? After all, he too was only doing his job."

Hazard, beet red from his anger and high blood pressure, marched over to the guard and uncuffed him. He pulled the guard's gun from his jacket pocket, unchambered it and then emptied the few bullets left in the mag, handing the guard his unloaded gun. Then the detective turned back to me, and seethed. "We're not done with this, Baker."

The Man walked up to Hazard, trying to calm him down. "Please, Detective, as I said, Haim is a friend of mine, and I wouldn't want to see anything happen to him. So please, forgive our friend and let's just pretend nothing happened here tonight, shall we?"

Hazard looked over at me, then back to him. "Whatever you say, Mr. Scattina. Whatever you say."

Hazard exited the door in a huff, leaving me agape. I now realized the man who just saved my ass from jail was the very man who had literally screwed that same ass, and had fucked his own sister as well.

Before I knew it I was at the doorway, about to pull my gun and blow away *El Dorado,* but Scattina smiled at me, like we went way back, grabbing my right hand, holding it with both of his own soft hands, like a grandmother would do, setting me at ease. Certainly to assuage me and my rising anger. Probably to keep me from pulling my gun.

"Haim, if you wanted to see my warehouse, all you had to do was ask. I'd gladly let you see anything you wish." Then he released my hand, turning to his guard, who seemed just as perplexed as me, and told him: "As I said, this man is a good friend of mine. He has my permission to be here, so please do not ever be hostile towards him again. Do you understand?"

There was an intensity in Scattina's soft voice, a warning that the guard took very seriously.

The guard was trembling when he said, "Yes sir, Mr. Scattina. I'm very sorry, sir. I didn't know."

"It's quite all right. Don't let it happen again," Scattina warned.

Then Scattina turned to Andy and Willy, who were now standing, with Andy slipping his phone into his pocket after no doubt recording as much of the fun as possible, and Willy beaming at the sight of one of his apparent Hollywood idols.

Willy suddenly turned on the charm after ripping off the rest of his mustache. Shaking Scattina's hand with aplomb.

"Mr. Scattina, I'm Will Anooshian, and I'm so thrilled to meet you. I read all about you in *Variety*. Great article, by the way. This was all just an audition, that's all. We're here on an audition. I mean, I'm here auditioning for Mr. Baker. For his TV show." Then Will turned to me. "How'd I do?"

I gave him a thumbs up. "Mark Hamill."

Will beamed as Scattina looked him over, like he was judging a used car, then smiled. "You have a nice look, Will. And a bright future. Please excuse us." Then he turned away from Willy's effervescent eyes, and focused on me.

"Haim, could you please send your friends away, I'd like to talk to you in private." He said that as if Andy and Will suddenly didn't exist. Or they were too far below him to matter. There was both power and pomposity behind Scattina's soft, threatening demeanor.

I told Andy I'd call him, then said the same to Will. They nodded and left me alone with Gato Scattina, who brought me outside to the parking lot, as Andy and Will drove away with the sound of ambulance sirens coming close.

Gato opened the scissor door of his uber-fast, uber-rare $3,000,000 Koenigsegg Jesko. The same car I saw at his party. He slid inside, then turned to me. "I have a condo in downtown Long Beach. If you don't mind, please meet me there. I think we may have a few things to discuss."

With that he pulled the door closed, punched the starter and the 1200 horsepower supercar drove away with the insane growl of a twin turbocharged V8. I suddenly got a text on my phone from him with the address to Gato's condo, along with the security gate code for the underground garage.

I opened the mundane door of my dented, 90 horsepower V4 and puttered away towards the tall glass tower lording over the city of Long Beach, looming in the near distance.

CHAPTER TWENTY-FIVE

After I punched in the code, the metal gate opened and allowed me and my Saab inside the bowels of the tallest skyscraper in Long Beach. By the time I'd parked and walked to the elevator, a man was waiting. He wore a scar on his creased face along with a nice silk and wool blend suit and no doubt carried a large gun. He didn't say a word, but motioned me inside and punched the top button, 39th floor, waved a fob on his keychain over a sensor, and the long journey upwards began. The scarred man made sure to keep a distance of at least three feet between him and me, just in case I wanted to cause trouble. He'd no doubt have time to draw his gun or knife and counter any move I might try to make. I thought about offering a joke, but he looked like he wasn't there to talk or listen or laugh.

The elevator was surprisingly fast, and in less than fifteen seconds, the door opened and the man waved me inside a huge, windowed space. Another large man was waiting near the door, just in case I'd taken out guy #1, I was guessing, and when I walked into the room he stopped me. Then I heard Gato's voice. The thin, bald cartel leader was wearing a sort of red silk smoking-jacket-robe-thing and was lounging on a couch in the sunken living room, nursing a drink. I guessed it was bourbon. He stood up and smiled.

"Haim. Welcome. Come join me for a drink. But first I must insist you hand Aldo your gun. Just a formality, of course."

Aldo had his legs slightly spread, his arms at ready. He was close enough to disarm me if I tried to do anything with my HK other than hand it to him. He was also standing between me and Gato, making it hard for me to get a line on Scattina, even if I were to somehow get the business end of my .45

out and my finger on the trigger. Besides, I knew the other guy was ready to plug me in the back if the situation ever got to that point. Gato's men knew their job, and they'd no doubt seen hooligans like me before. I reached in my jacket and handed the pistol to Aldo. He held it at his side as I stepped down into the living room. Gato was already fixing me a drink. Mr. Scar was now standing near Aldo. Both of them absently watching me. I wasn't comfortable having these goons behind me, especially the way Aldo was palming my Mk23. Scattina saw that I was keeping my peripheral on them. He came up and handed me a tumbler of bourbon on the rocks.

"Don't mind Aldo and Rodrigo. They're just earning their pay." Then Gato said in an offhand way, "Besides, if I wanted you dead, Haim, I'd never have invited you up here."

He was right. I would have been killed after I parked the Saab, if not before. Gato turned to his men. "In fact, why don't you boys take the night off. Have a late dinner, catch a movie, spend the night with your wives or your girlfriends. Your choice." The heavies weren't sure what to do, eying Gato questionably, as if this were some sort of test. "Go on, Haim's okay. I promise." With Gato's assurance, both dudes nodded and moved to the elevator. "And Aldo, just leave Haim's gun on the table."

Aldo set my H&K on a small granite entryway table next to a vase filled with fresh tulips and tiger lilies, which was making the place smell like vanilla and cinnamon. As soon as Heckle and Jeckle left the room, I felt more at ease and took a healthy sip of the drink in my glass. It was fantastic. Gato could see the pleasure on my face as I immediately downed another gulp.

"Great bourbon you got here," I said between "sips." I'd already drained the glass before Gato moved to me with a white label bottle and filled my glass with more liquid pleasure.

"It's Weller. Limited edition. One of my favorites. I'm happy to share it with you."

Gato Scattina was within arm's reach. I knew I could easily take the glass in my hand, cup it on his face, jamming his eyes and nose with the broken pieces, then punch him in the throat. If he wasn't dead already, I'd walk over, grab my gun and put a bullet in his brain. Heck, I'd probably do it even if he were dead. This was *El Dorado*, after all, the man I'd come for. The man responsible for misery and death all over the continent, if not the world. And here I was drinking bourbon with him and admiring the view. Why didn't I hate this guy?

Gato seemed to read the conflict on my face and immediately walked back to his bar, setting down the bottle after topping off his own glass. "I bet you'd like to kill me, wouldn't you, Haim?"

"The thought had crossed my mind."

He took a drink. As did I.

"Do keep in mind there are cameras everywhere, recording our little tête-à-tête. Yes, I'm sure after murdering me you could eliminate the guard downstairs, but trying to erase the images of your car entering and leaving and of whatever gruesomeness you'd planned for me up here would be quite the challenge. All this stuff is sent to the cloud, and frankly you'd need some world class techie to rid yourself of it. Believe me, I'm on display 24/7 and don't think that I'm happy to be such a security video star, but it comes with the territory, unfortunately."

I realized he was right. This wasn't the time or place for death, this shiny glass box on top of the world. I took another drink and let the sweet, smoky liquid set me at ease. I rid my mind of all the jumbled thoughts of punching and shooting and killing as I allowed the 95 proof alcohol to relax my jumpy nerves and looked around Gato's giant, spectacular condo.

The floor-to-ceiling glass that ringed the full-floor apartment allowed a 360-degree view of the port and the city. From our height, I could even see the twinkling lights of LA far away in the northern distance. There was a balcony with a huge deck, and the sliding door was open, letting in a soft, cool breeze on this warm Southern California night.

On the interior walls, Gato or his sister or whomever had hung a series of original Impressionist paintings by Edgar Degas. They were all beautiful pictures of ballerinas and I assumed they were original and probably priceless. There was also a bronze sculpture of a ballerina bent over, doing some sort of ballet dance move, set in the middle of the coffee table. Gato moved over to it and stroked it like he would a favorite house cat.

"We all have our lot in life, don't we?" Gato said as he admired the bronze. "I was born into a family that was known for supremacy, power, and ruthlessness. Certainly not for art or music or anything like that." Gato took one last look at his bronze and moved to the window, staring out at the twinkling city lights, and sipped his bourbon. "And I was expected to be supremely powerful and without any ruth at all," he said, as if making a sad joke. I saw that there was indeed a ring of sorrow that hung around Gato Scattina like a melancholy halo, this man who was supposed to be the Lord of Los Angeles. Then he moved to a trunk-sized wooden box and opened up his massive humidor, producing two long, beautiful cigars.

"Care for a Churchill?"

Of course I nodded. These weren't just cigars. I could tell by the red and gold rings that they were Cubans. Romeo Anejados. A rare treat.

He cut the ends, handed me a silver torch lighter, and invited me out to the balcony to smoke in front of a sweeping view of his SoCal domain. I lit my cigar and immediately savored the spicy, sweet, aged leather taste of the tobacco as I allowed the wonderful smoke to billow out into the night, watching it ride away on the evening wind.

Gato drew on his cigar, enjoying it at first, but then he seemed to withdraw inside himself as he watched the ships in the ocean chugging away from the docks, heading out to the Pacific Ocean. He took another long draw from his cigar, and when it had cleared his mouth he wondered aloud.

"What did you want to be when you were a child?"

I thought about the question, immediately remembering one my mom's boyfriends named Dennis (this was after Turin Baker, my ne'er-do-well father, left for Japan and was never heard from again). Dennis was a great guy and would have been a perfect surrogate dad had my mother not quickly dumped him once she saw he was devoid of the usual attributes that attracted her: narcissism, alcoholism, and abusive behavior. But Dennis doted on me, buying me model cars, taking me to Indycar races, and once he took me to a theatrical screening of *Le Mans* with Steve McQueen. That's what started my affair and fantasies with Porsches. I began to think about my old '73 911 Carrera RS. The car I lost in a haze of cocaine and hookers and gambling debts. The car I got again from Patterson Nobel, the man who should be in jail, but instead became the person who took my car back into his collection and is right now awaiting the death of the man standing next to me, leaning on the metal railing of his balcony.

"Race car driver," I said with a wispy smile.

"I can see that. I wager you could no doubt handle my Jesko better than I."

"I'd sure love to try." I flicked a long turn of ash onto Gato's pristine balcony floor. "I'm guessing you didn't always want to be a human trafficker."

Gato's face then turned hard as he stared at me. "Let's be clear. I am a businessman. And I'm a pornographer. And other things. But I only sign the papers and sign the checks."

I thought back to the warehouse. And guessed that there was more than art being shipped in from East Asia.

"You forgot to mention heroin smuggler. You're lucky Detective Hazard didn't look closer at those wooden statues."

Gato bent over the railing and looked down at the ground, far below, as if in shame.

"I wasn't always the man I am now." He took another draw from his Romeo, stared at the cigar, then smiled at me as he recalled a fond memory.

"When I was a boy, my mother took me to New York while my father was meeting with other heads of the crime families in Queens. We went into Manhattan to Lincoln Center to see ABT perform *Swan Lake.* And I was stunned when I witnessed Baryshnikov floating like a feather, jumping with such ease, as if he could defy gravity itself, dancing with perfection. He was perfect. And right then I knew that's what I wanted. What I wanted to be. My mother appreciated my passion and secretly indulged me, setting me up with private classes. I wasn't half bad and my teacher, who was Russian, thought I might actually have a future on stage.

The wind had blown out Gato's cigar. He fired his torch, staring at the triple flame as he lit the tobacco.

"But when my father found out that his only son wanted to hop around in tights and makeup in front of an audience, he put a quick stop to it." Then Gato drank the rest of his bourbon, chewing on an ice cube as he talked. "I mean, I had shot my first gun by the age of five and learned all places a human is vulnerable to the blade of a knife before I was ten. I wanted to please my father, so I put dancing out of my mind." Gato stared at his Cuban.

"But then..." Gato's face changed as if the ice he was chewing contained bitter cyanide. He put the cigar to his lips and pulled from it, but Scattina looked like he suddenly didn't like the flavor anymore.

He filled his mouth with more ice, then chewed and swallowed, as if cleansing his palate so he could continue to talk, talk about things that were less than clean.

"You know, when I was a young man, my best friend was a boy named Sergio. We met in school and were immediately inseparable. Like brothers. His infectious laugh sounded like jingle bells. He had dark wavy hair, and always sported a large curl that would droop over his big, bright eyes. Sometimes I wondered how he could see." Gato laughed, smiling along with his memories, then sat his chin on his hands on the railing of the balcony.

"One day, we were in my bedroom, playing monopoly of all things, when Sergio suddenly leaned over and kissed me. I'd never done such a thing with a boy. Sure, I'd had girlfriends, and promiscuity with women was encouraged for the manly son of the Scattina empire. I'd even kissed my sister, as we were a Sicilian family and affection was part of our culture. But to kiss a boy? It was innocent enough, but my father suddenly burst through the door. This was the first time I realized I was the star of my own security camera. I later learned cameras were all over our house. A way to keep tabs on friends, family and enemies. But for me, it was sort of like I'd been living my own *Truman Show*. My life wasn't mine. And I was about to learn that very terrible lesson."

"That's gotta suck." I could't imagine being spied on all my life. All the things I've done. Thank God only my own eyes have recorded my sordid deeds. I hope, anyway.

"Oh, it did suck," Gato said, trying to plaster a smile over a horrible memory. "They took Sergio to the basement. I was crying incessantly until my father slapped me hard. So I toughened up." Gato paused, flicking away some ash on the end of his Churchill, then continued as if the story were rote.

"Before I knew it my father and his men had Sergio's clothes stripped off, while four of father's guards held down the poor boy's arms and legs on our hardwood floor. Then father went up the stairs to the kitchen and returned with a steak knife. He proceeded to saw off Sergio's penis and testicles and another family guard, I think it was Luca, forced open Sergio's wailing mouth as my father stuffed Serge's genitals down his throat. Then father handed me the knife, ordering me to finish off my best friend. I'll never forget Sergio's frantic, crying eyes as he watched me slip the knife between his ribs and into his heart, which I pierced, ending the whole unsavory business as quickly as possible."

After chewing the rest of his ice, Gato suddenly tossed his glass off the balcony, down towards the Long Beach shipyards.

"That was the last time I ever kissed a man, at least on the lips. But after that, when I kissed my sister, I made sure it meant something. For some reason, kissing her was okay with father. I kept it in the family, after all." Gato took another drag from his cigar, then tossed it too over the edge of the balcony, like he was trying to throw away the memory.

I couldn't look at Gato. His nightmarish story was so very Hollywood in its crazy admission, something a normal person would only confess to his therapist or his priest, but not a man he barely knew.

Then Gato put his arm around me, as if he needed to comfort me after such a tale. "But let's talk good news." He sat me down on a reclining deck chair, taking the other one next to it. "I wanted to tell you that my company is financing your movie and streaming series project. Tom's almost finished with the script, and even if Chris gets cold feet, we've been talking to James Franco, who is totally into it. Netflix is even holding a spot for us next summer." Gato reached over and put his hand on my shoulder. "You're going to be a player."

I slipped out of Gato's grip, suddenly wanting to get as far away of him as I could, standing up, looking down on this tortured mob boss.

"Why'd you bring me up here, anyway?"

Gato stood, then backed away. "Good question."

Gato pulled his robe tighter around his waist, keeping out the wind that was beginning to get colder. "I guess I wanted to apologize for what happened in Clara's bedroom. My sister enjoys being quite ruthless in her desires, in her goals. In her ambition. If she only had a penis, my father would have been so very happy."

I glared at him. "She wasn't the one who made my ass sore."

Gato nodded with a slight smile of guilt. "I am often a victim of my desires, and I admit I have my vices. I'm sorry if you too were a victim of my carnality. I hope it wasn't all too displeasurable."

Suddenly the wonderful flavor of the Churchill seemed to burn my mouth. I set it down on the railing.

"Just about everything I've experienced here has been displeasurable."

Scattina then took my Churchill and tossed it over the railing. "To be honest, Haim, I know why you're in LA."

My face became grim as I imagined putting a bullet in Gato's thin, bald, sad face. I finally began to hate him.

"Then you know what I have to do."

Gato moved to his wooden lounge chairs and rearranged them, as if they were a touch off-axis.

"I know more than you think. And I've decided I want to help you in some small way. Perhaps to make up for your aching anus." Then he stepped up and leaned against the railing.

I moved closer. Maybe he was expecting me to snap his neck. I figured I'd be able to get out of the building before the alarms went off—even though there were those pesky cameras. But then, as if Gato knew exactly what I was thinking, he shook his bald head.

"Let me tell you God's honest truth."

"You believe in God?" I interrupted, my voice filled with sarcasm.

"I wish I did." Gato stared me in the eyes. "Haim, I'm not the person you're looking for." I saw in his face that he was sincere. I realized I actually felt relieved. I really didn't want to kill this would-be ballerina. But I knew he had the answer to the one mystery that had been burning in me since I'd been in LA.

"Then who is El Dorado?"

Gato ignored my question as he tapped on the balcony railing again. He looked out, as if he could see the shining sign atop the Hollywood hills. Then he turned to me.

"Care for another drink?"

I shook my head.

He looked back out into the night and sighed. "You know, I've often fantasized about dancing a *pas de deux* by myself here on the railing, then jumping a pirouette into the sky. The landing would be glorious."

I knew Gato wouldn't give me any names, but he did give me a hint when he finally turned to me and said:

"El Dorado is above us all, Haim. We all work for El Dorado. Even you."

"That all you can give me?"

Gato put his hand on my shoulder. "Actually, I'd hoped you'd learn an important lesson from my story about Sergio."

"What? Don't kiss dudes?"

Gato shook his head like I was an ignorant rube. Then he inched closer and whispered an ominous warning into my ear, as if his cameras were also recording sound.

"Be careful who you love. And be even more careful of who knows who you love."

Something about his tone worried me.

I was already walking to the elevator when he called to to me from the balcony.

"Don't forget your gun." Then he walked into the living room towards me, deadly serious as I picked my HK off the table. He nodded to me. "And make sure you have plenty of ammo."

CHAPTER TWENTY-SIX

As I drove away from Gato's gleaming tower, I couldn't stop thinking about Gato's warning. *"Be careful who you love. And be even more careful of who knows who you love."* But how did it apply to me? I convinced myself his words of caution didn't matter. Gato didn't know shit. I didn't love anyone. Not even myself. Last girl I really loved was Mary Rossi, and that didn't end well. She was back in Brooklyn living with my former best friend Mikey Quinn. They might even be married by now.

Of course I've had feelings for women, lots of feelings for women. Certainly Jen, but she stopped answering my texts months ago. I might have fallen for Mrs. Nobel, but she had a fifty cal bullet through her heart. Catharine was long dead after drinking herself to an early grave. And so was our son Thomas. I hadn't thought about them for awhile. I looked in the rearview and saw tears in my eyes. I wiped them away with my sleeve. I was in the clear, I was certain. Heck, by now I was completely incapable of love.

I certainly didn't love Jessie. Sure, she was spunky and pretty and sexy. Moreover, she was tolerant. Tolerant of me—up to a point. Up to knowing that I was trying to hurt her. Sure I slept with Clara. I wanted to sleep with Clara, I needed to sleep with Clara, if only to simply prove who I was. What I was. Just like I wanted to turn off my phone when I got Jessie's calls and messages. I wanted to hurt Jessie. Because Jessie needed to know the truth. Jessie cared, sure, she cared enough to call and text and worry. But she made the mistake of caring about me. I mean, when was the last time anyone really cared? For real. What an idiot she was. I had to punish her. She had to know what kind of man I was. Am. Hell, I'd stolen from her. Lied to her. And I'd hurt her. And I felt nothing. Nothing. Not a thing. I didn't feel a fucking thing. I was sure of that.

My face was wet. My nose was running. I had trouble breathing. I was gasping for air. It was the drugs, the lack of drugs, I told myself, trying to convince myself of something other than the truth. But when I looked back in the mirror, I could barely see through the thick tears, filling my eyes, rolling down my cheeks.

I'd hurt Jessie. And by hurting her I'd hurt myself. What the hell had I done? Just to prove what an ass I was? How could I hurt such a wonderful person? I didn't even give her a chance. Didn't give us a chance.

Before I knew it, I'd pulled over into the emergency lane of the 405 and was frantically calling her. But she didn't pick up. Nothing. I immediately texted. *"Please call me. You may be in danger. Please. I'm so sorry."* I was ready to hit 'send'. But I wasn't done. Then I added, *"I love you."* It took me several minutes to push the button, but after I finally sent it, my tears burst forth again. But these were tears of cleansing. These were tears of joy. Maybe I could love again? Maybe? After Cathy and Thomas and the booze and the drugs and staring down at the San Diego bay on the edge of the Coronado bridge. I'd come through all of it. I'd come to Jessie. And now she was at risk. In trouble. Because of me.

Fuck that.

I was in the fast lane, pushing the Saab past 80mph, screaming the little engine. I called her again and again. It was almost midnight and traffic was light, thank God. I got to her house in about 20 minutes.

I had my pistol out as I fumbled with the keys, bursting through the door. Running up the stairs.

As I feared, Jessie's front door was unlocked. It was eerily dark. I flicked on as many lights as I could, gun ready.

I found Jessie's iPhone on the floor. My calls and texts unanswered, unopened, the screen cracked. The bed was in shambles, blankets and sheets on the floor. Her little table was upended. A few chairs kicked over.

She had fought them. That realization gave me a little smile. She was tough.

But then I saw the note nailed to the wall.

"I told you to get out of LA. Now we do it the hard way."

CHAPTER TWENTY-SEVEN

I drove up the Pacific Coast Highway and parked in the Jack in the Box parking lot. It was now about midnight, which I found ironic, since the last time I'd had a run-in with Eddie and his/her/they goons was essentially around the same time of night.

I made sure my H&K had two full extra mags loaded with Fort Scott .45ACP rounds, which gave me 36 bullets of total killing power. I made sure my fedora was on tight, as I knew I was in for a fight, then quietly made my way down and over to the Malibu Inn.

I saw Latin King, wearing a thick cast on his right hand, standing guard in front of the door, holding a Beretta 9mm in his left hand.

I quietly swept around the side, peeking in a window. Inside I saw Jessie, scared, crying, wearing her flower pajamas, sitting on a chair in the rear of the space, on a small, raised performance stage that the local cover bands play on. Behind her was Eddie Schwarma, holding my 10mm Sig in his hand. I couldn't see the front of the place, but my bet was Black Bobby was somewhere ready to cap me when I came in the door.

I crept around back and found a rear door. It was locked, but I quietly picked it. Too easy. I stepped immediately to the side and sure enough the door swung open and Caucasian King hobbled out, a big cast on his right leg, a Glock in his hand. He must have been waiting for me. But he wasn't moving very fast and I moved in, grabbed his Glock hand, while kicking out his good left knee. Crack! BAM! He went down, but he fired off a round before I could try to twist his gun away. His hand was strong and I went down with him, trying to wrench it away. But by now he had his other hand to help and was holding onto his black plastic gat for dear life with his gym-hardened muscles. I had to end this quick before Eddie's calvary arrived, so I had no choice and pulled my HK, putting a round into his head point blank.

One down.

Now they knew I was here. So instead of waiting for trouble, I went to make my own.

I hustled around to the front, only to find Latin King nearly running into me, heading for the sound of gunshots. We both surprised each other. He fired first, but he was obviously right handed and missed wildly with his left trigger finger. I fired and hit him twice, aiming for center mass—one in the stomach, the other in the chest. He dropped like a sack of rocks. One of those .45s must have cut his aorta, as blood began pooling and soaking the pavement beneath his now-lifeless body.

"Drop it, Baker"

Ratso stood in front of the door, pointing his pistol at me. "I don't wanna kill ya, but I will."

I slipped my gun back into my shoulder holster like I couldn't care less. I could see Ratso's hands twitching. Odds of him hitting me with his shaky Smith & Wesson M&P were not great, so I casually began walking towards my former friend.

"I don't want to kill you either, Ratso, but I should."

"Eddie wants to talk. Just go in and toss him your piece and nobody gets hurt."

I looked over at the lifeless Caucasian King, staring up at the sky with dead eyes. "Too late for that."

I walked closer, playing my bet. I didn't think Rizzo had the guts to fire, and even if he did, I doubted his aim was going to get a 9mm anywhere near my center mass. But then again, the closer I got the bigger, the easier target I became. At some point Ratso just had to point and shoot and I'd get it in the stomach no matter what. I was now about ten feet away. Ratso's eyes were glassy. His head twitched. He was on coke or meth, so who knows what he might do. I counted on a few more feet out of friendship, but then I had to play my cards.

Eight feet.

"I mean it, Baker! You wanna save that chick, you better listen!"

Seven feet.

"Stop right there, Baker!"

Suddenly I sprinted at a diagonal towards Ratso's left side, figuring it would force him to fire at an angle at a moving target, giving me better odds.

I needed't have worried. He never fired.

Ratso dropped his gun as soon as I hit him. I drove him like a linebacker into the front door, slamming his face into the wood. He was stunned, so I put him in a half-nelson, opened the door and waited for the gunshots.

Six rounds went off—BLAM BLAM BLAM BLAM BLAM BLAM, filling poor Ratso Rizzo with lead. I then let my Ratso-shield fall to the floor and rolled left, behind a circular rack of colorful t-shirts. It provided concealment but no cover.

BLAM BLAM BLAM BLAM BLAM—more rounds came my way, ripping through the shirts.

I fell to the floor, hearing the bullets speed over my head and lodge themselves in the wall behind me.

I had no idea who was shooting, but I didn't have time to ponder that. I quickly spied a small round table to my left and sprinted for it, knocking it down. Now at least I had some cover. Then I heard Eddie clapping.

"Good job little dick. Thanks for coming to see me. But here's the deal. I'll give you five seconds to toss your gun or your girlfriend gets it." He put his/my gun to Jessie's head.

I peeked over and saw Black Bobby behind the bar with two pistols— one in each hand. He was crouching down a bit, giving himself cover. Schwarma was to my right and had positioned himself behind Jessie, kneeling down behind her chair, using her as a shield. He had my 10mm pushing into the side of her head.

"Help me, Happy, Please!" She begged.

Eddie looked at her quizzically, then bellowed, "Happy? Now that's fresh! *The Happy Little Dick!*" Eddie laughed heartily at his own lousy joke.

"Let her go, Eddie. This is between you and me."

"Fuck you, Baker. We play this my way... ONE!"

I began to sweat. I couldn't get a line on Eddie. He was at least twenty feet away. I didn't have a good target with him hiding behind Jessie, other than his arm and hand holding the gun to the side of her head. On a good day I might be able to hit his hand from that distance with a .45, but I ran the risk of Black Bobby on my left unloading on me, plus there was the very real possibility of plugging my girlfriend with my own bullet. My pumping adrenaline made a tight shot even less likely.

Wait. Did I call Jessie my girlfriend? I did. Fuck. I did...

"TWO!" Eddie cocked the Sig, putting it into single action. Now it would take only 3 pounds of pressure to pull the trigger and kill my girlfriend. Yes, I did say "girlfriend." "THREE!"

"Alright, just let her go!"

"Toss the gun and hands up!"

"You promise to let her go?"

"FOUR!"

I had no choice.

I threw my HK into the middle of the room and stood with my hands up. I squinted, waiting for Black Bobby to plug me. I saw him stand tall, aiming both of his Glocks, each with a 30 round "fun stick" magazine. But he didn't pull either trigger, looking to Eddie for orders.

Knowing Eddie's theatrics, I had the feeling this all had been rehearsed earlier. Eddie stood up, suddenly full of bravado now that I was unarmed. Jessie had tears streaming down her cheeks, shaking her head at me, willing me to run away with her frightened eyes. I saw the concern, the worry in her face. I nodded an okay to her, as if I had some sort of plan.

But to be honest, I had no idea what I was going to do. I was pretty much fucked. All I could see was to stall for time before Eddie realized he could kill me at any moment. But maybe that was to my advantage. Eddie seemed like the sort that needed to prove himself. Needed to prove that this little girl in a suit was tough. He/She had somehow needed to earn the title of tough *guy*. No. Eddie was going to relish this moment. Take his time. Take his time killing me. It wouldn't come quickly. Eddie'd want me to bleed out so he could stand over my body and gloat—preferably with an audience to see it. He might even let Jessie live so she could also tell the tall tale of the day the Great Eddie Schwarma finally ended the miserable life of the legendary Haim "Little Dick" Baker.

"If you're so tough, Eddie, why don't you and I go mano-a-mano?" I said casually. "C'mon Eddie. You and me."

I could see Eddie seriously thinking about it as he waived his gun under his nose while he briefly considered having at it with me. But he let his brains get the better of his emotions and he finally shook his head, walking out in front of Jessie.

"I've got a better idea. I'm gonna let you dance. With a friend of mine." Then he said with a smug smile: "Baker, I want you to meet my little friend Ryo..."

CHAPTER TWENTY-EIGHT

Suddenly, out of the shadows on the right side of the room emerged a huge guy wearing a red Gucci tracksuit. I hadn't seen him, as I'd been concentrating on Eddie and Black Bobby, but this dude was hard to miss. He was Asian, probably Japanese, with his long, black hair done up in a knot like some sort of samurai. He was the size of a sumo wrestler, maybe 300 pounds, and the way he walked, wide-legged and slow, it was as if he wasn't afraid of anything or anyone. He was walking towards me, eating what seemed to be a yellow mango. But he was eating it like an apple, skin and all, with the juice running down his face. He smiled at me, put the entire thing in his mouth, then spit out the pit into his hand. He reared back, and threw it at me like a hard fastball. I barely had time to move as it sailed inches past my face.

As I turned back to him, I saw he was now holding a big samurai sword that he'd pulled from a sheath on his back. He started moving faster, right at me, sword out, walking fast in a sort of circular stride, so I couldn't flank him.

All I could hope for was to somehow get past this big guy, pick up my gun and start blazing. But Ryo Grandé wasn't about to let that happen. Before I knew it Ryo had his sword held high over his head and was sprinting right at me.

I barely had time to jump out of the way as his sharp Katana came down hard, slicing right through the table, shattering and splintering the wood. He was quick, and took another hard swing right away. I quickly picked up one of the broken table legs just as the sword came down, inches from my head, and impaled the wooden leg. Luckily it was stuck, so I kicked at Ryo's knee. But he was expecting that and lifted his big leg up, striking my foot as it connected, knocking me down. My foot was throbbing. Rio-Grandé smiled, enjoying his beat down of me. But I was in reach of another table leg and bashed his big thigh with it. The table leg broke in two. The guy's giant leg barely flinched. But his smile turned upside down, because that had to have stung, even a guy his size.

He set the embedded sword on the floor, put his foot atop the wood, and yanked his blade free from the broken table leg like King Arthur pulling Excalibur from the stone.

I think I heard him snort as he reared back for another strike, but I wasn't waiting around for him to chop me in two as I scrambled back behind the circular clothes rack. I could hear Eddie laughing, and then I glanced at Black Bobby, who was laughing too. He had set his Glocks down on the bar and was pouring himself a beer as he enjoyed the show. For a moment I'd forgotten about the Big Guy. Big mistake.

SWISH! Godzilla sliced through about fifty shirts with his sharp sword. Fortunately I ducked when I heard the attack, and saw that the Asian monster had sliced off the top of my fedora! Only centimeters from my scalp. In fact he'd gotten a bit of my hair too. Damn, that was a close shave.

The swing had cut right through the metal post, causing it to fall into the Giant, who quickly dislodged himself from shreds of rainbow-colored cotton blends.

I tossed what was left of my Stetson at Sumo, hitting him harmlessly in the face. He looked down at my dead fedora, and smiled at the small victory, then stepped on it, as if he knew that my similar demise was only moments away.

I had enough time to dart to another rack—of pants this time—but I was also working my way towards my gun. I was only ten feet away from it as Ryo's sword turned the display into a rack of cut-offs, and I arced around, moving the wheeled display with me as I got within five feet of the Mk23. Eddie suddenly realized what I was doing and ran to the gun, kicking it away.

Dammit!

"Huh-uh, little dick, only me and Bobby get guns," Eddie said as he backed safely out of range.

I looked back at Mr. Grandé charging at me, sword high, ready to cut me in two. I knew I had to get that thing out of his hand or I was going to go the way of my Stetson. And I had to think fast, because he was nearly on me.

I pretended to back up and slip, falling to the floor, cowering. The Big Guy, now smiling with confidence and relishing the impending kill, took a little more time and lifted up his Katana for an extra hard swing, coming down full force to split me in two.

I timed it best I could, and rolled away at the last second, with the samurai sword arcing down inches from my back as I quickly got to my feet and charged Mr. Sumo. Since he'd used all his strength and weight in the blow, he'd lodged the sword about four inches into the hardwood floor. I quickly kicked as hard as I could at his hands, using all my weight, catching him on his right wrist. I heard a CRACK as his wrist bent inward, forcing him to release the sword handle.

I'd broken his wrist alright, but unfortunately my blow had also dislodged the sword, which flew past Black Bobby over near the stage.

I then moved behind Ryo Grandé, strung my arm around his thick neck, and put him into a headlock. I used all my strength, pulling tight to cut off the blood flow to his brain. But he simply stood up like I was a toddler trying to get a camel ride. He reached back with his left hand, but I wiggled out of the way, keeping pressure on his neck. I saw the Big Man turning red. Eventually I was going to win this one if I could just hold on tight for a little longer. But Samurai Sam wasn't about to let me do that.

Ryo began backing up, faster and faster, until SMASH, he buried me into the wooden wall. It knocked the wind out of my lungs and I crashed to the floor. I tried to gather my breath but Ryo saw what he'd done to me and smiled again. With his big left hand he picked me up and before I knew it, he had me in a bear hug. I was face-to-face with the Japanese demon. I could smell the soy sauce from his bento box lunch on his breath. Then he spoke.

"Good-night."

I was gasping for breath as he squeezed the remaining air from my lungs. I could feel my ribs starting to give way. Soon they'd be cracking and I'd be dead. He had my arms pinned at my sides, so I couldn't thumb his eyes or cup his ears (I've popped a few ear drums with that move). I was lucky if I could even get my hands into my pants pocket. And as the vision started to fade from my eyes, and Eddie's roaring laughter reached a crescendo, I suddenly remembered...

The Bersa Thunder!

I had Clara's little compact gun in my pocket all this time and had completely forgotten about it. I smiled at Ryo, and squeezed out my own two words.

"Good-night." I said.

With my remaining oxygen starting to wane, I reached into my front pocket, flicked up the safety, angled the gun upwards, and fired three shots. BLAM BLAM BLAM.

I fell to the floor as Ryo dropped his arms and stumbled backwards, his face in shock, turning pale; blood was already leaking from the three new holes in his chest. I fired once more, hitting him in the forehead, putting the Big Guy out of his misery.

As he fell backwards into the wall and slumped down, I quickly turned and fired at Black Bobby, hitting him in the cheek and face. He fell behind the bar. I wasn't sure if I'd finished him or not, but I didn't have time to check as I heard Jessie scream.

"Happy watch out!!!"

I'd forgotten about Eddie, and heard BLAM BLAM BLAM! Three 10mm rounds fired wildly, missing me completely. I spun around to see that Jessie had pushed Eddie from behind, saving my life.

Eddie quickly turned to her and fired.

BLAM.

"NO!!!"

I shot Eddie with the Bersa, hitting him in the shoulder. He screamed in agony as he spun back.

I aimed the kill shot right between his eyes. He looked at me with total fear, knowing what was coming. I could see the complete dread in his wide eyes ringed with smudged mascara, as if he were seeing his death coming in slow motion—the death of Eddie Schwarma and whatever his female name was. I could't wait to see him go.

But when I pulled the trigger-

-CLUNK. The damn little gun had jammed!

Eddie suddenly realized what had happened and knew he now had the upper hand again. He switched his gun into his left hand, now that his right shoulder had a .380 round lodged in it.

"Gotcha now, little dick!" He laughed as he aimed the Sig at me, turning the black gun on its side like a ghetto gangster.

I had one move.

I threw the Bersa at him, temporarily distracting Eddie, as I ran for the samurai sword, which was only about four feet from his feet. As Eddie fired, I somersaulted, grabbed the sword and came up swinging. Eddie fired again. Thankfully he missed with his gun hand doing the ghetto thang, like he saw it on some rap video. His bullets went wild. But all I could see in my adrenaline and oxygen deprived tunnel vision was my Sig, spitting fire. Eventually one of those bullets was going to hit me. I had to eliminate the threat.

I charged Eddie, sword high, and brought the big katana down on Eddie's left forearm. The velocity of the strike cut right through his bone, just below the elbow.

It was like watching a movie in slow motion. His hand still gripping the gun, but falling away to the floor, chopped clean off his arm. Eddie's face screaming in pain.

And then I saw Jessie. On the floor. Not moving.

Rage. All I felt was rage.

Before I knew it, I had the sword in the air, swinging horizontal, pushing hard on the handle with my right hand on top, pulling with my left holding tight with all my strength below it.

As soon as I connected, Eddie's small head flew from his shoulders. Eddie's blood began to spurt from the severed artery in his severed neck. And then what was left of his body fell away like a mannequin without strings.

I didn't have time to enjoy the death of Eddie Schwarma.

I tossed the sword and in seconds was holding Jessie on the floor, helping her to sit up. I held her close, feeling her warm blood on my hand as I gripped her back. She held on tight to my other hand, looked up at me and smiled.

"Happy, you saved me."

"No. You saved me."

She smiled. "We saved each other."

"Oh, Jessie..." There was so much to say. But I couldn't utter anything. I just wanted to look in her eyes and hold her close.

She then reached up and touched my face. "You, you lost your hat."

"I'll get another one."

"But it won't smell like you."

"Give it some time."

She chuckled. Then coughed. Then looked at me, her face now contrite.

"Happy, I need to tell you something. I lied to you."

"I lie all the time. I don't care."

"Happy, I have cancer."

"It's okay. It'll be fine."

"I'm so afraid."

"Don't worry."

"But I don't want to lose my breasts. I know you like my breasts."

"You can always get new ones. Just like getting a new hat. But I don't care. It's you I like. Breasts are nothing without you. Nothing else matters."

"That's so sweet." She smiled. Then she coughed again.

"I don't want the chemo. That's why I've been putting this off."

I stroked her head, running my fingers through her hair. "Listen. My mom went through this. I was with her the whole time. It was fine."

"Is she, is she okay now?"

"She's fine." I lied. "She's totally fine."

"I'm so glad." Then she shivered. "I don't want to be alone. Oh, Happy, I'm so scared."

"Don't be afraid. Please."

"I so scared of being alone."

"I'll be here. You'll never be alone. I promise."

"I know it sounds stupid, but I don't want to lose my hair. Losing my hair and being alone. I'm so scared."

I held her tighter. "You listen to me. I won't leave you. Ever. I'll hold your hand. I'll take you to the doctor, I'll make you meals, I'll clean your house, I'll wash your clothes, I'll make sure you're happy and safe and I won't leave your side. Ever. I promise. I promise you that, Jessie."

"You'd, you'd do that for me?"

"I'd do that forever."

Jessie's face relaxed and she began to smile again. She looked like she was glowing—as if she'd been waiting to hear those words all her life.

"And you can always wear a wig." I said. "Any style you want. You can even be a redhead."

"I've always wanted to be a redhead." Her face twitched, then she grabbed my hand again.

"Oh, Happy, you're so cold. It must be freezing in here."

I held her even tighter. "We'll keep each other warm."

"Please don't leave me."

"I'll never leave you, Jessie."

Her voice got quiet. "That's so beautiful." Then she formed a serene smile on her soft face.

"Thank you," she whispered as she closed her eyes. "Thank you, Happy."

I looked at her beautiful, glowing visage, and something within me bubbled up to the surface. I was emotional. The truth suddenly cut through my usual bullshit. I could only reveal to this beautiful woman the truth. The truth that I couldn't even tell myself.

"Jessie, I lied to you too. I, I stole pills from your bathroom... Because... Because I'm a drug addict."

And then I thought for a second, and knew what else I needed to say.

"But I don't want to be that guy anymore."

Suddenly something rose up my spine, like a light. Like warm wings. And a dark weight within me flew away and I actually felt lighter. I felt liberated.

I realized I still had the heroin in my coat pocket. I reached in, pulled the bundle out, and quickly tossed it away before I could change my mind. Then I promised this angel lying beneath me, I promised her with words I thought I'd never hear myself utter:

"And I'm going to get better. I'm getting clean. For you. Because of you, Jessie."

And then I started to cry, and as I wiped my eyes I said, "I'm going to be happy. I'm going to be 'Happy.'"

Then I bent down and put my mouth to her ear and finally told her how I really felt. What I knew was the truth all along:

"I love you, Jessie."

I kissed her.

But her lips were cold.

She was cold. Her warmth was gone.

Jessie was gone.

I gently set her down, kissed her forehead and stepped back.

I looked at her serene, dead face for a few moments. Maybe it was a few minutes. Maybe it was longer. I don't know.

Then I nodded goodbye to this emoji-drawing, sexy pole-dancing woman with angels and flowers and yellow and a fading gold halo around her head.

I had tried to fool myself into thinking that a 10mm penetrator bullet wouldn't kill her, but there was nothing we could have done. Eddie had murdered the woman I loved with my own gun.

I was too numb to cry anymore.

I glared at Eddie's severed head, the expression of dread and pain still plastered on that dead face. I thought I might have felt a bit of vengeance by chopping off his/her/they head. But I felt nothing. Nothing but sorrow.

I slowly walked over to Ratso's body, lying face down. I wiped my prints from the Bersa. I also kicked the .380 shells towards his body, and set the gun in his hand, sliding away his Smith and Wesson. I wiped my prints from the sword and tossed it back towards Grandé's body. I then remembered to check on Black Bobby. His body lay in a pool of blood on the floor behind the bar. I should have known he wasn't getting up with two rounds through his face and out the back of his head. Bits of his brain had splattered on the wall behind him.

I walked through the door, stepping outside into the salty air. I could hear the waves crashing on the private sand just beyond the multi-million dollar beachfront homes sitting across the street. I imagined what kind of people must live there—celebrities, corporate cronies, crypto kings. All sleeping on fine cotton sheets, living charmed lives unbeknownst that the underworld was creeping all around them in the night. They'll wake up to their perfect day and walk on the beach and maybe go to their high paying job or fuck their high-paid husbands or wives or girlfriends or boyfriends. But the woman who really deserved all that joy and happiness and perfectness will never get up again.

I looked back at the carnage inside the open door of Eddie's restaurant/bar/retail shop. I was hoping the cops would think my old pal Ricardo "Ratso" Rizzo was the doomed, would-be hero who had attempted to rescue Jessie Debost from her kidnappers. I picked up the three .45 shells from the bullets that took out Latin King and Caucasian King, so I couldn't be traced back to the crime scene, and walked back up to the Saab, which was still sitting in the Jack in the Box parking lot. I tossed the shells into a plastic trashcan and looked in the window of the fast food joint.

The place was closed and the crew were cleaning up inside, oblivious that five assholes were dead next door. They also didn't know that a beautiful woman had been needlessly murdered.

But I knew what had happened here in Malibu in the waning hours of the night. And I wasn't going to leave LA until I made sure that the person ultimately responsible for Jessie's death was six feet under. I promised myself and promised Jessie's soul that within the day, which was now breaking the darkness with its sharp rays of burgeoning dawn, that *El Dorado* would be gone, and Jessie's death would be avenged.

Or I'd be joining her in the afterlife.

CHAPTER TWENTY-NINE

I was feeling heavy and morbid as I drove south down the Pacific Coast Highway as the sun slowly rose into the sky. I was also feeling tired, and the combination led me back to the Wilshire Motel. The green bungalow was still taped off from the Sicario killing, but I was able to get one of the blue bungalows set back in the parking lot. The young male clerk told me that I wouldn't have to check out until tomorrow at eleven. I assured him that I'd probably be gone by then.

I slept a few hours until noon, then showered and brushed my teeth. I looked in the mirror and noticed I was starting to sweat and my muscles were quivering. My addict demon was hungry, but the only thing I could do was placate it with caffeine, so I made three cups of pod coffee. I was still feeling the need, but my will was stronger.

I distracted myself by loading all three magazines for my H&K with .45 Fort Scott tumbling rounds. Then I left the motel key at the desk, along with a few hundred dollar bills, got into the Saab, and headed out to the Sunset Strip. I tried to call Andy, but he wasn't answering. The guy was smart, so I hoped he was also sensible and prayed he'd finally driven himself back down to the safety of San Diego.

I drove down the Sunset Strip and found a busy In-N-Out Burger. I ate my double-double in the parking lot, then stopped in at an overpriced clothing store called Ron Dorff. They had a $700 fedora in the window and I figured I'd better blow the rest of this wad of money before I got my brains blown out. But when I tried the hat on, it just didn't feel right.

Out on the sidewalk, I found a street vendor who barely spoke English and was selling all types of hats for twenty bucks. I found a navy blue straw porkpie that looked pretty boss. It fit perfectly. I gave the immigrant lady $40 for the hat plus tip and got back into my Saab, ready to go. But I knew I needed to do one more thing before heading off into the netherworld.

I drove through traffic to Hollywood and Vine and was lucky to find a parking space on the street right in front of one of my favorite haunts, The Bourbon Room. I know I'd promised Jessie I'd kick the drugs, but, well, I never said anything about grain alcohol. Especially since she and I had met over Irish single malt. I had a feeling Jessie might even approve of me toasting her with a Yellowspot. That's what I convinced myself anyway.

But when I walked inside, the vibrant scene looked downright dull. The stage was empty and only a few old alcoholic men were drinking this early at the big bar that looked like the bar scene from *The Shining*.

I walked back out and strolled up Hollywood Boulevard instead, taking in the crazy scene here in the heart of La la land. Tourists of all types were trying to find their favorite stars on the Walk of Fame, leaving flowers, taking selfies, or in the case of Donald Trump, stepping on, spitting, or, as one shirtless man was doing, urinating on it to the applause of several onlookers.

I walked over to Humphrey Bogart, his engraved name gracing the middle of his little star. I gave him a bit of silent reverence until I heard a voice.

"Staaaar maps! Find your stars on the ground and in your car!" Willis walked up to me. "Find your star, pal?"

"Yeah," I said with certainty.

He looked as disheveled as ever, his wild, balding, red hair blowing in the warm breeze. "You changed your hat, Baker." He said, staring at my porkpie. He seemed almost perplexed. I figured it must be a spectrum thing. Like he'd never imagined me without a Stetson.

"Had to."

"Don't like it. Don't like it." Willis began looking around in his paranoid way.

"Hey Willis," I said as I pulled a can of cold Bud from my pocket. "I bought you a beer."

He took it and stared at it like it was made of gold.

"Been five years, two months and seventeen days and four hours." Then he looked at me and smiled, his face full of joy.

"You got me a beer." He said in reverence.

"I'm leaving LA."

"Gonna miss you, Baker."

"Miss you too, Willis." We stared at one another as if we'd never meet again. I knew better than to hug him or shake his hand—he usually recoiled if you touched him. So I nodded. So did he.

"And thanks for the tip." I said.

"What tip?"

"Tyler Hintzman. I'm gonna go get El Dorado now."

Willis backed away, like I'd just pulled out a gun and was aiming for his face. A sort of protective insanity veil instantly seemed to cover his eyes, and the Willis I knew retreated into his tormented mind.

"No. Nonononononononono..." He continued to back away in fear.

"Willis!" I said loudly.

"...C, Charlie Sheen, N, Nikki Sixx, they wanna kick me out of SAG!"

"Willis..." I stepped towards him.

He stopped talking, looking at me like I was a stranger, like he was trying to figure out what I was doing there, if I were a friend or foe.

I looked into his troubled eyes, trying to reach the Willis I knew.

"Thank you," I said

Then, for a moment, as if Willis somehow willed it, his veil of torment retreated and Old Willis began to smile back. He suddenly held up his can of Bud as a sort of farewell salute. "See ya, Baker."

"See ya later, pal." I tipped my hat.

I think he nodded as he carefully put his beer back into his ratty coat pocket, turned, grabbed his yellow maps from another dirty pocket, and trotted off down Hollywood Boulevard like he'd forgotten I was ever there, yelling,

"Star maps! Staaaaar Maaaaaaaps!..."

CHAPTER THIRTY

Beverly Hills is not what most people think it is. It's a small enclave of LA, less than six square miles, and is actually a city in and of itself, with its own police force and government and high taxes and school system, a virtual island of opulence surrounded on all sides by the behemoth of the City of Los Angeles.

There's the famous downtown Beverly Hills, below Santa Monica Boulevard, with the ritzy stores and restaurants and hotels, where Hillers and posers and wannabes strut their stuff. There you'll see people wearing clothes that cost more than many of the cars we drive, and faces plastered with the de rigueur botox injections and plastic surgery and implants that cost as much as a single family home in a normal American city—creating those weird visages that set the swells apart from the commoners. You'll also see gaggles of uber-expensive automobiles sitting in traffic or jockeying for limited parking spaces, all interspersed with gawking tourists, buying $100-$500 bottles of Chanel perfume, packed in pretty little paper plastic Chanel bags that they will use later for makeshift gift bags for their mundane friends.

Most of the ordinary people who get to claim to be from Beverly Hills live in the remodeled ranch style homes and the multiple apartments and condos down here, allowing folks to brag to their friends that they actually live in the 'Hills, and more importantly, they have the gold-plated address that allows their children to attend the small city's high achieving schools, including the famous Beverly Hills High.

But the real Beverly Hills and the real Hillers live above Santa Monica Boulevard, the higher the better, far away from the mundane low-dwellers who are often forced to rub elbows with the plebes from La la land—the rest of us dregs who don't have that famous 90210 stamp on our driver's licenses. No, the scions who reside above California State Route 2, and especially the Lords who live near the top of the mountain, in the actual mountain-high Hills, with their multi-million dollar mansions and jetliner views and tiny winding roads—this is where the Masters of the City (and you could argue, the Masters of the Universe) dwell and play and scheme in complete privacy and splendor.

And high up above Canon Drive, after it winds upwards into a nosebleed and turns into Benedict Canyon Drive and then into a private drive at the summit of the Santa Monica Mountains, exists one of the most exclusive properties in the world—a sprawling estate of at least 70,000 square feet set high upon 157 acres of sweeping mountaintop views, lording over the entirety of Los Angeles County. The property is called *Heaven* and I found myself driving there in my Saab with the windows rolled down on this sunny, hot, SoCal afternoon.

After I left Willis, I got an excited call from Tyler, informing me that Gold Studios had finally set up a deal for the "Haim" project, giving me Executive Producing and Story credit for a movie and streaming series based on my recent case in El Cajon. They wanted me to come in and sign a few contracts, where I'd be getting a check for $90,000 to sign my rights away, but I'd also get a separate, unspecified amount when the movie was officially greenlit, and for each episode of any series. He didn't mention what the other contract was for.

Normally such transactions are done at a talent agency, such as Annotated, but for some reason Nash Gold requested I come to his personal residence in Beverly Hills. Tyler said it was an honor for me to be invited, and that it proved the show was a go. Now, I didn't really give a damn about being some sort of producer or story person, whatever that was, but I was sure interested in talking to one of the wealthiest men in the world.

CHAPTER THIRTY-ONE

The Saab chugged, struggling up the steepest parts of Benedict Canyon, rumbling past Cielo Drive where the infamous Manson murders took place (and which was also the setting for the great Tarantino flick *Once Upon a Time in Hollywood*), and maybe fifteen minutes later, nearly at the top of the high hills, right before hitting Mulholland, I took a right-hander onto an unnamed private drive, running into a tall, solid, black metal gate. I couldn't see a thing behind it. The gate was maybe thirty feet high, with a smattering of ccv cameras sitting atop it, reminding me of some sort of border wall built to keep out all but the most determined breachers. No doubt armed security would be waiting nearby even if someone were to get over or breach these black castle walls.

There was nothing on the gate but a camera lens aimed at my face on the small intercom, and a red button. I pushed it, expecting to say something flippant, but instead I heard an electronic motor begin to buzz and the heavy metal wall began to slide to the left, revealing a long, steep drive about a quarter mile long, ringed by tall trees. The estate no doubt had facial rec or some AI software or both, telling the powers-that-be that one Haim Baker was attempting to grace the presence of Lord Gold.

I shifted the Saab and began the slog up the steep drive, which looked like a massive 21 degree grade incline. I kept the car in first gear as it strained against the hill, noting that the gate quickly closed behind me as soon as I cleared the threshold. I could see the extension of the gate winding around the giant property facing the street. I had the feeling that the towering metal wall was built not only to keep out the unwanted masses, but could also function as an unbreakable prison for those inside this lap of luxury.

And as I drove past the line of tall palm trees, I saw a black armored SUV sitting at the end of a dirt path, ready to pounce if needed. Since the Saab was going so slowly up the hill, I could see that the security vehicle was not just a typical 4x4, it was a rare Rezvani Gladiator, a six-wheeled bulletproof pickup truck worth probably half a million bucks that could easily be part of a Navy SEAL operation. Anything but typical security services here in the Hills. But then again, Nash Gold's net worth was thought to be in the Elon Musk and Jeff Bezos territory, a man who had more money in his bank than many countries could muster, so it made sense that Mr. Gold would have the kind of determined security detail that a head of state might require. You could probably make the case that Nash was at the very least the real head of state of Beverly Hills, California.

The private drive leveled off and I could see the sprawling estate come into view behind massive acres of manicured English gardens. We were so high up that the mansion seemed to be haloed in clouds as I approached it. Since we were at the summit of the mountain, one side of the estate overlooked Los Angeles, while the other offered a bird's eye view of the San Fernando Valley.

I drove to the semi-circle driveway and puttered past several parked cars—a few more Rezvanis—these were the Tank versions, and a Ferrari and one of those exotic, limited edition, 3 million dollar Aston Martin Valkyries. Only a multi-billionaire would have such a stable.

I walked over near the unfenced edge of the property and took another glance at the Mt. Olympus view of LA, and felt like a god staring down upon the little moving human ants and fleas down below. And the only way back down to mundanity was Gold's private drive, unless you had a hang glider, a parachute, or felt like rappelling at least 500 feet down to the winding Benedict Canyon street blow.

I was surprised no one had come out to meet me, but then again I was certain I was being watched by video eyes inside that estate. And the estate was huge, more like a hotel than a house. I couldn't see the rear of the building, but I imagined it went on and on, straddling the edge of the mountain.

I strolled up to the heavy wooden front doors of the surprisingly staid, prosaic, Italianesque architecture, replete with acres of red tile roofing. As soon as I got close, I heard the click of a bolt being released from an automatic lock, probably triggered by the small intercom camera next to the door. I pulled the thick handle open and walked inside.

CHAPTER THIRTY-TWO

I was expecting a house that echoed a modern art museum, like the art-filled expanse I found at the Nobel estate. Instead I was greeted by an interior that resembled something that could have been transported from the Hearst mansion—Old Masters graced the walls—Rembrandts, Goyas, and Vermeers stared back from the curiously small living room, interspersed with furniture from mixed eras and styles—a Louis XIV chair there, a Tiffany lamp here, a Ming vase over there. They didn't match in style, but somehow all fit in together—maybe because the incalculable value and pristine condition of all the artifacts in this domestic setting was a proud testament to conspicuous consumption. You could make the case that this home was a sort of American version of an English estate held by a duke or an earl.

I was struck by the feeling that this huge building was honeycombed by a plethora of smallish rooms—the kind of place you could get lost in.

A hallway led to an open area where I saw a huge circular stairway leading upstairs and several doors no doubt heading into the bowels of this overpriced and rather ugly architectural monstrosity. The entryway's tiled floors echoed with my footsteps as I made my way forward towards a double door, which was opened before I reached it by the hand of a tall, fit black guy in a black suit.

"Right this way, sir." He said, appearing like a combination butler/security dude—polite but a little threatening at the same time—as he motioned for me to move past him down an even longer hallway, graced on either side by a number of framed Old Master still lifes. I obliged and slipped past his open arm, curious the he didn't frisk me and take away my Mk23.

But then again, this was a business meeting, wasn't it? But, so was the meeting at Annotated Agency, and they took my gun?

I began fixating on the weapon holstered under the left armpit of my sport coat, the two extra mags secured on the right, feeling comfy and happy that I had this metal and gunpowder protection to keep me safe. I thanked the gun gods they were with me and hoped they'd grace me with their blessings. My mind kept drifting away from the present, so I forced it back, focusing on pushing forward, one step at a time. The cheap Chinese-made porkpie didn't breathe very well, making my hair limp and matted under the synthetic material. It was hot in here, for some reason, and as I brushed away a drip rolling down my forehead, I discovered I was sweating. Then I checked my shaking hand and was reminded by the sudden ache in my forehead that my addiction demon was starting to bite again.

I looked back and saw the Black Butler following me, several steps behind—giving him the appearance of subservience, but also plenty of time to react in case I made any sudden moves. When he saw me turn back, he swept his arm forward again, nodding me to continue down the hallway. Then, as I got close to another double door, the guy spoke up again.

"Through here, please, Mr. Baker."

Before I got to the door, my escort had suddenly, somehow moved ahead of me, opening it before I could reach the handle, motioning me into a huge office space ringed by open windows.

Behind a large, antique wooden desk sat a man who looked like he was right out of the roaring twenties. He appeared to be about as old as that as well. Well, maybe not *that* old, but he was certainly in his seventies. Even though he was sitting down I could tell he was tall, perhaps six-three or four, and thin, with a shock of white hair parted perfectly on the side, wearing a custom, tuxedo-like suit jacket over an argyle sweater with a colorful bow tie and not a lick of facial hair on his well-scrubbed face. I could tell he had expensive, manicured nails as he lit up a light brown cigar as soon as I entered the room. The label wrapped on the stogie gave it away as a Cohiba Double Robusto. I knew that Cohibas were what Castro smoked, and this guy certainly looked like he would fit right in running a country or a politburo or a corporation. The Cohiba had come from a small, open cedar humidor set on the desk, and in front of the wood box sat a stack of legal papers which appeared to be two stapled contracts.

The dapper man nodded to me, took a puff of the aromatic tobacco, and set the wafting cigar down on a gold metal ashtray. After he'd carefully balanced the cigar on the edge of the tray, he stood. He was taller than I guessed, maybe six-five as he leaned forward, offering his right hand over the giant desk. I shook it. His grip was firm for an old guy.

"Welcome, Mr. Baker. It's a pleasure to finally meet you. Please, have a seat."

I looked behind me and found there was a leather chair, magically placed for me to sit by the butler guy. Before I knew it, the dude was already back standing near the door. He was good.

"Oh how rude of me," the dapper man said, as he offered a choice from his humidor. "Please, have a cigar. I believe you'll find them acceptable."

I peered inside the wooden box and saw a sprinkling of colored rings displaying a variety of Cuban offerings—different sizes from long to short, from thin to fat. I reached in and picked out the longest one I could find—a Trinidad Fundadores, almost 8 inches. He passed me a torch. I lit it up. It was amazing. But I wasn't here to pretend I could live the high life with cigars and mansions, and black butlers.

"Who the hell are you, anyway?" I asked as I puffed.

The guy sat back down in his big tufted burgundy leather chair and leaned back.

"My name is Haskell."

He sucked on his cigar, then gently rolled off some ash into the metal ashtray. "They call me Dr. Revenue."

"Doctor Revenue? What are you, a Bond villain?"

Haskell seemed to ignore my comment, wheeling his chair to a nearby liquor cabinet, pouring a crystal glass filled with bourbon and ice. "This will pair nicely with that excellent cigar." He leaned over and me handed the amber liquid.

I took a sip. I don't know what it was but it was damn smooth and smoky. And it did pair nicely with the Trinidad. I sat the glass down on the wooden desk.

"Where the hell is Nash Gold." I wondered aloud.

Haskell frowned, quickly slipping a metal coaster underneath my glass before the condensation could mar the vintage oak. Then he took a pull from his Cohiba, exhaled and smiled again.

"Mr. Gold is indisposed at the moment." He then slid the contracts in front of me. "If you don't mind. I'd like you to sign these. Mr. Gold has already countersigned."

He then opened a drawer and pulled out a checkbook ledger, ready to cut me a cheque as soon as I finished with the pen.

I was beginning to think that this "Dr. Revenue" was the real brains behind the organization, that maybe Nash Gold was just a front. Maybe this old man version of Dr. No sitting in front of me was the man I'd been searching for. Gunning for.

I arced the chair to the side, so I could keep Black Butler in my peripheral as I thought about pulling my gun and plugging both of them. I figured I'd have to take out the Butler first, who no doubt carried a weapon, but that'd give Dr. No a jump on me. I assumed he had quick access to a firearm as well. It was too risky. In fact, I could see the Butler easing forward, putting his weight onto the front of his feet, as this would enable him to sprint or move quickly on my mark. He was anticipating my arm moving to my holster, which would no doubt trigger his reaction.

Haskell, on the other hand, seemed far too at ease. Like he had everything in hand. The Doctor wasn't nervous at all. But he did stand up, moving back to the liquor cabinet, pouring himself a healthy glass of whiskey. He knew what he was doing.

Moving to my left, the old man had made himself a much harder target. I'd have to do a complete 180 after shooting the Butler, giving Mr. Revenue enough time to take me out. I decided to stop playing mind games and look at the contracts. They were as thick as a small phone book.

"What's in these things?"

"Oh, just the standard deal. For the production you'll have EP credit, story credit, and an option for spinoffs."

"And what am I giving up for all of this?"

He looked at me deadpan. "Your life rights."

That didn't sound good.

"Not bloody likely," I said, tensing.

"Oh, Mr. Baker, we must insist." Haskell then turned to look out the window at the LA cityscape down below us on this Mount Olympus. "This project is has taken on a certain momentum."

He turned back, blowing a smoke ring. "Chris Pratt is ready to sign. We've got Antoine Fuqua to direct." We traded gazes. Haskell didn't give anything away. I'd hate to play him in poker. "All we need to move the project ahead is your signature."

I knew what I had to do. My cigar was sitting in the metal ash tray. I picked it up, stood, and turned to Black Butler, who was still waiting expectantly in the shadows near the door. This had to work perfectly.

"Hey pal, you gotta light?"

The Trinidad was still smoldering, but Mr. Butler obliged, pulling a 7th Cav Zippo from his pocket—giving his Army background away.

I held the cigar to my mouth. He flicked the lighter open and leaned near me, holding it up to the end, expecting me to draw in the tobacco and pull in the flame.

But I had other plans.

With his face only inches away from the long stick, and as the flame touched the burning coal of the cigar, making it hotter, I suddenly gabbed his right arm with my left hand, pulling him closer. At the same time I thrust the hot burning tip of the Trinidad into his right eye, as far as I could—assuming that this was his dominant side.

"AAAAARGGGGGHHHHH!" He screamed as the hot Cuban burnt right through the Butler's thin eyelid, sizzling his eyeball. I could smell the melting flesh as the skin began to smoke. The cigar snapped in half from the brute force as his right eye burned into blindness. Thankfully he automatically reached to his eye with his left hand, while I twisted his right arm clockwise, forcing him to bend over, giving me a few seconds to pull my HK and fire three bullets BLAM BLAM BLAM into the top of his head. Bye-bye-butler.

I knew I only had moments before Dr. No was going to draw on me, so I spun as fast as I could, before the Black Butler's body even dropped to the ground. But instead of Haskell's hand pointing a gun at me...

...He was *clapping*.

A little smile twinkled on Dr. No's face.

"Mr. Baker, that was quite inventive."

I held my gun, ready to put a bullet into the Old Man's heart. But then the Doctor stopped clapping and another door opened behind him, and two huge black men stepped in, also wearing expensive suits. I could see that both of them wore the imprint of automatic pistols, like a Mac 10 or an Uzzi, holstered under their sportcoats. These were not butlers. These were soldiers.

I tried to keep all three men within my sights, as I carefully arced left. My nerves and my addiction caused me to start sweating again. I tried to calm myself, but the situation was not in my favor, as they say. I realized my hand was shaking, the HK quivering. My palm was sweating, making the grip slick. I was having trouble holding it on target. But which target?

Haskell nodded to the twitching gun. "You can put that down, Mr. Baker."

I wasn't about to holster my HK, but as I was training it on one of the dapper thugs, he casually walked past me, picked up the Butler, dragged the body to the hallway door, and opened it.

Another black man in a black suit was waiting to retrieve the body. He dragged it into the hallway, and then procured a white cotton towel and wiped up all the blood from the tile floor before backing out and closing the door.

The Big Guard then walked up to me and stood, staring. Stone faced.

Haskell pulled from his cigar, and said matter-of-factly, "You'll need to hand Mr. Robinson your firearm. You won't require it any further. "

I hesitated, quickly calculating the odds of me plugging the giant standing in front of me, who didn't seem to care a wit about the fact that I was pointing a .45 at him point blank. I then considered the odds of me spinning and taking out the other guy before he drew and cut me in half with his Uzzi. Then there was Haskell, well within reach of a gun in his desk or a holster. I looked back to the guy staring me down. Something about the way Mr. Robinson didn't even flinch suggested he might also have soft body armor under his jacket. In fact, I was almost certain he did. That lowered my chances of survival even more. Haskell could sense my internal debate.

"Please, Mr. Baker, if we wanted you to die, you'd never have made it this far."

I figured he was right. I handed my MK23 to the Big Guy, who took it, then frisked me with his other hand, finding the syringe and spoon. He showed them to Dr. Revenue, who smiled knowingly

"Why, Mr. Baker will need that. Oh yes he will."

The guy dropped them back in my pocket and walked past me like I was little more than a flea on the floor. Then he gave Haskell my gun, who put it in his desk drawer for safe keeping. Mr. Robinson then joined his friend, standing on either side of the other door that lead to whoknowswhere. I moved to a different angle so I could see past the big black men to spot a stairway that appeared to go down to another level.

Haskell picked up the contracts and was already through the door when he turned back and motioned for me to follow.

"Come, Mr. Baker, time for you to meet Mr. Gold."

I figured I didn't really have much of a choice. So I strode past the two black Gargoyles who turned and followed behind me, out of range in case I decided to play any martial arts games.

"Here we go, Baker," I said to myself as I walked towards the stairs...

CHAPTER THIRTY-THREE

I descended down a long circular staircase that led out into a huge lower level living room, decorated in what seemed like 14 carat gold. The walls, chairs, and curtains were gold. The room ringed a gold rectangular swimming pool that also extended outside under the giant glass window into an infinity pool that overlooked all of Los Angeles, which was partially obscured by the low hanging clouds wafting just below us here atop the mountain.

I heard a splashing.

Swimming laps in the pool was none other than Nash Gold, the same short, bald, stocky guy from the party. He was completely naked as he moved effortlessly through the water, his muscles rippling.

Then I heard a smoky voice.

"Hello, Haim."

I turned to see Clara, sitting at a nearby wooden table drinking a margarita from a gold-rimmed glass. She was wearing some sort of high-collared Asian blouse and a long skirt, slit up the side with no underwear. She gave me a smile and a brief nod, then turned to Nash, who was now exiting the pool, dripping wet. Clara stood, retrieved a towel from a shelf near the pool, and immediately began drying off Mr. Gold, who looked over to Dr. Revenue.

"What's the story, Haskell?"

"Baker refused to sign. But he did show initiative and resolve. In fact he exhibited the hallmarks of professional training. I must say he quite ingeniously eliminated Mr. Arthur."

Clara retrieved a large cigar from a wooden case near the towels, clipped the end, lit it, then put it in Gold's mouth. He sucked on the tobacco, then exhaled.

"What's that going to cost us?"

Haskell set the contracts on the table, pulled a calculator from his pocket, hit some keys and smiled. "Actually, Mr. Arthur's contract was up and we were facing an extension. That invalidates his life insurance policy. Mr. Baker actually saved us seven figures."

"Excellent!" Gold blew some smoke and smiled his pearly white, veneer teeth.

Clara was now on her knees before the Golden Man drying his thighs and his genitals.

She looked at him.

He nodded to her.

She then began to give him fellatio. Right in front of us. Gold didn't flinch. I don't know how he kept his attention. It was as if this was part of his daily health routine.

"That's why we call you Dr. Revenue." He said, as if the blowjob was a mere formality. Like it was nothing more than a scheduled oil change. His voice didn't even waver. He puffed his cigar as Clara worked him. "I'd say my instincts were right."

"Right as always, Mr. Gold." Haskell said.

Gold paused a second, losing just a brief moment of concentration as Clara finished him off. Then she handed him a robe, helped him into it, and sat back down, briefly glancing at me with her sultry eyes as she wiped her lips with a gold napkin.

Gold cinched up his thin silk robe, then moved to the contracts and glanced through them.

"Are these not to your liking, Haim?" He said without looking at me.

"Haven't read them."

"You don't need to read them," he said.

"You're right. Answer's no."

Mr. Gold turned to Dr. Revenue. "Haskell, didn't you explain to our friend the opportunity before him?"

"I gave him our deal option for the movie and streaming project. Based on his reaction, I assumed he'd want to hear the rest from you."

Gold turned, giving me another once-over, sucking on his cigar. He saw my sweating hands flinching from the heroin withdrawal.

"Care for a cigar? A drink?"

I shook my head. "No, thanks."

"How about something stronger?" He turned to Clara. "What do we have for Mr. Baker?"

"Anything he wants. As always." She smiled at me, peering dangerously into my dark pupils. I could feel myself moved by her big, black, hypnotic eyes. I was getting hard, licking my dry lips. I wanted her. Wanted her mouth. Her body. I wanted the shot, the warmth. The drugs. The bliss...

From her pocket, she pulled out a small wad of brown wrapped in cellophane. Heroin.

I stared at it. I could smell it. I could smell her. The drugs, the sex...

But then I thought of Jessie.

I turned away and forced myself to focus on Gold, trying my best to break Clara Kali's spell.

"I'm fine."

Gold smiled.

"Just so you know, Haim, we offer any vice you wish. All forms of opium—from heroin to Oxy. Fentanyl. Or perhaps you prefer cocaine? Only the purest." Nash Gold studied my reaction. "Women. Men, any age. You name it." He moved closer to me. "It's yours."

"I'll make do." I said from tense lips.

Gold stepped past me and flipped open the contract on top to the signature page. "I at least expected you to sign this one. Is it that you want more money? I mean, for your first project, 90k is generous." Then he tapped the table with his finger. "Perhaps I could up it to 100?" He looked over to Dr. Revenue, who nodded.

"Not interested." I said tersely. I figured Gold was a deal-maker. And the only way to play a guy like this was to keep him from getting your John Hancock. The longer I could do this, the better the deal, and the more time I had to figure out what I was going to do next. More importantly it gave me the time to discover how the hell I was gonna get out of here alive.

"I have to warn you, Haim. We don't take no for an answer."

I shrugged. "I'm also wondering why you have a contract as thick as a phone book for a deal that just gives me story and producing credit."

He interrupted me. "*Executive Producer* credit. There's a difference." Gold stepped closer, trying to gauge my reaction. Like we were playing poker. "You'll still have power. And money."

"What's in the other contract?"

"Opportunity, Haim. Opportunity."

"This isn't just about some movie deal, is it?"

Gold stepped over to a leather loveseat and sat down. I could see his johnson slipping out of his loosely tied robe. This guy loved to show off.

"We've had our eye on you for a long time. And you've lived up to expectations. I must say you've passed every test." Then he looked over to Clara, who was now sipping some tequila. "Hasn't he, Clara?"

"Oh yes. Yes he has."

I stepped over to the papers, lazily flipping through them. There were two contracts. The one on the bottom was between me and "Global Inc." and had a bunch of redacted pages, except for the last page, which required my signature.

"How am I supposed to sign something I can't read?

"You sign it, that's that."

"I'm guessing I can't have my lawyer look this over, the unredacted version?"

"You don't have a lawyer."

Gold took another draw from his cigar. He then walked over to Clara and drank some of her tequila. "Opportunities like this rarely come around in one's life, Haim. I hope you understand that fact."

Haskell, standing next to me, suddenly offered me a pen he'd pulled from his navy sportcoat. I took it, then opened the first contract, the one between me and Gold Studios, crossing out the $90k fee for my story.

"I want one-seventy-five. And Andy gets 100k for writing the treatment."

Gold stared at me. Haskell stared at Gold, waiting for his answer. Finally Nash turned to Dr. Revenue. "Okay. Give Haim one-fifty."

Haskell nodded and made some notes on the contract.

"What about Andy?" I asked.

Nash turned to me. "Mr. Candy's fee won't be a problem. How about a bourbon, Haim, to celebrate?"

I shook my head. "What if I don't sign?"

Nash ignored me, found a fancy bottle of bourbon and poured himself a glass. "I have a feeling you're smart enough to know better."

"You don't know me very well," I said with a smirk.

Gold drank his dark, amber alcohol. Then nodded slightly to Haskell, who turned to me and smiled ominously.

"It was a pleasure to meet you, Mr. Baker. I hope we see you again." Then Dr. Revenue walked up the long set of curving stairs and exited the room.

I noticed the two black guards were now animated and stepping closer. Out of instinct I tried to calculate how I was going to get to the stairway and out of here before the shit went down.

"Hey," I said. "We're just negotiating, here," as I began moving to my side.

"Negotiations are over." Gold took a draw of his cigar, then suddenly crushed it into a gold-plated ashtray. Gold turned away and walked through a metal door as if he were finished with me.

"Hey!" I said.

I didn't have time to say anything else...

CHAPTER THIRTY-FOUR

Before I knew it, a black burlap bag was yanked over my head. I tried to throw an elbow strike, but both my arms were quickly grabbed by what felt like King Kong himself—no doubt it was one of the two giant guards who anticipated my move. Now I was fairly strong for a man of a certain age who spends far too much time drinking, carousing, smoking, and as of late, injecting heroin into his tired body. But these two trolls were solid muscle, each looking like they could easily bench press 500 pounds. And while one of them had my hands in a vice grip, the other threw a thick zip tie around them and pulled tight. I was fucked.

"Hey, this is a pretty aggressive negotiation tactic!" I yelled.

No one answered as I was unceremoniously thrown over the guard's huge shoulder and he began to carry me out of the room. I could smell his lathered-on Ralph Lauren cologne. I needed to get myself free, so I tried to throw a kick, but my legs were immediately grabbed by arms of steel, and another zip was fastened around my ankles. I scolded myself for not playing limp. Now I was really fucked, with no recourse but to enjoy the ride on the Polo train.

I was carried through a door, then down a hallway and another set of stairs, this time a spiral staircase. The air became colder as we descended, and I became dizzy as we went down and around over and over. Finally we made it to solid ground, and I heard footsteps echoing on a solid floor— perhaps tile or concrete.

I heard a metal door unlatch, and even colder air from an active HVAC system met me along with music that seemed to echo off the floor as I was dropped onto a cold metal chair. In the air was a Bobby Darin tune, *Beyond the Sea.* The guards backed away, but I could tell they were still in the room. At least I wasn't fastened or bound to the chair, but I knew my options were limited.

"Hey, maybe I'll have that bourbon after all," I said to whomever was listening. No reply, of course. But then I heard another sound over the music, like a faint hum. It wasn't the A/C, no, it was as someone trying to talk, someone who'd been gagged. Not a good sign.

I hoped no one had seen me palm the pen that Dr. No wanted me to use to sign the contract. I'd slipped it into my pocket and thanked heaven that the guard zipped my hands in front instead of behind my back. Since I was seemingly left alone here in the chair, and since I'd heard the Guards step back behind me, I decided to take the risk of slowly moving my hand to my coat pocket, slipping the pen up into my sleeve. I couldn't risk attempting to free myself until I was certain no one was watching me.

"What happens if I have to pee?" I blurted out. Nothing. "This is my last pair of clean pants." Still nothing.

I then sat there for what seemed like ten minutes, trying to figure my next move, trying to make a plan on how I was going to get out of this one, when the bag was suddenly pullud off my head.

My eyes adjusted to see that I was in a dark room sitting under a pool of light. I noticed the plain, grey, unfinished concrete floor, which was contrary to the opulence of Nash's mansion. And worse, I saw a large grated drain at the center of it. That meant it could easily be cleaned by a hose. Cleaned of blood. Shit. If I didn't know better, I'd say I was in an interrogation room. But why would a Hollywood mogul have an interrogation room in the basement of his billion dollar estate? I knew the answer but didn't want to admit it. That's when I heard footsteps and saw Nash move into the edge of the light. He was now fully dressed in a dark suit with a white shirt and an untied gold bowtie hanging off his collar. He pulled out his phone and tapped it. The music stopped. Then Nash Gold talked.

"Paco worked for me for over a decade. I picked him specifically for his particular talents, for his cleverness, for his dedication and tenacity, and particularly for his effectiveness. The young man quickly earned the nickname 'The Mongoose' because he never missed dispatching a target, no matter how difficult." Gold then moved closer. "That is until you terminated him in a hotel room." Gold lightened up a bit and smiled as if admiring my handiwork. "Pretty clever."

"I've just got one question," I said, as I adjusted my arms and legs trying to get comfortable, while also moving my bound wrists closer to my pocket. "Why *El Dorado?* I mean, is it because your last name is 'Gold,' and El Dorado is the city of gold?" I shook my head, trying to goad the short, bald, billionaire. "Kind of cheesy, if you ask me."

Nash took it in stride. "No, no. Not at all. First of all, my real name is Lipshitz. Lenny Lipshitz. That name was the only thing my fucking drunk of a father ever gave me. My whore mother, she gave herself to everyone else, that is, when she wasn't fucking me too. And when I moved to Hollywood from the Lower East Side when I was 14, I changed my name to Gold. And it's been Gold ever since."

I was shocked. This guy was a potential thesis project for a psych student.

"Your parents just let you pick up and go to California at 14?"

"They didn't have a choice." Then he gave me a wicked smile that sent chills down my spine. "Before I jumped a greyhound to LA, I went into their bedroom and cut off their heads with a butcher knife. Best thing they ever did was watch their blood run away and soak their dirty sheets." He stared at me chillingly. "They couldn't scream of course, because I'd cut out their throats. Which is the only thing I regret. Would have loved to hear them scream."

Then he bent close, as if relating a secret, "But that's also when I found out how much I really loved knives."

Something about the offhand way he said that. Like a psychopath. I began to understand the myth of *El Dorado.* Hell, he *was* a real-life Keyser Soze.

One of the guards gave him a chair. Mr. Lipshitz sat right down in front of me. *"El Dorado."* He said wistfully as he clipped the end of another cigar and lit it. "The name had nothing to do with gold." He stared at the ceiling, thinking, recalling some fond old memory.

"No. It was a song. The Jim Croce song. Always liked that one. That *Leroy Brown.* Would have loved to call myself 'Leroy Brown.' But a Jew from Baruch and East Houston couldn't pull that off, no matter how much he was trying to reinvent himself. But I did consider it. I worked a bit for Meyer Lansky, and he definitely put a stop to me using any schvartze names. Didn't stop me from hiring a bunch of them, though...I love the schvartzes."

Then he started singing, *"He got a custom Continental and an El Dorado too..."*

His tone was way off. I broke in.

"So, you have a .32 in your pocket and a razor in your shoe?"

He puffed on his Cuban, then chuckled. He lifted his leg, kicked it on the side of the chair, and a 4 inch blade flicked out from the tip, like the KGB agents used to use, or that female Bond villain from that old Sean Connery flick.

Gold clicked it again and the blade slipped back inside. "I carry something a little bigger than a .32 in my pocket, however."

I nodded, having already seen too much of the guy's johnson.

Nash stood up, changing the subject. "So, now we have a conundrum." Nash walked around behind me. "What are we going to do with you, Mr. Baker?"

"How about letting me out of these zips?"

He walked over to a metal desk near the wall. It was shrouded in shadows. I heard him pull out a drawer.

"I apologize for the restraints, but you've proven yourself to be a capable man. Which I admire, by the way. And though Smoky Robinson and Jackie Robinson are also quite capable, I find you interestingly capricious and unpredictable, which dictates caution until I'm satisfied with your allegiance."

"You hired two black guys you call Smoky and Jackie... *Robinson?* Isn't that kinda racist?"

"I pay them handsomely. And if I want to call them *Robinson,* I will damn well do as I please. Ask them if they care."

I craned my head back, barely able to make the well-dressed muscle guys out in the shadows, standing on either side of the door, reeking of cologne. Far out of reach from me.

"You guys mind that your boss is racist?"

Nothing from them as they stared ahead like good, trained, attack dogs. But then I heard Nash moving towards me.

I turned back to see the short, stocky, bald man walking into the pool of light edging my chair. He was now carrying something big and shiny.

It was a blade. Not a sword like Ryo Grandé wielded, but almost. It was a very long custom knife, longer than a bowie for sure. And covered in pure 14 carat gold right down to the wickedly sharp edge. I shuddered when I realized I was staring at the infamous weapon of "*El Dorado."* The name was even inscribed on the gold metal. And it was well within striking range.

I quickly went over in my head all the moves available to me in this situation—and they were few. I could try to kick Nash back, but he'd just get back up and attack me. Plus the Robinson boys would be on me in seconds. I could get up and jump him, but the odds were too far against me with my feet and hands secured.

As I searched my troubled mind for another option, I suddenly heard a *swishhhh* CLANG! Mr. El Dorado had quickly arced his big blade right at me, slicing through the zips around my ankles like butter, missing my legs by millimeters, sparking and nearly embedding into the concrete below my toes. I immediately spread my feet, then looked up to see the gold blade now held inches from my face. Nash gave me a smirk then motioned to me with his finger.

"Lend me your assistance." He ordered.

I stood as he withdrew the blade to his side and nodded to one of the Robinsons.

Suddenly the lights all came on, nearly blinding me.

Then, as they adjusted, I saw a short, rotund man sitting at the back of the room, in an area that was previously completely dark. A muffled voice came from him. It didn't take me long to realize that it was Andy Candy sitting on that wooden slatted chair, bound to it by thick leather restraints on his wrists and ankles. He had a black burlap bag on his head, but I could hear faint muffles coming from his mouth. He must have been gagged too. He also had pissed his pants, with big black stains on the crotch and legs staining his black joggers. I could smell the urine, along with the stench of his body odor that wet his armpits and chest, which no doubt came from sitting for hours with intense fear and terror.

"What the hell is Andy doing here?" I asked.

Nash walked over and pulled the bag off Andy's head. His face was moist with sweat and tears. He had an eye mask and headphones strapped on, along with a gimp gag in his mouth. He couldn't see, hear, or talk.

"This man has been causing me trouble with his speculative journalism."

I shook my head. "Andy's an idiot. He doesn't need to be here. He should be ogling Larpers at comic-con."

As I stepped towards Andy, I quickly reached into my pocket and palmed the stolen pen, clicking the top, opening the tip.

Gold's face soured. "Maybe you don't read his man's little blog, but I do. And so do my friends. And that is beginning to cause the partners in my organization some concern."

Fortunately Gold seemed to be focused on Andy. And once I was certain no one had seen me palm the pen. I began to try to push the tip against the little plastic cog that held my zip tight. Nash moved around Andy, ending up behind him, holding the big blade over Andy's shoulder, seemingly ready to saw off Andy's head.

Nash's face turned serious as he continued. "Mr. Candy linked my name not only to Patterson Nobel, but he's exposed some of the operations of our worldwide syndicate, not to mention my association with the ruination of Jeffery and Sean."

My face dropped as I forgot about the zip tie. "Jeffery Epstein?"

"Jeff ran the East Coast operations. But he became sloppy. And like Patterson, Epstein had certain behavioral issues that had been causing us problems for years. While we control most of the media and the courts, people like your associate here started shining daylight on places that need to remain opaque.

I couldn't believe it. "*You* had Epstein killed?" I didn't need to ask, I could see it in Gold's eyes as he sucked on his cigar. "What about P. Diddy? You took him down too?"

Nash picked up his sword and did a practice swing above Andy's head. "Sean went freelance. He forgot who he was working for," he said, off-handedly.

"Who's that?"

"The same people we all work for, if you really think about it."

"The IRS?"

That got a chuckle out of Gold. He lifted up the big, redacted stack of paper he wanted me to sign. "No. The name on this contract. I call it 'Global, Inc.'"

"What the hell is Global Inc?" To me it sounded like a bad video game.

"WEF, WHO, World Bank. Bilderberg. The people in charge, in charge of government. Of all governments. You've probably heard of some of the names, others you've never heard of."

"You mean, like Bill Gates? Blackrock? The Rothchilds and Rockefellers? Like something from an Alex Jones rant?"

"Yes. Like an Alex Jones rant."

"How come you didn't kill Alex Jones?"

"We neutered him in court. Besides, he's amusing. We keep Jones around for shits and giggles."

"So...You want me to work for the... The World Economic Forum? Klaus Schwab? That fucking Nazi?"

Gold shrugged. "It's complicated. But very lucrative. And like I said. We all work for Global, Inc. anyway, one way or another. So why not make a profit? A hell of a profit."

Nash left his Cuban in his mouth as he hefted his gold blade and walked to a door with a combo lock on it. He punched a series of buttons and opened the door to a large deck made of thick glass, motioning me to tag along.

I followed him outside. The glass deck was sticking out some twenty feet into the smoggy air overlooking the San Fernando Valley, on the other side of the house, on the other side of the mountaintop. I could see tiny cars negotiating Mulholland Drive below me and the colored ants moving up and down the 405 and the 101 and the infinite dots of suburban ranch homes and palm trees that stretched out to the San Gabriel mountains. It felt like we were demigods, looking over all of SoCal. I guess that was the point. I could look down through the glass and see we were hundreds of feet in the air. It felt like I was standing on a cloud.

Gold seemed to marvel at the vista, at the majesty below us, while keeping a keen eye on me and a hand on his blade, just in case I might get the idea of tossing this bald fireplug of a Hollywood gangster over the railing.

And I have to admit I certainly ran over in my head the odds of me succeeding.

"This could all be yours, Haim." He said as he flicked ash hundreds of feet below.

"I'm guessing just having my detective cases turned into a TV show isn't quite going to punch that ticket."

"It's a start, but no. More of an enticement." Then he turned to me, studying my face, seeing if I were at all amenable, playable. Pliable. He saw my sweat, my quivering hands. He saw my weakness. Which is what I wanted him to see.

"We want you to be part of our organization."

"And all I have to do is sign away my life to a blank page." I said sarcastically. "I'm guessing this is a contract I don't walk away from."

"You won't want to. Imagine, Haim, all your debts erased. You can ditch your old car and have whatever automobiles you desire."

"I like my Saab."

"And you like your previous Carrera RS, a car recently repossessed from what I understand.

"Well, it was a nice car." I didn't tell him how much I loved that Porsche, but he could see it in my eyes. He nodded to me, expectantly.

"I surmised as much. And I'm happy to tell you that the car is yours again. It's waiting for you back in San Diego."

"Yeah? So is a murder rap."

Nash puffed away. "I can take care of that with one phone call. In fact you'll never face problems with the authorities again. You can do whatever you wish with impunity."

"Is that what you told Puff Daddy?"

Nash took a breath and sighed. Then he smiled again.

"You know, Haim, we've been keeping an eye on you a long time."

"The hell does that mean?"

"You fit our profile. Capable. Impulsive. You think it was dumb luck that Mrs. Nobel found you and set you upon her husband?"

I stared at Gold's eyes. He was serious.

"But... My client, Constantillo, he told her."

"Constantillo worked for me. I guided him to you. He guided you to Nobel. Now you're here."

"And the little fact that he was tossed over a cliff onto the rocks in Encinitas, that was just a little collateral damage, right?"

"Constantillo had become a bit too... religious for his own good. "

"I guess injecting God into a human trafficking ring makes things a bit sticky."

"Unfortunately you can't serve two masters." Then Gold looked up at the scattered clouds above.

"Do you believe in God, Haim?"

I took his question and thought about it. Did I? No. I didn't believe. Didn't I? I thought about it some more. Thought about all the people I've lost. The pain. The tears.

"No." I said. A little unsure. Gold nodded with approval.

I then turned away from him as I remembered how I felt when I was with Jessie. That picture of Jesus on the wall. Like maybe he approved of us. I thought about how much I loved her. Besides, wasn't Love supposed to be God or something like that? I knew there was evil in the world. But didn't that mean there was also good too?

Oh hell, I didn't know what the fuck I thought. But Nash seemed to be placated and I wasn't quite ready to decide or admit that I was becoming one of those crazy believer nut jobs.

"No. There's no God." I said, mostly to reassure the Lord of the Manor. Gold seemed to smile at my answer, then he turned to me and began to look serious.

"I need a replacement for Paco. And then, perhaps someone to run operations. At the moment we have an opening in Malibu. Perhaps San Diego."

Yeah. I could be the one profiting from all the little girls kidnapped off the street or purchased like cattle from their poor parents, plied with drugs, repeatedly raped and then forced for years to perform sex acts dozens of times a day. And when they're all used up, their bodies are cut open and their organs are sold for more profit. Yeah. I didn't have to think very hard about that one.

"Not bloody likely."

"But Haim, I can give you everything you want."

"You don't know what I want."

"Of course I do."

With that Nash Gold tossed his cigar off the balcony.

"Come, I have one more thing to show you." He walked back into the room, with me following curiously.

Nash moved past Andy as if the poor fat guy didn't even exist, opened another door, and strode into the darkness. I saw the fake Robinson twins still standing guard behind on the main door. No other way out I figured.

I followed El Dorado into the darkness, then I heard him stop near the center of the room.

"This is my gift to you."

Suddenly the overhead lights blinked on, throwing a center spot onto another man bound to another wooden slatted chair with leather restraints. He too had a black burlap bag on his head. Before Gold removed it, my heart had already started to pound with anticipation and my fists clenched in fury. I could see the large silver belt buckle over the expensive denim and dark red custom cowboy boots.

Gold pulled the bag to reveal a battered and bruised and unconscious Patterson Nobel, looking utterly defeated. His long grey hair matted and stringing over his broken nose and swollen eyes like he'd just reenacted the passion of Christ. For a moment, I actually felt sorry for the guy, even though I knew he was a monster.

Nash stood behind Nobel, like the old man was his personal trophy. Then he looked at me.

"I'm surprised you haven't broken free of your restraints by now, with that little pen in your pocket. I'm almost disappointed in you, Haim."

I'd forgotten about the pen, and immediately clicked open the zip. It fell off as I held the pen ready, like a weapon. I'd seen *John Wick*. But so had Gold, evidently, as he held his blade at the ready while he walked around me, out of fighting distance, and stood in the doorway.

"Can I have a blade like yours?" I asked.

Gold smiled again.

"I like you, Haim. You remind me of me. Fucked-up parents. Fucked-up life. Taking life into your hands. And removing it from others."

"I'm not like you." I uttered.

"But Haim, the way you sliced and diced Eddie Schwarma was magnificent. I couldn't have done a better job myself."

He started to go.

"How am I supposed to kill Nobel?"

Gold looked at me before he closed the door. "Be creative." He said. "You have a pen."

Then the door shut, leaving me in a small room with the person I detested more than any other.

CHAPTER THIRTY-FIVE

I stood and stared at the man I'd vowed to kill. The man who'd gruesomely murdered my best friend, who'd shot his beautiful wife to death. The man who'd kidnapped little girls and teens and shipped them to a warehouse and made them addicts and sex slaves.

And here he was, a captive. A prisoner. A dead man barely alive. And I finally had my chance to end his horrid presence. And I wanted to. Wanted to more than anything. Gold was right. I wanted Nobel's death.

I grabbed his head, ready to snap his neck. But then I realized I couldn't kill him without looking into his evil eyes. I needed him to be alive before I snuffed out his life. I needed him. I needed to destroy him. I had to avenge Maria. Avenge Mrs. Nobel. I needed to murder this monster who fucked up my life. Who shoved a 500 magnum revolver up my poor ass.

I thought again about taking his drooping head in my hands and twisting it quick until his neck snapped.

But I couldn't. Not yet.

SMACK!

I bitch-slapped Nobel's swollen visage, his hair flying with a spray of sweat and blood. His head lolled back and forth like some sort of '80s metal guitar maniac.

When his head finally settled, his unswollen eye began to open and I saw his red bloodshot eye and blue pupil glance up at me. He stretched a small grin with his swollen lips, lifting up his swollen cheek. Then he squeezed out words with a raspy voice:

"Baker..." He coughed. "You finish the job?"

"Oh, I plan on it."

He nodded as much as he was able with his hanging head. I could see a sense of relief in his good eye.

"I know you will." Then he used his strength to lift up his face again, looking at me in the eye with what could only be true remorse.

"Baker... listen. I'm sorry."

I couldn't hear it. I refused to hear it. He was a killer, a monster, he could't be allowed redemption.

"NO." Was all I could say.

"Please forgive me. For everything."

"What am I? Your fucking priest?"

Then he closed his good eye.

"Make it quick." He asked. "Please."

Then he hung his head and waited for his inevitable end.

"No, no, no, no!" I slapped him again—SMACK!

Nobel coughed. I could see blood in his spittle. He knew he wasn't walking out of here alive. And he was at peace with it. Expecting his executioner. Calmly waiting for the end.

Waiting for me.

But I stepped back. This was wrong. This was not the way it was supposed to happen. Not the way I imagined this moment. This was not very satisfying at all.

I was supposed to kill Patterson Nobel in mutual combat. I was supposed to prove that his sins were worse than mine and that good triumphs over evil. That I was better. He was evil and I was not. I was the better person. I was supposed to kill this man because of what he'd done to the world, and I was going to kill him because I'd promised myself that I would.

But I was going to kill Patterson Nobel for me. Not for Nash Gold.

I didn't know if Gold was watching me with his cameras or not, but then a song came on through the loudspeakers. Bobby Darin again: *Mack the Knife.* Maybe that was El Dorado's way to tell me to get on with it.

I pulled out the pen and imagined stabbing Nobel through the temple. Or thrusting it in his good eye and into his brain.

But then I felt what could only be nausea. It had to be the heroin withdrawal.

But maybe it was my conscience.

How the hell could that be?
I stood and stared at Nobel and suddenly an idea came to me.
Now I knew what I had to do...

CHAPTER THIRTY-SIX

I opened the door and yelled out into the room, where *Mack the Knife* was also playing on the speaker and Gold was waiting patiently, making notes on my contract at his desk while the Robinson twins continued to guard the outer door.

"Can someone please get rid of this goddamned body? I can't stand the sight of that rat bastard."

Gold stood, peered into the room and clapped, "Beautiful, Haim." Then he nodded to Jackie Robinson, who immediately strode across the concrete and into my room, where Patterson Nobel lay in a heap on the floor.

As Jackie picked up Nobel's limp body and slung it over his shoulder and headed for the exit, Gold held out the contract and pulled out another pen, expecting me to sign it. I nodded that I would. Later.

"How did you do it? Gold wondered.

"Broke the fucker's neck." I said, as I walked out into the room, behind Jackie, as Andy continued to whimper underneath his head bag on the chair in the back. It looked like he'd peed himself again, as urine was dripping from his pant legs.

"Can we get out of this room before I sign? It stinks." I said as I moved to the door and towards Smokey. "I'll take care of Andy later. That fucker's getting on my nerves." I promised.

"Excellent." Gold said as he gathered up the contact and the pen.

As soon as I got within arm's reach of huge Mr. Robinson, I said, loudly. "Let's go!"

Suddenly Patterson moved, pulling his arm back, revealing my pen palmed in his hand, and as swiftly and strongly as he could, he stabbed Jackie in the front of his neck, aiming for the jugular.

At the same time, while Smokey was momentarily distracted by Patterson's attack, I charged the big guy. I had grabbed the heroin syringe out of my pocket, pulling out the handle, filling the reservoir with air. I quickly stabbed Smokey in the thigh before his meaty palm smacked me silly. I flew to the ground, whacking my head on the concrete, temporarily rattling me dizzy. I didn't know if I had managed to plunge air into Smokey's vein or not. I'd know in less than a minute. Either the air bubble would hit his heart, blocking the blood flow, shutting it and him down, or he'd be on me like a junkyard dog.

I saw blood spouting out of Jackie's neck as he threw Patterson against the wall with a hard THUD

Trying to stanch the flow of copious blood pumping life out of his body, Jackie put his right hand to his neck, staggering to his feet, pulling his Uzi with his left hand.

I forced myself up, moving as close as possible to Smokey, getting in under his reach, giving me a bit more equal ground. With his long arms and legs, staying away from him would only be a death sentence.

I saw the needle sticking out from his thigh and strangely, it didn't look like he even knew it was there. The needle was sharp and he was thick and tough—probably didn't feel a thing. Only problem was the plunger was still up. I'd failed. And worse, Smokey followed my gaze to his thigh. Now he knew. Shit.

He reached down to pull it out, his eyes wide with fear. He knew what I was trying to do. He was attempting to pull it out as I reached down to plunge in the oxygen. Our right hands met before they got to the needle, gripping one another. Then I went for it with my other hand and so did he. They too met as we grabbed each other with both hands now. It was like a wrestling match as we struggled to the death—but this guy had 100 pounds on me with much more muscle—it didn't look good for yours truly.

Out of the corner of my eye, I saw Patterson struggling to stand, and then heard the RAT TAT TAT TAT TAT TAT TAT TAT TAT of Jackie's 9mm automatic pistol quickly and haphazardly rattling off what sounded like a few dozen rounds, spraying the wall with his shaky left hand. Chunks of tile and plaster flew out as a multitude of rounds went wild, creating a saw-like, staccato pattern on the plaster. Unfortunately for Patterson, several bullets hit home and plugged him in the stomach, as blood continued to shower from Big Robinson's neck, until Jackie finally stammered, falling down to his knees as blood and life left him in a stream of crimson, puddling onto the concrete.

I then realized two things:

One: *Mack the Knife* was annoyingly on a loop, continuing to play over and over, with Bobby Darin's smooth, sardonic voice and ironically violent lyrics endlessly sounding over the bloody violence unfolding before me.

Two: Out of my periphery I saw Nash Gold approaching from behind, his big blade held up, ready to slice me in two, a crazed look in his eyes and an even more crazed smile plastered on his face. In fact, as Smokey squeezed my hands until I couldn't feel them anymore, I heard Mr. El Dorado singing loudly and out of tune, along with the musical beat: *"...Just a jack-knife... You know when that shark bite, with it's teeth babe, scarlet billows, start to spread!"*

As Gold came upon me I knew there was no way I could hold Smokey off much longer. He was overwhelming me with his strength. I had one play and the timing had to be perfect.

I waited until I heard Gold get within striking range. Thankfully I could judge it from his loud, obnoxious singing: *"Now on the sidewalk, Ohhh Sunny morning ah-ha, Lies a body, just a' oozing life!"*

SCHWWWWINNNNNG!

I guessed he was going to wait until he finished the phrase and luckily I was right. I quickly went from pushing Smokey's left hand, to pulling it to me, using his strength to spin him 180 as I dropped and kicked out his leg. He immediately swung around just as the gold *El Dorado* blade struck— slicing deep into and through Smokey Robinson's shoulder-

AAAAAARRRRGHHH! Smokey screamed and fell, as the big Mac Daddy Knife had completely sawed off Robinson's huge arm and shoulder, with blood spouting out from a severed artery, like that Monty Python movie; as he was bleeding out, Smokey's blood was spraying Gold's face, who seemed to relish the mayhem. Gold didn't miss a beat, still singing:

"And someone's sneaking around the corner. Could that someone, be MACK THE KNIFE?!" He bellowed off-key.

El Dorado Gold rose up again like a madman, like he was having the time of his life, red dots splattered on his face, his hand gripping his gold blade coated in crimson, readying for another swing. A swing at me.

What could I do now?

It was then I realized I was still gripping Smokey's severed left arm and shoulder, which was dangling from my hand like a club. And as Mack the Knife swung again...

"And five'll get you ten..."

THUD! I swung up Smokey's arm in defense.

The knife sliced off Smokey's forearm, knocking the whole thing out of my hands. His severed hand went flying across the room.

I stood there, dumfounded, staring down at half an arm lying on the ground as Gold, with a Cheshire Cat smile of madness, stopped momentarily so he could finish the line as he yelled:

"'Ol Mackey's BACK IN TOWN!"

I bent over and picked up the arm club, sans hand, making sure the heavier shoulder was the business end, with blood leaking out from the emptying artery, drip drip drip.

This was the weirdest fight I'd ever been in. However, I didn't have time to think about that as El Dorado came at me again. But now it was my turn. Before he could bring down the knife...

SMACK!

I hit Gold straight in the face with the shoulder-club, stunning him.

And it was also my turn to sing along with Bobby Darin, which I found oddly satisfying:

"Macky'ssss back in town!" I yelled.

Gold quickly shook off my attack and charged me in anger, catching me off-guard. He was furious. Like this was <u>his</u> song and I was ruining <u>his</u> moment.

I stumbled back to avoid him and stepped into the pool of crimson bled out by Jackie, who was now hunched over, dead. I slipped and fell back as the madman swung.

SSSSSCHHHHWINGGGG!

I barely had time to shield myself with my Smokey Shoulderclub, rolling out of the way at the same time, as the blade crunched right through Smokey's former muscle and bones, slicing them in half and out of my hand, just missing my nose by a centimeter, as *"El Dorado"* cut into the concrete, nearly blinding me by spitting up chunks of concrete, dust, and pooled blood. I spun around on my back as I wiped my eyes and quickly kicked Gold hard, knocking him down, and better yet, knocking the knife away, clanging across the room, out of reach.

I saw Jackie's Uzi and dived for it, stumbling in the blood on the floor, coating my poor black Hugo Boss jacket in mottled red stains and losing my porkpie, which finally fell off my head, sinking into the puddle of crimson.

I could hear Gold scrambling to his feet as I grabbed the blood-soaked Uzi. And lying on the ground, I pointed the gun between my legs up at Gold, who was now staring down at me, his smile fading as he saw I had the upper hand.

I felt I needed to say something quippy, as this was the perfect moment. I had him. The legendary *El Dorado* was too stunned to move. But Bobby Darin's song was just starting over again with the drums and bass, so I couldn't sing along, and I didn't have time to wait for the right lyrics for the right moment. The only non-lyric words I could think of were from Ryo Grandé of all people.

They would have to do in a pinch.

"Good-night." I said.

I put my finger on the trigger as Gold's eyes registered fear—real fear coming from the legendary, infamous *El Dorado.*

"Take this mutherfucker!" I yelled.

I pulled the trigger.

CLICK.

Out of ammo. Fuck.

Jackie had shot all 20 rounds. Why couldn't he have used a 30 round mag?

I didn't have time to ponder whatmighthavebeens, as Gold started to smile at me again, looking down like a psycho.

"It's still daytime, Haim." Gold said, as he pulled out his phone. He clicked on it with his finger.

Shit, I assumed he was calling in reinforcements.

But no.

It was worse than that.

He had clicked off *Mack the Knife.*

And he'd replaced it with yet another song!

This guy was a maniac.

And as I carefully stood, ready to go mano-a-mano, the guy fucking started singing along.

Oh God. Not again.

I pleaded with him: "No! No, don't do it, Nash. Please don't...sing."

I'd heard the familiar piano keys pounding through the speakers and knew the song Gold was going to badly harmonize before he opened his mouth.

"Well, the south side of Chicago, is baddest part of town. And if you go down there you better just beware of a man named Leroy Brown!"

This psychopath was crooning louder than ever. And flatter than ever too. My ears were in pain from his voice.

"Please stop!" I yelled.

Gold kept singing, just to spite me, I think.

"He's bad, bad Leroy brown, the baddest man in the whole damn town..."

My turn to lose bravado, as Gold pulled out a .38 stubnose from his pocket, duetting with Jim Croce:

"He got a custom Continental. He got an El Dorado Too. He got a .32 gun in his pocket for fun..."

BLAM BLAM BLAM!

I dove behind the hunched-over body of Jackie, who absorbed two of the .38 rounds slotted for me.

"Gonna sign that contract, Haim!?" Gold screamed as he FIRED again, the bullet whizzing past my ear.

I looked for Smokey's body and his untouched Uzi, but Gold was standing in front of him. No chance.

The only play I had was to run out the door, but El Dorado was also in front of the exit.

Then I felt a cool breeze and looked to my right—the balcony door was still open! I had one chance...

I sprinted with all my might.

BLAM!

The force of the bullet knocked me down as I tried to dash out the exit, with the .38 round throwing me into the glass railing.

Shit, that fucker had good aim.

Adrenaline was coursing through my body, allowing me to temporarily ignore the burning pain in my left shoulder. The round had luckily gone right through, putting a hole in me and into the clear glass railing panel next to me, splintering it. But it also rendered my left arm useless.

I heard a CRACKLE. The glass was starting to spiderweb.

And then I heard Gold. He was cackling with deranged excitement.

I barely had time to turn around to see him sauntering towards me, giving himself time to finish the lyrics.

"He's bad, bad Leroy Brown, the baddest man in the whole damn town. Badder than old King Kong. Meaner than a junkyard dog."

He smiled, then fired again.

Oh shit.

CLICK.

Thank God those little revolvers only hold five rounds.

But before I could thank my lucky stars Gold had blown through all the bullets, he'd tossed the gun and clicked his right shoe sideways on the floor of the glass balcony, spitting out the 4-inch shoe-blade.

Shit. Here we go...

Usually in a knife fight you'd better have a knife yourself or at least some sort of defense. A chair or small table would do, but there was no patio furniture out here. The only thing I had was my jacket, which I quickly stripped off and rolled around my right hand and arm—the only arm that worked. It would give me several inches of protection and maybe blunt the blade. However, with my right being my only good arm, I had to play defense only. But that was better than getting stabbed.

I knew that Nash was built more like a linebacker than, say, a ballerina like Gato, or yoga star like Clara, so I doubted he could kick higher than my ribcage. But he had powerful thighs, and I was certain he'd strike me hard in the leg or stomach, which would end my day and probably my life, so I kept my jacket guard low as he slowly approached.

"We can start over, Haim. There's still time. Time to begin a new life. Time before your old life ends. Time before I kill you."

He suddenly swung his leg at me. He was quicker than I anticipated. I barely had time to parry it with my jacket-arm. The force of his kick knocked me back a bit and no doubt put a wicked bruise on my forearm. But I didn't feel a cut, thank goodness.

"You can take over Patterson's San Diego operation. You'll be a billionaire, Haim."

He suddenly kicked again. This time I jumped back on his move. He barely missed me.

"Imagine the money. The power."

He moved towards me again. I backed up.

"Don't think I'm cut out for it, Lenny." I slowly edged to my right.

"That's where you're wrong, Haim. You're perfect."

He swung his leg and scored a direct hit on my hand, which stopped him from embedding steel into my thigh, the pointed blade cutting my right palm before I yanked it away. "Ouch!" I could feel the blood soaking into my jacket from my new stigmata. Nash could smell blood. He could smell victory.

"What you don't understand, Haim. Is that you're just like me. I know how much you've suffered. How you lost your son, how you lost yourself. Come to your calling. You'll never suffer again."

I stepped to my side, situating my body in front of the splintered balcony railing.

"You see, Lenny, there's this little problem I have. Thanks to you, the woman I love is dead. And someone's gotta pay."

Nash lifted up his leg for a strike. There was nowhere for me to go as I backed up hard against the railing. I could feel it start to buckle and groan as Nash readied his death blow.

"Who needs love? When you've got power?... Whaddya say?"

"All I can say is that I'm not a Jim Croce fan."

I transferred all my weight to my right foot as he suddenly sprung a devastating fast and furious front kick, striking out his footblade like a cobra.

Thankfully I was ready for him and dove as fast as I could, the blade slicing part of my jeans and nicking my thigh as I jumped out of the way.

CRASH!

His blade embedded into the glass railing wall, just below the bullet hole. He tried to pull it free but he was stuck. Worse, the glass began to crack and the balcony began to shake, as the glass spiderweb now splintered and spread all over the sides and floor. The entire thing was ready to collapse.

I stood up and circled around, trading places with Nash. He couldn't move, so he craned his neck back to me, glanced at the breaking glass all around, and saw that his situation was splintering too. He tried to make the best of it.

"Everyone likes Jim Croce. Tell me you don't like *Cats in the Cradle?*"

"You got me there." I agreed.

"You see, I know who you are."

"Yeah, I'm Haim Baker." I said with bravado. "A fucked-up, half-Jew drug addict who also happens to be a mediocre private detective."

I stepped closer to him. "But I'm also the guy who's gonna put an end to *El Dorado.*"

"HA!" Gold yelled in disbelief.

"And you know what else?" I said.

"Better tell me before I slice you like a beef brisket." He made another attempt to yank out his shoe-knife from the thick glass.

"I think you're more Leroy Brown than *El Dorado.*"

"What do you mean?" That caught him off-guard.

I listened and waited for the right moment, as the song continued on the speaker.

"Now it's MY turn to sing."

"What?" Nash Gold lost his smile. Like he was the only one who got to croon along with the violence. "No..."

"Yes."

I began to sing, "*You're about to 'look like a jigsaw puzzle with a couple of pieces gone.'*"

"NO!" His eyes widened as he desperately tried to get his foot free.

I pulled up my right leg, cocking it back for a strike. "This is for Jessie..." I said, as I shove-kicked him with all my might.

CRRRRRAAAAAAACKKKK!

The railing shattered and gave way when I kicked him hard into it. He flailed at the edge and managed to grab onto the floor as he tumbled back into the air and the glass behind him fell away and the the structure began to sway without the railing to support it; the entire structure beginning to splinter.

Gold was now precariously hanging onto his life by his hands, fear riding his face.

As I watched Gold helplessly dangling, it occurred to me that this little stocky Jewish man, who'd made some of my favorite movies, and was responsible for many of the best films in modern history, was also responsible for running several of the worst, most powerful cartels in the world. I thought of all the girls kidnapped in the middle of the night or off the street in some small village and forced to do terrible things and all the drugs he'd put into the world that infect millions of people, people like me.

But, as much as I hated this evil person, all I saw in front of me now was a victim. A man fighting for his life. A man afraid. A man helpless.

And then I decided in my mind to strip away all the labels and evil deeds attributed to *El Dorado*. Instead, I simply saw a human being whose life was literally hanging by his bleeding, failing fingers.

And then I began to see Nash Gold in a new light. Not the dangerous killer known as *El Dorado*. I instead saw little Lenny Lipshitz. Raised by fucked-up, abusive parents. Turned into the monster he infamously became.

I stepped up to him, thinking I should kick his hands away and send him to his death.

He looked up, expecting me to finish him off. Almost hoping I would do the task. The task he wanted me to do.

"Just remember..." He said, swinging precariously over the canyon below, blood from his cut up hands and fingers rolling down his arms, dripping onto his face and eyes as he held onto the broken glass balcony and tried to blink away the crimson.

He looked up at me with a sort of pride, pride that I was his executioner. As if he was happy with himself for choosing me to be here. Perhaps he even expected it. Expected me to kill him.

He smiled, like a father would to a son, as he nodded.

"You're me. You're *El Dorado...*"

"Like hell." I stepped near his fingers, remembering the scene from one of Nash's early films, where the bad guy steps on Cary Grant's fingers as he hung from a cliff. But I didn't want to be the bad guy. Did I? Then I also remembered another famous Nash Gold movie, where a dying android grabs onto the hand of the dangling man who'd been sent to kill him, saving his assassin's life before his own life ebbs away.

No. I decided I didn't want to be *El Dorado*. I wanted to be *Haim Baker.*

I bent down to save him. "Grab my hand."

Nash saw the sudden compassion in my eyes and shook his head with disappointment.

And then with a deflated look, the infamous crime lord suddenly let go of the balcony, falling three hundred feet to his death.

THUMP.

I didn't have time to watch the show as the balcony began to give way. I scrambled towards the door as the glass structure twisted and broke, falling away below me. I barely managed to leap inside the room before the entire glass floor dropped down the cliff, no doubt crushing and encasing Lenny Lipshitz's flattened, broken body in thick, clear glass splinters.

CHAPTER THIRTY-SEVEN

Thankfully when El Dorado crashed below, so did his phone, killing the damn music along with him.

I unwrapped my hand, seeing a ½ inch cut in the center of my palm. I was lucky it wasn't bleeding too much. But I was going to need medical assistance. My left shoulder was starting to really hurt and I was dizzy and shaking and sweating from the melee and from opiate withdrawal. I tried to put my jacket back on, getting my right arm through, but the pain was too much for the left, so I let my arm dangle under the Hugo Boss.

I looked around and knew I'd better figure out how to get out of here soon, but oddly, the only thing that came to my attention was Patterson Nobel.

I saw him lying on the floor against the wall, blood seeping out of his wounds. I kneeled down. He was still breathing. Barely.

He must have sensed my presence as he opened his good eye. He was struggling to breathe, but he managed to push out a few words.

"Baker." He coughed. Blood leaked out of his mouth.

"Yeah?"

"You finish the job?"

I nodded. "Yeah."

He relaxed, exhaled, smiled. "I knew you would."

Then he narrowed his eye and coughed up blood again.

"Baker…"

"Yeah?"

"They'll be coming. You've got to run."

"I know."

Then he shook his head, ominously, "No, you don't. Get out of California. They'll come for you…Hide…hide…"

Then he closed his eye and let out his last breath.

I looked at the broken, dead man in front of me. The man that had started my entire journey into this miasma of darkness and death. The man who for some reason helped save me in the last minutes of his life. I wanted to kick him. And I wanted to hug him. So I just left him there.

I realized that I'd totally forgotten about Andy. I got myself to my feet, picked up the El Dorado blade and cut him free.

As soon as I pulled off his headphones and eye mask, Andy used his unbound hands to pull out the ball in his mouth.

"What the fuck!" He stood up. "Where am I?"

Then he suddenly noticed all the carnage and blood. "What the hell happened, Baker?" Then he saw my shoulder and hand. "You've been shot. What did you do?"

"I killed El Dorado." I showed him the engraved gold blade.

"You did? Wow. Scattina?

I shook my head.

It was Nash Gold, right? He was El Dorado?"

I nodded.

"I knew it!" Andy exclaimed. Then he saw Patterson's body.

"You killed Patterson Nobel too?"

"It's a long story."

Andy stood up and smiled. "You are a badass!"

"Both our asses are going to be dead if we don't get out of here."

I grabbed Smokey's Uzi, checked the chamber, making sure it was loaded. I stuffed it in my pants. I decided, for some reason, to take the El Dorado knife with me too. I ran out the door, holding the gold knife in my good hand. I looked back.

Andy was still in the room.

"Hey!"

The fat man was bent over, stretching, trying to touch his toes.

"Come on!" I yelled.

"I'm a little stiff from sitting in that chair, Baker, Jeez."

Finally after a few side bends and twists, he stumbled, then trotted after me, his big stomach bouncing above his legs.

"Do we have to run?" He coughed, already out of breath as we approached the spiral staircase.

"Just do your best." I shook my head. I wondered how the bloated blogger was even going to make it up the stairs.

I was expecting an alarm to start ringing, alerting all the pseudo-soldier-butler-guards to come down on us like a hard rain. But as we trundled up the spiral, I felt lucky, as all I heard was Andy's huffing and puffing interspersed with his constant complaining. No alarm. Yet.

By the time we made it to the ornate door that led to the golden living room, Andy was sweating and gulping air—more than usual.

"You okay?"

He bent over, trying to catch his breath. Finally he nodded. I pulled out the Uzi and handed it to him.

"Know how to use one of these?"

Andy shook his head and held the gun like it was a Star Trek phaser or something. He didn't have a clue.

"Here's the safety. Click it off, then point and pull the trigger."

Before the little walrus could hand it back, I opened the door and walked into the large room.

In the middle the the gold space, Clara was doing some sort of yoga thing on a gold mat. Maybe downward dog. Through her legs she saw me emerge into the room, with Andy stumbling in behind me.

She did a quick, effortless roll forward and before I knew it she was standing, sweaty and hot. Boy was she hot. Her smile faded quick when she saw Andy holding the Uzi, and me the gold blade. And all the blood.

"Where's Nash?" She commanded.

"You won't be giving him anymore blowjobs."

I could see the anger brewing inside her. Suddenly she did a cartwheel, and kicked me hard in the stomach before I had a chance to react. I fell down backwards. Dropping the knife. She picked it up. I struggled to get up with only one working arm as she approached with malice. I tried to scoot back.

"I'm going to gut you like *El Dorado* should have." She spat. I could see the fury burning in her demon-dark eyes.

I squirmed and pushed myself back some more, scooting away on the floor as she swung, barely missing my leg. She came at me again. I couldn't get away fast enough.

This wasn't going to end well...

Until I heard RATATATATATATATATATATATTATAT!

Clara stopped swinging the blade in mid-air and fell lifeless, nearly cut in two by a chainsaw of 9mm bullets slicing across her chest, fired from Andy's Uzi.

Problem was, Andy had a loose grip and was shooting wild and wouldn't or couldn't stop, spitting bullets all over the living room—smashing windows, including the large glass over the pool, which crashed into the water. There were bullet holes peppering all over the walls and even several light fixtures dropped down into the smoke and mayhem. Chairs, tables, plaster, wood. The expensive bottles of brandy on the bar shattered and leaked aged amber. Andy sprayed everything. He missed me by inches as I turned and flattened myself to the floor, hearing lead whizzing overhead.

Finally fatman ran out of bullets. I risked a peek, seeing his wide eyes through the barrage of gunsmoke, looking totally bewildered, leaning backwards from the recoil. His face in shock. He kept pulling the trigger, bending back, nearly falling on his ass until: CLICK CLICK CLICK. His mag was finally empty.

"Andy! You can stop now!" I yelled.

That seemed to pull him out of his trance. He looked at the gun as if it were alive, quickly dropping it and backing away like he'd been petting a snake.

"W, what did I do?" He stammered.

"You saved my ass." I said as I got back on my feet. I bent down and picked up the El Dorado blade from the floor next to what was left of Clara. Her ribs and lungs and heart were ripped open and bleeding into a pool of crimson. Her large black eyes were dead and looking into the netherworld.

Andy gazed over at her body.

"I... I did THAT?"

"Thanks, man. You're pretty badass yourself."

He couldn't take his eyes off the carnage. I think I heard him piss his pants again. Or maybe it was a fart. But I grabbed him by the shoulder, turned him around and steered him up the large staircase, holding my nose.

When I opened the door to Haskell's office, I was immediately greeted by the tall dapper man casually pointing my H&K Mk23 right at my heart. I could see he had security monitors behind his desk—showing little video pictures of the melée—the dead Robinsons, dead Patterson, the missing balcony, cut-down-Clara. He knew exactly what had gone down. He'd watched the whole show. And he had me dead.

But he didn't pull the trigger. Instead, he slid a copy of the damn contract towards me. Again. Then a pen. Again.

"You will provide your signature. We've put too much into this project for you to fuck it up."

I didn't have a choice. I sighed. Then I signed.

"And give me back my pen, please."

I did.

He smiled and lowered the gun.

I looked at him incredulously. "You aren't gonna shoot me?"

"Why no, Mr. Baker. You've just singed the contract." He said matter-of-factly as he checked the signature. "That was the whole reason for you being here."

Satisfied with my John Hancock, he diligently pulled out a drawer and placed the papers safely in his desk.

"Besides, I told you. You wouldn't be here if I wanted you dead."

He then opened a ledger, pulled out a check, and slid it to me. It was made out for $150,000. He turned to Andy, still stunned by his accidental gunplay. "And you sir, you'll find your check in the mail. To be frank, I'm a bit unprepared to remit your funds. Frankly, I wasn't quite expecting you to walk out of here today."

I could hear Andy gulp, as he began to realize the gravity of our situation. Haskell saw my own confused face as he sat down in his chair, leaning back with a Cheshire grin, his feet on his desk.

"I'm the CFO of Gold Studios and Gold Enterprises, both subsidiaries of Global, Inc. And according to my contract, in the event that Mr. Gold is incapacitated and unable to carry out his duties and responsibilities, I then become acting CEO."

He righted himself and poured a glass of Sauternes, sipped it, smiled and put his feet back up on his desk. "You see, Mr. Baker, you've just increased my net worth by a very substantial amount."

"You guys are worse than the Sith," I said under my breath.

Haskell already had one of his cigars in his mouth and was lighting it. "I'd ask you to share a Cuban and some delicious liquor to celebrate my good fortune, but unfortunately, it'd be far more prudent for both of you to leave the premises. You see, in my new duties as CEO, I'm required to call security and tell them the unfortunate news about their former employer. They'll be quite upset, I suspect."

I pulled Andy across the room, heading for the exit.

"Wait," Haskell said. "You might need this."

He stood up, walked over, and handed me my gun.

"Gee, thanks." I said as I swung open the door, peeking each way to make sure no butlers were lurking in the hallway.

"Have fun on your way out." Haskell said, ominously. Then he shut the door on us.

CHAPTER THIRTY-EIGHT

I pulled Andy down the hallway with my right hand, which also held my gun. I found my left hand could grasp the big blade, but couldn't wield it without massive pain. Hell, I'd fought hard for that knife and I wasn't about to let that trophy go. The thought of the gold prize hung up on my wall gave me a bit of cheer, enough to overcome the pain of holding onto it.

Andy, on the other hand, was not happy. In fact I could tell his anxiety was reaching new heights. I think I heard him start to cry or whimper, but I wouldn't allow myself look back at him. I needed the little egghead to help us get out of here and didn't want to deal with having to console him. Besides, I didn't have the time. Especially when I saw a Black Butler open a side door and stare at us in shock. He saw my HK pointing at him and reached for a gun in his belt. As he pulled out a Glock I shot him twice. He crumpled into a heap of dead. I quickly gave the Glock to Andy, who held it in his limp hand. He looked at me again with that bewildered face.

"Same drill. Only this one doesn't have a safety. Just point and pull the trigger."

Suddenly his eyes went wide. He then began shooting behind me BLAM BLAM BLAM BLAM.

I spun around and saw that he'd plugged another Butler. Most of the lead had gone wild, but at least one round had found a home, center mass. The dude was dead, bleeding out from a hole in his heart.

I nodded to him. "Yeah, like that."

I stepped over both bodies, and headed towards the double-door at the end. I looked back. Andy was still standing, unmoving, staring at his Glock and the dead men.

"Come on!"

That jolted Andy enough to run towards me.

That's when the alarm started blaring.

"That's not good!" I yelled over the BEEP BEEP BEEP.

I heard footsteps and realized I only had five rounds left in my mag. I found the nearest door and opened it. It led to a bedroom suite that had its own kitchen, deck and shower. I pulled Andy inside and locked the door as a jumble of footsteps pounded past outside in the hallway.

"What are we gonna do?" Andy said, his voice filled with anxiety. I saw he was unwittingly pointing his Glock at me. I pushed it aside.

"Only point that at the bad guys."

Then I noticed the kitchenette. Better yet, the emergency sprinklers above. Andy, on the other hand, had found a bowl of fruit and was peeling a banana. He noticed my incredulous face as he took a huge bite.

"I'm a stress eater." He said with his mouth full.

"Never woulda guessed," I said as I jumped onto the counter, flicked my lighter, and waved it under the sprinklers. Suddenly three of them began spraying us with water as another alarm began HONKING. Adding confusion to the mayhem.

Then I turned on the gas to the burners but didn't light them. I wadded up some aluminum foil and put it in the small microwave. I set it for 10 minutes and hit the start button.

Andy's eyes went wide. "Hey! That's gonna..." I pulled him to the door, opened it, and we ran out into the chaos.

Several doors were opened and black dudes in suits were everywhere, frantically heading towards the main exit as water sprayed down on everything. We were soaked as we joined the fracas, hoping the dudes wouldn't notice us in their haste, and wouldn't care that we didn't quite fit the description of hired help or honored guests of the establishment.

We were able to make it to the small living room and to the open main door, when someone yelled "Stop!"

That got the attention of three dudes in front of us, and suddenly we were surrounded by five dudes with Glocks who didn't appreciate the fact that I was carrying the infamous gold blade of their former employer.

"Hey, didn't you hear the fire alarm? Let's get outta here!"

They all pointed their guns with grim, determined faces.

"Drop your weapons!" The biggest dude said with an authoritative voice. Andy immediately threw him his Glock.

"Now fellas, let's be reasonable." I tried to be gregarious. Then I leaned my head towards my little partner. "Andy, please don't piss yourself again."

"I'll t-try."

Then I looked at the Big Guy. "You mind if we borrow one of those cool Rezvanis outside there?"

"You ain't borrowing shit, asshole. Now, last time, drop your weapons and get on your knees or you both dead."

Andy dropped to his knees as fast as he could.

"Now wait a minute, pal. You didn't tell us to get on our knees before. Unlike my little pal here, I don't just get on my knees for anyone."

I was playing for time, of course. Because right after I said that, KA-BOOOOOOM!!!!!

A huge explosion rocked the house. It felt like a small earthquake. All the dudes dove for cover, and even Andy fell down. But I was ready for it and held my ground. I immediately fired a bullet at each dude, dropped my mag, slotted in a new one, pulled up Andy and pushed him outside. About a dozen guys were running in various directions as smoke began to rise from the far side of the house. Thankfully no one noticed us in the chaos.

"Andy, can you drive a stick?"

He shook his head. Then I saw that I had parked the Saab on a slight incline. I opened the door to the Saab, turned over the engine, and put Andy in the driver's seat.

"Okay, here's what you do. Just release the emergency brake, and coast back down the hill. It's all downhill. You'll just have to do it backwards."

"No way!"

"Yes way."

I released the brake. The Saab began to roll to its rear.

"Shiiiiiiiitttt!" I heard him scream. The Saab weaved to and fro as it began to pick up speed backwards, undulating down the steep incline. I silently wished him best as I got into one of the Rezvanis.

I set my gun and the blade on the passenger seat, said a silent prayer, and pushed the "Start" button. The big motor started right up. I thanked my lucky stars. Then I thanked God. Maybe I did believe in God after all?

I didn't have time to contemplate my luck as I put the rig into 4 wheel drive and punched it, throwing a u-turn, scattering dudes and running over several bewildered guards, as I headed for the errant Saab, still weaving down the incline. One guard grabbed the door. I quickly pushed a toggle switch labeled "Shocking door handles." I heard the guy scream as he fell away from the car, holding his electrified hand. Cool!

I heard a few bullets hit the big SUV, but I knew the the thing was bullet-proof. Even the tires were run-flats. I looked back at the bank of switches and flicked the one that said "Smokescreen." A bank of white smoke spewed out from the rear of the car, obliterating any view by the remaining angry guards of Global, Inc.

I got close to the Saab but then saw the big Rezvani security truck blocking the path ahead with an armed Guard wielding an AR15 in the rear of the pickup.

Thankfully, Andy's weaving gave the truck an impossible target, and somehow the Saab wove around it unscathed. The guy with the long gun took some shots at him but missed. Then I came upon them. They figured my Rezvani was one of theirs—until I sped up and rammed the rear of the Hercules, knocking the guard out of the flatbed. I went around the side of the big 6-wheel pickup and tried to do a PIT maneuver by hitting it hard on the rear quarter panel. The big truck slid sideways as I flew past it, but then righted itself and came after me.

I hit the smokescreen button again and also flicked on the "blinding lights" switch, causing the pickup to slam on its brakes, then slide sideways and roll, tumbling down the side of the mountain. Goodbye. Or should I say Good-night...

As I passed Andy in the Saab, I sped up, heading towards the big metal gate. I made sure the harness was clicked in and braced myself as the 4x4 crashed into the steel wall. SMASH!

The hardened bumper rammed right into the metal and tore the giant gate right off its track, as it ripped away and flew over the smashed SUV, just missing the Saab swerving behind me.

I could see Andy was out of control—his eyes wide as saucers, as the Saab was moving to and fro ever more erratically. A few moments more and the car would flip and roll. I pulled up in front of it until the little car slammed into the rear of the Rezvani, stopping my poor old Saab, putting a huge dent on the rear bumper.

Andy happily moved to the shotgun seat as I got in, tossing Gold's big knife in the back. Only problem was that I couldn't steer with my left hand, meaning I had to shift and steer with my right—quite a challenge.

"Andy, I'm gonna need your help again."

"Oh, please, don't say that."

"I need you to steer as I shift."

I didn't give Andy any time to say no again. I put the car into reverse, then first gear, then I began the drive down Benedict Canyon, and with Andy's help, sweating and complaining and somehow steering, we drove down Canon Drive and onto Sunset Boulevard.

CHAPTER THIRTY-NINE

Andy and I both needed new clothes—I couldn't tell what was worse—my blood-stained threads or Andy's urine and sweat-soaked joggers. The first place I saw was some upscale men's store called H. Lorenzo. It was beyond bougie, with a bunch of expensive rag racks in a big industrial-looking space, made to service the young, wealthy, privileged kids and wannabe rich young adults who live up in the Hills. I didn't want to go there, but I didn't have the time or patience to drive to Target.

I walked in, picked out some new black pants and a sport coat, with a crinkled grey collared shirt and a new black Borsalino fedora. Andy found some baggy parachute pants and a tight 2XL t-shirt that had the word "PUNK" emblazoned on the front, along with a bright green hoodie. He also insisted on getting a white trucker cap that said "*Keep on Truckin.*" This guy was something else.

I agreed to the hat as long as he got new shoes and socks to replace the pee-filled ones. He picked out some sort of ribbed silver sneakers that cost $500. In fact our combined outfits totaled over $7k. A very tolerant, patient and quiet Hispanic woman helped us with our purchases and happily agreed to toss our soiled cotton, wool and poly, no questions asked. However, I wasn't about to let my Hugo Boss go without a fight, so I rolled it up and promised myself I'd clean it.

We walked out, looking and feeling like cool dudes in overpriced duds. My roll of cash from the dead sicario was itself looking dead. I only had a few hundred left. Fortunately we were close to a City National Bank, where my freshly cut Dr. Revenue check was from. So I walked in, signed the back and asked for $150,000 in cash. After many hems and haws and phone calls and after speaking to the branch manager, they somehow agreed to hand me over 1,500 one hundred dollar bills. Fortunately I had my wheelie suitcase in the back of the Saab and filled it up with the dead presidents.

Next I walked into an urgent care facility. Since I didn't have to dick around with insurance and paid them 2k cash up front, they were happy to help. They took x-rays and found I had a bullet hole in my shoulder that had somehow missed my clavicle. I lied and told them I was a victim of a car jacking. They didn't believe me and kept insisting on calling the police. I made them more suspicious when I ordered them not to. They at least cleaned the wound and sewed it up, along with the cut in my hand. About an hour later I was good to go, but was told to wait in the little room. Andy had bought himself a new laptop and was furiously writing his new blog entry. I decided we didn't have a lot of time to waste, so I slipped on my clothes, doing the best I could with my arm in a sling, and opened the door to the hallway. I looked down it and saw two cops speaking to the nurse, who was pointing in my direction. I grabbed Andy and we started walking the opposite way, towards the stairs.

We hustled down to the Saab and got the hell out of there. Thankfully I could now at least use my left hand, and being able to both steer and shift, I took over complete driving duties. I quickly dropped Andy off at his motel so he could check out and pick up his black firebird. Then I forced him to clean out the trash in his car and used some wet wipes to sanitize the passenger seat. I had him drive to a self-storage warehouse on Olympic Boulevard that I knew offered spaces for car storage. That's where I left the Saab, figuring, now that I'd killed the King of Beverly Hills, and thoroughly fucked up his mansion, every cop in town would be on the lookout for me and my brown beater. I got in Andy's semi-clean Pontiac and settled in for a long ride.

It took almost three and a half hours to drive down the crowded 405, then onto the horrid, bumper-to-bumper I5, and back to San Diego. Andy dropped me off in front of my apartment in La Mesa and I was amazed to see Patterson Nobel's beautiful orange 1973 Carrera RS sitting out in the driveway—just as promised. It was the very same car I'd bought from an auction and the same one that was taken back by the dead billionaire. And here it was again. El Dorado Lipshitz was true to his word.

But I wasn't taking any chances and pulled my gun out as I opened the door to my apartment and carefully moved up the stairs. I cleared the entire place, room by room until I was satisfied that no bad guys were lurking about. I found my old laptop and opened it up. Yahoo News told me that the famous movie mogul Nash Gold had died at his home from a sudden heart attack brought on by an accidental gas stove explosion. Then below that article was the tragic story of movie financier and producer, Gato Scattina, who apparently had jumped to his death from his Long Beach condo after he heard the news that his sister, Clara Scattina had died suddenly and unexpectedly.

I figured Gato finally did the jump and pirouette after all. I actually felt sorry for the guy.

But I didn't have time to mourn as I quickly gathered up what little stuff I had and packed it up into the Porsche. I'd left Sushi the Cat with Auri, the gal who'd been my "friend with benefits" until she figured out I wasn't as much of a benefit or friend as she had initially surmised. I was only supposed to be gone a week but I decided that Sushi was better off with her than on the run with me.

Thankfully, since Thomas died, I'd been living the life of a nomad. It it didn't take long to pack up most things I owned and put them into a single suitcase. I took one last hot bath, careful to keep my surgical wounds dry. I stuffed my new bougie clothes into a bag and felt more comfortable dressing in sensible threads—including my one pair of vintage Levi commuter jeans, the kind with enough stretch and a special crotch to allow any number of leg kicks and knee strikes. However, I had grown rather fond of my new $350 fedora and decided to keep it as the latest addition to my hipster private dick outfit.

I packed up the frunk of the Porsche, but as soon as I was finished I had the sudden urge to vomit. My head started pounding again and I knew I didn't have much time.

I got into the RS, but I didn't have even a moment to enjoy the smell of vintage leather, the throw of a crisp manual transmission and the sound of a rear engine boxer six.

I barely made it to La Jolla, as the pain in my head was like someone stabbing me with daggers and I could barely see from the throbbing behind my eyes and the cramps in my stomach.

I drove into the private detox facility and stumbled to the desk, telling them that I was suffering heroin withdrawal, and that I had plenty of cash in my suitcase, and that I needed and wanted to get clean.

I woke up in bed in a small but clean modern room. A male nurse named George had me sign some documents, and before I knew it I was given shot of Naltrexone, which eased some of my migraine.

But it wasn't enough. My legs had been shaking uncontrollably and I wanted to claw my eyes out. I sat there in bed, feeling like death itself. I didn't care anymore about the Nobels and El Dorados of the world. I didn't care about anything, and thought about getting up, going out to the Porsche, opening up the glove compartment where I'd put my HK, putting it into my mouth and pulling the trigger.

I stood up, seeing that I was in some sort of medical gown. All the easier, I thought, since I wouldn't be soiling my clothes when I put an end to my fucked-up existence.

I looked out the small window and saw the orange Carrera sitting right outside. I walked down the hallway. The receptionist tried to stop me but I told her to fuck off as I shuffled past, out the front door. I knew that, since I'd admitted myself and wasn't here by court or doctor's orders, they couldn't stop me.

I staggered and stumbled and almost fell into my car as I opened the door. I sat and stared at the glove compartment. I had nothing left to lose. My son was long dead. The woman I loved was freshly dead. And even though I'd killed all the people responsible for Jessie's murder, I still felt guilty and a tinge of sorry. I felt like shit. I rationalized that my mission, my life, was now over. I just needed to end the pain for it to all end.

"Hey, Mr. Baker..."

I was sitting in the passenger seat, with the door open, still staring at the glovebox. I decided I'd do it right here in the car. But then I looked up and saw the receptionist. She was blonde and pretty and had an ever-present smile. They must have taught her that one. It sorta worked. But I was still determined to plug a hole in the back of my head from the inside.

"Mr. Baker, I know you want to leave, but your belongings are still in your room."

"I don't give a damn."

"Well, last night you asked me to clean your jacket—the one with blood on it. I figured it must have meant something to you, so I just got it back from the dry cleaner. They even sewed up the hole in the shoulder."

I looked up at her, the bright San Diego sun shining into my eyes, giving her a sort of eye-burning halo. She was holding my Hugo Boss. It was on a hanger, covered in that clear dry-cleaning plastic, looking good as new. For some reason it made me smile. Or maybe it was the sun in my eye. I don't know.

I took the jacket and hung it next to me inside the car. At least the plastic would protect it from the blood splatters, so some lucky sap could wear it again someday. I saw that my new fedora was in the back seat. I thought about putting it on, allowing me to die in my trademark uniform. Well, part of my uniform, anyway.

I reached back and set the hat on my head, looking silly in an overpriced wool cap whilst wearing a powder green hospital gown with a slit up the back, but for some reason it felt good. Like an old friend. My naked butt was enjoying the vintage brown leather seat, but the hot leather was also sticking to my sweaty ass. For some reason that made me chuckle.

I then noticed the receptionist was kneeling down, next to the open door. She was holding something else. It was a piece of paper.

"Mr. Baker, I found this in your jacket pocket. I thought you might want it."

She smiled in that professional way, and walked back into the building. She looked pretty hot in her white pants. But then I decided it was silly, thinking about sex when I was ready to blow my brains out. It didn't matter. It shouldn't matter.

I opened the glove compartment. My HK was lying there, loaded with 10 rounds of .45 caliber bullets. I'd only need one of course, but it was waiting. Waiting for my final trigger pull.

I picked it up, caressing the familiar G10 grip in my good hand. The thought came to me that I had just wasted 2,000 dollars fixing my shoulder. Why? Why did I get new clothes? Fuck it. Who cares. I needed to fix the pain in my head. The cravings that would never go away. I had to end all of the bullshit. All my mistakes.

I put the gun to my head. Then I remembered I was gonna put it in my mouth. Yeah. Make it phallic. I deserve that.

I peered down at the black barrel, now encircled by my lips. The metal caressing my tongue.

It felt familiar. It was familiar. Only then it was Clara's finger on the trigger. But it was like I could now hear her ringing laugh echoing in my head, her strange tone both high and low.

"Yes," I imagined her voice to say. *"Do it."*

Her breathy echo in my ear. Her husky voice. I wanted to please her. I wanted her. And I knew I'd see her again if I did this last thing she commanded of me.

I placed my finger on the trigger.

"Yes, Haim... Pull it. Do it."

"Yes." I said to the voice in my head.

"Yes..." she said as I heard her laugh. Felt her intoxication eating at my soul. I moved my finger up and down the trigger, caressing it. The curved metal, cold to the touch. Just four pounds of pressure needed and it would all be over.

"Yes." I began to pull against the metal. The trigger began to move...

"Yes!"

But before I committed completely. Before I gave myself over, pulling the trigger one final time, I noticed the pretty blonde had put a piece of paper on my lap. It was small, and blank.

"Finish it... Finish it!"

Yes, fuck it. Time to die. Clara was right. I needed to end this, end the misery.

But then I thought, what the hell? Maybe this paper was a sign? Might as well see what it was, right? I mean, why was this in my lap all of a sudden? I didn't even see the blonde chick put it there. Maybe it was the bill to this stupid rehab clinic, maybe they wanted all their money before I left. Fuck them. That would really give me the courage to pull that trigger quick. And I needed courage, no matter what the voices in my head told me.

I decided, just for the moment, to slide the gun out of my mouth and set it next to the blank paper.

I looked down at my Mk23. Sitting there. Waiting. The black dragon. Big, powerful, intimidating. Beautiful. Full of ammo. Heavy. It had saved my life on countless occasions. Now it was going to save it one last time, right? Save my life from misery.

"Yes..."

I'd almost forgotten about the paper as I reached over to pick the gun back up and put it in my mouth. I missed the metal taste, the spicy residual gun powder. The gun oil. I wanted it. I wanted it in me.

But then I saw the paper.

Oh, that paper. The blank piece of paper.

I picked it up and left the gun waiting on the seat.

"No..."

It was a heavier piece of paper than a normal bill you'd get from a rehab clinic.

"Pick up the gun..."

Something was on the other side...

"Don't!"

I turned it over.

It was a drawing.

It was a picture.

A picture of me.

Jessie's picture of me.

It was my portrait, with my little sardonic smile.

And below, it, she'd written,

"Happy."

Happy. Oh God. Oh damn. Oh... God.

I sat there for I don't know how long, as water poured from my eyes. I was crying. No, I was balling. Wailing. Staring at that portrait. Staring at myself. My happy self.

And that word.

It was like she knew. Somehow she fucking knew....

Happy.

"Happy."

EPILOGUE

I lived at the La Jolla rehab clinic for five weeks, paying them $50,000 for the privilege. Detox was one of the most difficult things I'd ever done. But what did I expect, after dozens of years addicted to little white pills and booze, and finally, to the big *H* of heroin? They'd given me counseling and introduced me to the twelve step program. I actually had a date with Doris Gooch, the hot blonde receptionist, but of course it didn't work out, since all I talked about was Jessie, and so we amicably agreed to just "be friends."

I was given a sponsor named Russ, who was a former Gypsy Joker biker, who dropped out of the gang when he got married and then became a long haul truck driver. Russ retired a few years ago and attends twelve step meetings every week. He's been clean for ten years.

At one time, Russ had lived two lives, with a family in Pocatello, Idaho and another one in Portland, Oregon. He'd spend a few weeks with one and then spend a week with the other. For a decade they didn't know about one another, until Russ OD'd and was arrested for transporting narcotics. He lost all contact with his four kids and two wives, but eventually was allowed back in their lives after his recovery. If he could do it, I sure as hell could, he'd always tell me.

Russ knew about El Dorado from his biker days, and was genuinely worried about me, especially after I told him the entire yarn leading up to Nash's death. He was curious about the movie Netflix was going to make about my detective work. I had gotten a text from Jason, Tyler's assistant, that Netflix had made some changes to the upcoming movie and TV pilot "*Haim.*" Someone high up in Netflix had decided that Chris Pratt wasn't the right actor for the story, and in fact, an exec decided the movie needed some major revision—Netflix wanted a "new direction" more consistent with the Netflix mission to meet DEI standards. Instead of *"Haim,"* the flick and potential TV series was now to be called *"Her,"* starring Alfre Woodard. It wasn't a story about someone like yours truly trying to put an end to a human trafficking ring in a small town—no, now it was about an African American lesbian female detective fighting her racist boss and a racist small town to stop a group of white supremacists attempting to kidnap the governor and overthrow the local government.

I didn't have high hopes for the project. At least I heard Willy got a supporting role in the cast as the "non-binary confidant with comic relief."

Russ wasn't impressed either, but he was sure interested and concerned about what I did to Nash Gold.

"You don't make a play with organizations like that and get away with it, Hammy." Russ always called me Hammy for some reason. "They'll be coming for ya."

I knew I needed to lay low for awhile, and Russ agreed with Nobel's warning that I had to get out of California. I needed cover and also a job, since most of my cash was already gone, having sent a huge chunk of it to cover the cost of Jessie's funeral, as well as about 25k to a lonely divorcée living by herself in an old Santa Monica apartment. Besides, Russ insisted on me working a regular gig to keep my mind busy and off the drug demons.

Russ had a former biker pal, Justin, who was now a manager at a grocery store in Portland, and contacted him about hiring me up there, but there weren't any openings, and frankly, when I spoke to him, he sounded like he didn't want my stink around him either. I couldn't blame the guy. At least he gave me the name of another manager in Eugene named Waldo, who did have a need for another crew member in his store. Justin set me up, and with his recommendation, Waldo agreed to hire me on a probationary status.

I drove the Carrera up to LA, but Russ warned me that the Porsche was too conspicuous, and that I'd be better off in the Saab.

I drove to the storage place on Olympic and swapped cars. In my paranoia (I swore I was being followed by cops or feds), I decided to take the Saab over to Earl Scheib on Venice Boulevard. There I paid a young guy named Hernandez to do a cheap bondo job to cover the bullet holes and dents, and then ordered the whole car sprayed in quick-drying blood red paint to cover up all the memories I wanted to forget.

The Saab seemed to like the new, pretty red makeup, and I swore she had a little more pep in her v4 than usual. I needed all the power I could get as I made the long drive up I-5 and across the border into Oregon, then over the mountain pass and up to Eugene, the second biggest city in the state, known for the University of Oregon, Nike running shoes, and as the city with the highest percentage of lesbians per capita.

I fought daily urges for booze and pills and the feel-good. I accepted that there was a Higher Power, and somehow I knew I was going to keep the demons and the bad guys away. At least that's what I thought...

THE END

Opiate addiction is not fun, and worse, opiates, heroin and fentanyl kill hundreds of thousands of Americans every year. If you're addicted, you really need to get some help. Please call 1-800-662-4357 and someone will be there for you. If you don't like talking on the phone, just type this into your browser—https://dpt2.samhsa.gov/treatment/directory.aspx and they'll help you get clean.

And along with drug addiction, suicide is also a serious and growing tragedy. If you need talk to someone, please call the National Suicide Prevention Hotline at 1-800-273-8255. No judgment, only help.

And we all need help now and then. Even Haim Baker.